FEARLESS

Broken Love Series

BOOK FIVE

B.B. REID

FEARLESS by B.B. Reid

ISBN-13: 978-1540768605
ISBN-10: 1540768600

Second Edition 2016

Manuscript Analysis & Editing by
Rogena Mitchell-Jones, Literary Editor
Final Proofread by Ami Hadley
RMJ-Manuscript Service LLC
www.rogenamitchell.com

Cover Design by Amanda Simpson of Pixel Mischief Design.

TABLE OF CONTENTS

Dedication

To our monsters.
May you run to hell and stay there.

PROLOGUE

LAKE

I NEVER THOUGHT I'd find a new reason never to want summer to end. "Baby," I moaned against his sucking lips once more before pulling away. "You have to let me go at some point, you know."

"No." And to make his point clear, he gripped my ass tighter, pulling me closer to him while I sat on his lap. I couldn't help but smile against his chest.

"You're being unreasonable."

"You think I give a fuck?" His sharp tone was replaced with a softly worded plea. "Stay with me."

Now how was I supposed to resist that? He so wasn't playing fair and he knew it. To make it worse, he leaned down and rubbed his nose against mine. I could feel the sweet scent of his breath against my face.

Keiran had always been possessive, but this felt different. He was clinging to me in a desperate attempt to delay or stop what was already happening.

Tomorrow, I would be leaving Six Forks behind for

Nebraska. A few months ago, leaving this place and the unrelenting torment he unleashed on me had been all I wanted. I never thought he would be the reason I would want to stay. He and I would be attending separate schools thirteen hundred miles away.

It felt like our fairytale was ending. Uneasiness turned my body cold. Would he go to his school in Arizona and forget about me? What if he realized I wasn't what he wanted? What if he found someone stronger, fiercer, and better equipped to handle him?

The answer to his weird behavior was an epiphany brought on by my fears. A tidal wave of unwanted emotions shattered the light bulb and I found myself clutching him back. What if he felt as insecure as I did?

"Are you afraid?" I breathed evidence of our shared insecurities into the night air, letting it hang between us.

"Yes."

I hadn't expected honesty. Keiran had just admitted he was afraid. The idea that I could make him feel vulnerable made me both elated and afraid. We have been together for only a few months now, but I feel like I've been his forever.

In a way, I guess I have.

Before I could tell him I shared his fears, he emitted a sound between a growl and a grunt and abruptly lifted me to my feet. "Fine. Go then."

I had no idea what set him off. Without another word or backward glance, he was gone, and I was left standing alone in the playground that had become our meeting place when we needed to be alone.

"What the fuck just happened?" I whispered aloud.

I stomped to the parking lot but found his car already gone. His behavior was unlike the possessiveness he'd shown since he claimed me as his for good. I hopped in my car confused and feeling a little bit played.

The next day, I was pulling up to the airport with Willow and Aunt Carissa feeling angry and hurt. I hadn't heard from Keiran since he left me alone at the playground.

I was getting ready to leave my home behind for the first time, and he was off somewhere pacing like an angry, caged lion. I knew he wouldn't be pouting. It just wasn't his style, but it didn't make him any less childish. I moved my suitcase and carry-on from the car with short angry movements. From the corner of my eye, I could see my aunt and best friend lift their eyebrows.

"Are you okay, honey?"

"Fine," I barely pushed through my teeth. I didn't want to be rude to my aunt, but Keiran's absence had already consumed me. Each minute that stretched by, my anger rose. To avoid making eye contact, I stared at my shaking hand.

I heard Willow mumble something to my aunt. I wished they would leave so I could have a moment alone. It was getting harder to get on that plane knowing how we had left things.

"Hey."

I tore my attention from my twitching hand to find a worried green gaze staring back at me. "What did he do?" I could tell by her sharp tone she wouldn't leave it alone, so I looked around for my aunt, who seemed to have disappeared, before answering.

"What makes you think it was him and not me?" I wasn't going to take the blame for our fight, but I was sick of people treating me with kid gloves when it came to Keiran.

"It doesn't matter now, does it? You're here and he's not. He should be here."

"We got into a fight last night."

"About?"

"I wish I knew."

"I'm not following," she said impatiently.

"Keiran doesn't want me to leave. I guess it was too much for him." As if he's the only one feeling it. My sudden awareness of how selfish he was acting did nothing to abate my anger.

"Are you sure you're prepared for a long distance relationship?"

"I don't know, Will. A few months ago, I was a target, not a girlfriend. I have no experience, but I always knew he'd be right there." For fuck's sake… why was I talking as if we'd broken up instead of had a fight?

"He needs a stiff kick in the dick."

I didn't want to laugh, but I did. I held my sides as I bent over from the hard laugh that shook my body. It wasn't what she said but the level of frustration on her face as she said it. Her brow was pulled so tight she could have had a unibrow.

"Girls?" my aunt called as she approached with a fresh bottle of water. "It's time to board."

I took one last look around the busy parking garage and gave up the hope that he would change his mind and rescue my breaking heart.

Ten minutes later, I was waving goodbye to my aunt. Willow and I found our seats. She immediately pulled out a sketchpad, and I leaned my head back and closed my eyes.

When a loud shout and an even louder commotion erupted from the front of the plane, I was saved from the shame of a major breakdown by one Keiran Masters.

"Sir! Sir, you cannot board this plane without a ticket. Sir!"

Willow turned wide eyes on me at the same moment.

"No," she groaned with disbelief and slammed her head against the headrest.

I swallowed hard and fought hard not to smile. She read my emotions immediately and shot me a look that said I was crazed. Maybe I was, but I knew in my gut who was the cause of the havoc.

My suspicions were confirmed when he rounded the corner at the exact moment my heavy heart picked up its beat again.

His hair was disheveled and his eyes crazed as he wildly searched the cabin. His chest moved up and down as if he'd just run a race. When his eyes were finally connected to mine, he froze. His expression quickly morphed from desperate to unsure and then to possessive. I never even realized he was moving until he was right in front of me and on his knees.

"Lake."

"The next words out of your mouth better be in the form of begging," Willow grumbled next to me. Her eyes were closed and her face finally relaxed as if his presence was as much a healing balm for her as it was for me.

"If she'll listen, then yes." I searched his eyes as he held mine. "I want to beg, baby."

* * *

ONE MONTH LATER

I BOUNCED FROM one foot to the other, waiting for Willow to collect her colorful pens. Some things never change.

Since we were freshmen and taking general courses, we were able to take three out of five courses together. I didn't know what I would do if I had to start my first year of college thirteen hundred miles away from my boyfriend and without my best friend, too.

"Willow, hurry, will you?"

"Ugh. God, Lake. As if he wouldn't wait or call you a million times if you're even a minute late for your Skype date."

"He's not that bad."

"Oh, yes he is. But it's kind of cute, I guess."

Keiran had always been possessive, but the distance separating us had brought a vulnerable side to him that I never thought I'd see.

Sheldon said it was normal for guys who think something or someone belongs to them. He had already marked his territory but was now unable to defend it, which is the reason he'd become agitated.

Those were her words.

I didn't know whether to take her advice as the truth or if it was a result of pregnancy hormones talking. I still couldn't believe she was going to have a baby and my crazy fuck of a boyfriend was the one to convince her to go through with it when she wanted to terminate.

If possible, I fell in love with him even more because he had. He's grown up knowing only death. I never thought he would value life in any way other than living.

She finally finished packing her stuff and met me at the door.

"Sorry, I can't do lunch today. I have a test in my next class, and I need all the studying I can get."

"Nerd," I teased.

"Whatever. You'd be the same if you weren't so stuck up Keiran's as—"

"Hey."

Willow and I both jumped at the sudden sound of Keiran's deep rumble. He stood across the expansive hallway with his hands shoved in his jeans wearing a pleased grin.

"Hi, Willow," he taunted. It was evident he caught her remark.

She rolled her eyes and wiggled her fingers dismissively. He knew her well enough by now not to be offended by her pissy attitude. Willow was hurting. We all knew it, and so did she.

His eyes finally shifted to me and instant heat assaulted me. We stood frozen on opposite sides of the hallway, content to drink one another in. "Hey, you."

It took me a few extra seconds too long to realize he'd spoken. "Hi." Breathe. It's all the one syllable word managed to be, and yet I felt completely breathless.

My first romantic relationship.

My first boyfriend.

My first love.

What a sap I turned out to be.

"Turn down the sexual energy, will you? I feel pregnant just looking at you two."

"Willow!"

I had no reason to be surprised. Willow usually said exactly what came to mind. Her attitude was as flamboyant as her dress code.

She rolled her eyes at my shock. "I'm off to the land of the nerds. I bought a fresh can of Lysol. Please be sure to clean every surface after use. You know... 'cause people gotta eat on 'em."

Willow quickly retreated, her laughter trailing behind her. I looked over to Keiran, who was noticeably holding in his own.

"Don't encourage her."

He regarded me with hooded eyes, letting the heat in them consume me.

"Would you rather I didn't fuck you on every surface?"

Oh. My. Fuck.

"Then stop staring at me like you want to be fucked."

"So how should I look at you?"

He chuckled and finally moved to touch me. "As much as I want to," he fingered my hair, "a responsible man feeds his woman first."

"Fine time for you to be chivalrous."

His smile only widened at my quip. "Maybe I want to be better for you." He lifted his hand, palm up for mine to take. It took longer than necessary for me to oblige. I was lost in the sincere emotion in his eyes.

Hand in hand, he made me show him to the nearest dining facility. Unfortunately, Brady Hall was the closest. I didn't like eating there because it was jock haven, but I figured Keiran would fit right in. The guys were always rambunctious and rude. Willow and I had been subjected to many catcalls and lewd suggestions.

On second thought...

"Babe?"

"Yeah?" He was pulling the door open and waiting for me to go in.

"I'm not very hungry."

He looked at me suspiciously and then cracked a smile. "Nice try," he said, thinking I was seeking a shortcut to sex. He pulled me inside by my wrist, and we made our way to the cashier where I swiped my meal card and Keiran paid cash. As we grabbed food, I prayed the jocks had already come and gone. We had a game tomorrow, which was when they were usually the rowdiest.

As we made our way to a table, I realized my prayers had gone unanswered. Why, why, why would I pick this stupid cafeteria? There were two more on campus, yet I had to pick this one.

"Baby, if I have to call your name again, you might just get my hands on your ass, but not in the way you had imagined."

"Huh? Oh... what?"

"What's up? Why are you so tense?"

"Oh, nothing."

His jaw clenched, and I knew my lie hadn't gone unnoticed. He usually read me like an open book.

"You don't lie to me. Ever. You keep looking around like you're waiting for someone to jump out at you." If it were possible, his jaw seemed to clench even more. "Has someone been fucking with you?" It was his turn to look around as if he knew who the culprit would be. When his gaze landed on the tables full of football players, his eyes narrowed. I should have known he would know. "Have they?" His voice was full of grit and fire as he nodded at the table of players.

"I don't understand your question." It was another lie. I understood him—just as I knew what would happen next if I confirmed his suspicions. Keiran was thousands of miles away from home in Arizona. He was alone, and there were too many of them for him to take. Jocks stuck together—right or wrong. I was sure Keiran knew that considering he was a jock, but the way his chest heaved, I knew defending my honor would be more important.

"Lake, I would never let anyone hurt you. Do you believe me?"

"I do, Keiran, but that's what scares me. It's okay to walk away sometimes."

As soon as the words left my lips, the school's quarterback planted himself in the seat next to me.

"Hot girl."

I rolled my eyes at his obnoxious greeting. Don't get me wrong. He's asked me for my name many times, but I'd always denied him. The last thing he needed was encouragement to be an even bigger asshole.

"When are you going to let me have that date?"

"Would you like to take her out before or after I break your neck?"

Oh, shit.

Oh, shit.

Oh, shit.

Panic replaced irritation when I saw the infamous vein that meant trouble as it appeared near Keiran's forehead. Sean never bothered to take his eyes off my breasts, and then he made the catastrophic mistake of groping me. It was the first time he'd ever been so bold and, of course, he picked now.

Keiran rose from his seat, and I thought he would make his way to the other side of the table, but he didn't. He pulled Sean across the table with a grip on his throat.

I jumped from my seat at the same time the entire football team did. The cafeteria, including the staff, had gone quiet. Keiran was outnumbered, and now he had their star quarterback in his hands.

This would end badly for Keiran—I was sure of it.

I looked down and grabbed my fork. It was the best option, and if used in the right spots, it could do severe damage. I was prepared to protect Keiran as fiercely as he was determined to defend my honor.

"You're making a big mistake, bro. I suggest you let him go or our entire defensive line will make this very painful for you."

"Pain?" Keiran had transformed into his most sinister self right in front of every eye in the cafeteria. Without warning, he kicked out, sending the quarterback to his knees. His grip transferred to Sean's right arm, and with one motion, he forced it in an awkward angle just enough to make him cry out. I remembered another time, similar to this moment when Keiran had stopped Trevor from raping me in the girl's locker room. "Let me school you about pain. Pain for who I guess is your star quarterback here is when I break this bitch's throwing arm in two. Pain for you is when you lose your game tomorrow and break your winning streak because he doesn't know when pussy belongs to someone else."

"I don't believe you." The guy who I recognized as Jerald motioned to his team, and they moved to surround Keiran. My anxiety kicked into high gear as I held my weapon that seemed meager now and wondered if I could get across the table in time.

Keiran didn't move or speak as he was surrounded.

One of the biggest players in the circle stepped forward. I started to warn Keiran because I didn't think he would see him. Keiran jerked Sean's arm back infinitesimally. His cry was loud, causing Jerald to unload a string of threats to Keiran. Judging by the angle of Sean's arm, it wouldn't be long before his arm broke. I wasn't entirely sure his arm would even be useful tomorrow as it was.

This was not going to end well.

Even if Keiran managed to get out of this unscathed, I would officially be the school pariah and target.

Again.

"His arm isn't going to last much longer," Keiran taunted, voicing my thoughts.

"Fuck!" Jerald's face was red with rage while Keiran stood calm and cool as if he weren't threatening to break someone's bones in a room full of witnesses.

"Please," Sean yelped.

"You know what to do," Keiran stated.

"Stand down! Stand down!"

Everyone moved at the same time. I watched them back away and only then began to breathe easier. We weren't out of the woods yet.

Keiran had let him go, so what would stop them from pouncing now? Sean stumbled into the safety of his team

"Lake." I forced my gaze back to Keiran. "Head for the door, baby."

"No."

"Lake." His tone was no longer soft.

"I'm not leaving you."

"This will end much worse if you get hurt. Now go."

I let the distress I felt rip from me as a whimper.

What do I do? What do I do?

"What the hell is going on here?" The team's coach thundered by me leaving behind a gust of wind. Along with him were two members of the campus police. Everyone scattered, leaving us alone with a different kind of trouble.

Keiran's arrest was imminent, and suddenly, I was no longer afraid for him. I was crazy mad and wanted nothing more than to drive the fork into his brain and dig out his common sense.

I knew for sure someone would snitch—and wouldn't he deserve it? He did almost break a guy's arm... for groping me. The reminder of that sleaze ball's hands on me made my skin crawl.

"Nothing, coach. Just goofing around," Jerald spoke up though his glare never left Keiran.

"Why is my quarterback clutching his arm, and

who the fuck are you?" the coach bellowed between Jerald and Keiran.

"Misunderstanding," Sean whimpered.

Keiran smirked, and I knew if he could reach him, he would offer a pat on his head.

"Boy, your arm better not be broken! Security! Get this piece of shit out of my cafeteria."

Security moved forward to grab Keiran, but with one look, they backed away and reached for their sides. I prayed campus security didn't carry guns. Keiran ignored them and reached for my hand, leading me out of the cafeteria. I was still in shock by the time the building was out of sight.

"I have no idea where I'm going, baby. I need you to snap out of it."

His casual tone broke me out of my trance, and I quickly snatched my hand away from his. "I can't believe you did that."

"Are you defending him?"

"I'm defending me! I won't be able to show my face anymore. He's the star quarterback."

"So I'm supposed to let him put his hands on you because he can throw a ball? That will never fucking happen, Lake."

"You can be such an overbearing dick! Sean is harmless. You couldn't just walk away?"

"I'd never walk away from protecting you." His voice softened, and I willed myself not to break. Today could have ended badly. Keiran wouldn't have been able to win against an entire team, and if they had decided to rat him out, he'd be in jail right now.

"You sure it wasn't just your jealous ego?"

"That, too."

I couldn't help it. I laughed. He was so adorably cute and proud about the wrong things. "What am I going do now, Keiran? I'll be a pariah."

Rather than answer, he pulled me close. I didn't want to, but I wrapped my arms around his neck and inhaled his scent. "Run away with me."

"This is not the time to try to get into my pants. You lost that privilege when you were almost jumped and arrested."

"I'm serious."

"Why would we run away? Where are we going?"

"I want you to come to Arizona with me. I can't do this anymore, Lake. I tried. Fuck me, I tried."

"I can't just leave. What about school?"

"I want you with me. I want you in my bed. I want to see you and touch you every day.

"What about school," I repeated.

"Arizona has an outstanding education program."

CHAPTER ONE

FIVE YEARS LATER

LAKE

I FUCKED UP. For the last seven months, I felt as if I were living on borrowed time as a free woman. I was responsible for the death of Mitch Masters. The father of my former tormentor turned boyfriend. He was evil, and every second he lived, he was a danger to Keiran.

I had a love to protect and a point to prove.

Keiran wouldn't destroy me, but I might have destroyed him.

"If you cannot afford an attorney, one will be provided for you." The officer who had cuffed me continued to read me my rights, but my focus and worry wasn't for me. It was for what I knew would happen in five... four... three... two...

"Get your fucking hands off her!"

I clenched my eyes shut and willed him away. For once, the law wasn't after him. I was the one in deep shit, but if he came after the officers who were only doing their job, he would be in worse trouble than I was in.

"Son of a bitch!"

"Grab him!"

I twisted just enough to see Keenan and Dash leap over the porch railing and run after Keiran, who came after me with unsuppressed rage. The other officers had already drawn their guns on him and shouted a warning. I knew he wouldn't have heeded if it weren't for his brother and best friend. It took them both to bring him down, and they all hit the ground hard once they did. I winced at the impact, but Keiran didn't seem to notice. His gaze was fixated on me, and within its depths, I witnessed the anger and disbelief.

"Uncle Keke." Kennedy's broken cry ripped through the night air. The sounds of distress and what seemed like the entire police department's invasion had disturbed her slumber. Sheldon held her back, and I could see tears in both her and Willow's eyes. Willow held her very pregnant belly, and I silently prayed nothing would happen to the baby because of me. I'd never be able to survive the added guilt.

"You better get him under control if you don't want him going downtown, too. We've got plenty of room."

"We got this, officer," Keenan spat. I knew he had another word in mind to call the man but knew better with his fiancée and child standing a few feet behind. At least one of them was thinking clearly.

As I was loaded into the back of the cruiser, I glanced one last time at Keiran. I had no idea what would happen next, but I didn't regret what I had done. I just hoped he would forgive me.

* * *

EARLIER THAT DAY

"SO, WILL." KEENAN cleared his throat and grinned, and I knew—I just fucking knew—he was about to say something stupid. We'd all kind of gravitated here for the day and were now sitting around Keenan and Sheldon's living room. "How does it feel to be pregnant?"

I groaned remembering how sensitive Sheldon was at this stage of her pregnancy. Keenan had no clue what he was walking into. Keiran and I shared a look, but it was too late.

"Like there's an alien invasion happening in my uterus."

"Really? I always thought it would feel more like butterfly flutters in your belly."

Keiran groaned.

"You would because you don't have a uterus."

"True, but—"

"Nope," she continued as if he hadn't spoken. "You guys just poke your penis where it doesn't belong and your job is done for the next nine months."

"Babe—" Dash began but was cut off by a vicious glare from Willow.

"Don't 'babe' me. It's hot, and I feel like a whale swimming in a desert."

"You're beautiful."

"Can it, Chambers. You're getting laid tonight. You don't need to kiss my ass."

She'd gone too far that time—pregnant or not. Dash's nostrils flared as he leaned toward her to whisper in her ear. Unfortunately, I was close enough to hear. "If you don't watch your attitude, I'll be spanking that ass later instead of kissing it."

Willow blushed and ducked her head while Dash

sat back with a smug look. It was incredible how rightfully wrong two people could be for each other. It was evident Dash liked taking control, and Willow enjoyed pushing him to do it.

"So, I was thinking we could start teaching Ken to play basketball."

"Don't you think it's a little early? She still needs two hands to hold the ball," Sheldon argued.

"But she only needs one to dribble. We got to start somewhere, and if she's going to play power forward for Lynx, she'd need all the practice she can get."

"Whoa. What makes you think she's playing forward? She's playing guard."

"Oh, and which guard might that be?" Keiran asked with narrowed eyes.

"She's a shooter, of course." He shrugged as if it were a done deal.

"Funny. I think she's better on point. She's a leader."

"My kid. My say," Keenan answered smugly.

"Oh?" Sheldon snapped. The guys ignored her and continued to argue.

"Dude she's playing for Liberty," Dash growled, bringing the conversation full circle.

"I don't know, man. Lynx usually gets first pick over Liberty. She'd have a better team behind her."

"I agree, except she's playing forward not guard."

"I know how we settle this." Dash grinned.

"How?"

"Suit up."

They took off at once. Keenan ran upstairs while Keiran and Dash shoved each other to get to the back door first. Sheldon blew out a breath and pointed a thumb over her shoulder. "Can you believe them?"

"I hope Dash doesn't think he'll decide our son's

life."

"Of course, he has. Whether he likes it or not, he takes after our father. It's just that his methods don't require him to be as huge of an asshole."

"Have your parents brought up that custody issue again?"

She snorted, cast a nervous glance toward the stairs, and shook her head, apparently reluctant to discuss it with Keenan in hearing distance. I still couldn't believe her parents had demanded custody be given to them in the event of her death. When Sheldon refused, they threatened to remove her from the will until she conceded.

"Have you still not told him?"

"And give him more ammunition to make things worse when he sees them again? He's a hot head."

"Good point, but he may find out somehow."

"Keenan is a great father to Kennedy. What is your parent's issue?"

"They believe he's a flight risk, as my mother put it."

"So," Willow began, her eyebrows pinched sharply with confusion, "what's the deal? Did Keenan run when he found out you were pregnant?"

Sheldon shook her head with her eyes cast downward. "He left the night Kennedy was conceived."

"Do you think he would have stayed away if he knew about her?"

"I have no doubt nothing would have kept him away."

"Hey, Shelly!" Keenan came running down the stairs holding a sleepy Ken as if she were a bomb about to detonate. "Your daughter pissed all over her sheets again. Handle this, will you?" He passed her to her mother and jetted out the door before Sheldon could respond.

"Keenan, you jerk!"

"Oh yeah." Willow deadpanned. "Dad of the year award is definitely his."

Sheldon shook her head and took Kennedy back upstairs to clean her up, so I decided to head out back where I could already hear shouting and swearing and the rhythmic sound of a basketball dribble.

"Oh, my." I heard Willow gasp lustfully beside me. I was temporarily blinded by the sight of three impressive bare chests glistening with sweat as they savagely fought for the ball. I wasn't sure how well basketball could be played with only three players, but it was apparent the game was no longer the objective.

Keenan managed to steal the ball from Keiran and knock him down in the process. I winced at how hard he hit the ground. Just as quickly, he bounced up and stole the ball mid shot. Keenan cursed and took the offensive along with Dash.

I grew nervous watching. Sweat pooled between my breasts and my breathing escalated. Watching Keiran move and play—specifically without a shirt—was overwhelmingly stimulating.

Dash and Keenan closed in on him. His eyes shifted between the two, looking for weakness.

It didn't seem likely. I thought he was done for, but then his eyes found mine. He smiled, winked, and made his move.

The ball was thrown high in the air. He threw a fist into Dash's finely cut abs and an elbow into Keenan's regal nose and shoved past them as they groaned in pain in time to catch the ball.

"Hey!" Willow yelled. "He can't do that." She turned to me with eyes ablaze and as wild as her hair. "Can he do that?" I shook my head, feigning concern, and tried to hide my smile when he made the basket and turned with a cocky grin.

"Come on, pussies. We playing ball or having tea?"

Dash moved first and took Keiran to the ground. He managed to slam a fist across his jaw before Keenan surged forward, knocking Dash out of the way, and taking his shot at his face. I cringed at the sight and sound of Keiran getting pummeled. They began to exchange blows uninhibited.

"What's going on?" Sheldon asked as she entered the backyard.

"Keiran scored and they started beating the crap out of each other."

Sheldon's eyebrow lifted, and her eyes flashed with aggravation. "They do realize they're grown men and not teenagers anymore, right?"

I nodded toward the rumbling mass of hard male flesh. Keenan dick-punched Keiran and Dash tripped Keenan. "Good luck explaining it to them."

I then watched as Sheldon and Willow manipulated their men shamelessly.

Sheldon huffed and charged forward until she was close enough for them to hear. "Keenan, I want to fuck."

Her tone couldn't have been less sexual, but still, his head popped up from biting Dash, and just like that, his attention was redirected.

"I'm out," he said and untangled himself.

So much for his daughter's future.

When he wrapped his arm around Sheldon and began nibbling on her neck, it was her turn to smile. "Good luck with your men."

"Dash, my feet hurt and I'm hungry," Willow whined purposely.

"My lady says I can't play anymore." He hit Keiran one last time, causing his head to snap to the side, and then Dash jumped to his feet. I watched them leave and then turned back to see Keiran watching me. He had a light in his eyes that I recognized all too well. I could feel my temperature rise even now.

"I saw the way you were looking at me."

"How? Dash kept trying to give you a black eye."

"I saw you," he insisted, his tone husky. He closed the gap between us and pushed until my back was against the pole.

"You're sweating."

"You like it."

"Your smelly sweat all over me? Why would I like that?"

"Because it reminds you of when I fuck you so hard you can barely breathe or move when I'm done."

"Tease." I wanted to be disgusted by it. I really did, but he was so damn sexy when he was sweaty.

His smile came slow as he pushed his body against mine. The pole was now digging into my spine, but I didn't feel it. My entire body was distracted by the feel of his much more appealing hardness. He nibbled on my chin and whispered, "I could fuck you now."

"But you're all bruised," I flirted. "I could break you." I batted my lashes and peeked up at him. Despite the many leafs we'd turned, I knew he still craved the chase. Even more, I wanted to be his prey.

"Lift your arms and grip the pole."

My arms trembled as I obeyed. His eyes never left mine even when he reached for the button of my shorts. I gasped and gripped the pole tighter when I felt his finger caress the sensitive skin of my waist. With my arms stretched over my head, my thin t-shirt rose, exposing me for his torment.

"You have the softest skin."

God, his voice was like velvet. So deep and smooth.

He slid his hand inside my shorts, along my hips, and pushed my shorts and panties down until I was completely bare from the waist down.

"Someone could see."

"Let them." He slid down to his knees and lifted my leg over his shoulder. I was already threading my fingers through his hair. I wanted to close my eyes and let go but couldn't resist the urge to watch him.

"Kennedy could see." Shut up! Shut up!

He returned my hand to the pole with a stern look. "They won't let her back here."

"How do you know?"

"Because we didn't follow them in. They'll know."

"And does that turn you on?" I was joking, of course, but anything to get a rise out of him.

"You turn me on. Now shut up."

No, I wanted to keep him talking. The feel of his breath blowing across my skin was almost as good as the promise of his tongue. I needed him to devour me.

And devour me he did.

Right against the basketball pole, he sucked me into his mouth with a hungry passion that could have been witnessed by anyone. The chance of getting caught with his tongue deep in my pussy only made me hotter. More daring. I gasped and groaned and cried his name without care of who might hear.

"Keiran, please," I begged when I couldn't take him fucking me anymore.

His only answer was a groan and an assault on my clit that sent me over the edge and into screaming ecstasy. My leg weakened and shook, so he guided both of my legs around his neck as I came in his mouth and clung to the pole. His tongue continued to lap at my pulsing heat until my shaking subsided.

"Fuck me," I demanded through harsh breaths.

"Fuck me now."

He didn't utter a word as he ripped down his shorts, lifted me up so my legs rested in the crook of his arms, and plunged inside me unprotected. "Goddamn," he growled.

After he had fucked me hard enough to shake the pole seated firmly in the ground, we redressed and entered the house, but not before Keiran took one last opportunity to grope me. They were all back in the living room pretending not to know what we had just done. Kennedy was the first to spot us. She jumped up from playing with her ninja turtles and wrapped her arms around my legs.

"Hi, Auntie Lake."

"Hi, sweetie."

"Wanna play turtles?"

"Of course, I do." I followed her to her play area. In my peripheral, I saw Keiran take a seat where he could watch me unobstructed. I think it was a habit he picked up from when he tormented me. Ironically, it no longer felt threatening and, in turn, made me feel safe. "Can I be Mikey?"

"No, this one." She held up the turtle with the blue bandana and explained the rules in a way only a four-year-old could.

We spent the rest of the afternoon taking turns playing ninja turtles with Ken, who managed to hang for a few hours before she needed another nap.

Di even showed up out of the blue.

Sheldon had reluctantly begun to accept her, but there was still obvious tension.

No one had ever been able to figure out her problem with Di. I wasn't sure Sheldon even knew. Di was incredibly beautiful and desirable when she wasn't snarky.

For the rest of the day, we felt the need to be together, so we ordered pizza and wings and made it a movie night, but hanging out soon turned into a strategy meeting for survival.

"We still don't know who kidnapped Kennedy and then killed John."

"What are you talking about? It was that crazy whack job. Sorry, Di."

"None taken." When Keenan turned his attention away, she threw a chicken wing and hit him in the head.

"It wasn't Esmerelda. I questioned her about it when we were taken. If she didn't take the opportunity to brag about it to two people she was about to kill, she couldn't have done it. She only said she wished she had because then Kennedy wouldn't be alive, and I would be suffering much more than physical pain before I died."

"Damn," Keenan murmured. He turned to Di and said, "My mistake, Di. Your mother is a super crazy whack job."

She flipped him off and leaned forward. "So we still have a major problem on our hands."

"Fuck! I need answers now."

Just then, the door burst open and what seemed like the entire police force rushed in, shouting to everyone the order to get down.

Everyone put their hands up and probably assumed they were here for Keiran. Only I wasn't surprised when they bypassed him and placed me in handcuffs instead.

My borrowed time had just come to an end.

"Lake Monroe, you're wanted for questioning in the murder of Mitchell Masters. You have the right to remain silent..."

* * *

PRESENT

"I'VE GOT TO say, Miss Monroe. We don't get many like you in here. I'm also aware this isn't the first time you've been here because of murder." When I only stared back at him, he continued. "Five years ago, you were a witness to an atrocious crime committed against two of your classmates who were burned alive." He made a point of looking at the thick folder splayed out on the table. "Anya Risdell and Trevor Reynolds."

"I'm familiar with the case. What's your point?"

"My point is we both know you didn't murder Mitch Masters, so why don't you tell me the truth."

"I don't know what you mean."

"I think you do. Come on... you and I both know Keiran Masters killed his father so why don't you make this easier on yourself? You were brave back then. What's stopping you now?"

"I love him."

"Love?" he scoffed. "Love is about to cost you twenty to life without the possibility of parole. Don't let his cock ruin your life."

I was sure his mention of my boyfriend's cock violated his code of conduct, but I let it slide.

"He also didn't do it."

"Now why should I believe that? You just told me you wouldn't give him up because you love him. Why should I believe you aren't lying?"

I narrowed my eyes feeling as if I were led here under false pretenses. The interrogation felt too much like a trap. The detective seemed more focused on accusing Keiran than offering evidence against me. "Am I here because I'm suspected of murder, or am I here because my boyfriend is suspected of murder?"

"Oh, we're sure you're guilty. We're also certain you didn't act alone."

For the first time since the detective entered the room, I felt my heart rate quicken. My tongue was suddenly dry as I choked on unspoken words. I was suddenly very interested in what the detective had to say even though I remained silent. The detective took it as an invitation to continue. Plucking a single sheet of paper from the folder, he slid it across the table.

"Do you recognize this?"

I peered down at the sheet and immediately recognized the name written at the top of the chart. It was a visitor sign-in sheet for Summit Rehabilitation for Cancer Survivors.

The facility where Mitch had been residing for three years while he withered away from cancer.

"I find it interesting that you were visiting the center the same day your boyfriend's father was brutally murdered. Even more interesting, you signed in... but you never signed out."

If it were ever proven impossible that the entire body couldn't start to perspire at once, I'd just disproven that theory.

"I want a lawyer."

He didn't miss a beat and stood up straight. "Good. You're going to need one, Miss Monroe."

I let my gaze trail to where I had written my name. I wouldn't have been so stupid if I hadn't got caught that day.

CHAPTER TWO

SEVEN MONTHS AGO

LAKE

"SO SHE BEAT it? That's great!" Sheldon jumped up to hug me after I delivered the news. On top of Alzheimer's, my grandmother had been diagnosed with breast cancer three years ago. Because she was under strict medical care, it had been caught early on, but that small ray of hope was overshadowed by the aggressive growth of the cancer cells. Rather than get better, she had progressed to stage two in under two years.

When her condition seemed hopeless, Jackson and Keiran secured one of the best doctors in the country to oversee her case. It took a year of treatment, but she was finally cleared of all cancerous cells.

"We're going to get tears on the seating chart," I joked to break the emotional tension. We had been going over the last minute details of her wedding in two weeks when I decided to break the news.

"But it's so worth it. So will she be going back to Red Rock?"

"Actually, no. Aunt Carissa decided it would be better for her to spend time in a rehabilitation center specifically for cancer survivors so she could continue to get the aftercare she needed. There's a great one just four hours west."

I noticed Sheldon's expression fall. I was sure she was thinking the same I had thought at first, so I went on to reassure her the same way my aunt had. "I know it's further than Red Rock, but it's for the best."

"That's not—fuck—Lake... what is the center called?"

"Summit Rehabilitation for Cancer Survivors. Why? You know the place?"

Her face had completely lost color. "She's not safe there."

"What? Why wouldn't she be?"

"That's the treatment facility where Mitch is."

"I don't understand. John said Mitch was never cured of cancer. Why would he be at a facility for cancer survivors?"

"Because the center isn't just for survivors. It's also for cancer patients who have given up on treatment and are waiting to die."

I didn't have time to reflect on how horrible the idea of people suffering and waiting to die sounded. I'd just found out my defenseless grandmother was living in the same place with a demented, evil man. My mind was racing with more than one fear, and among them was the most dangerous of them all.

"Keiran doesn't know about the center where Mitch is, does he?"

"John never wanted him to know, and I assumed Keenan is still honoring his wish. We all know what will happen when he finds out exactly where Mitch is."

Keiran wouldn't hesitate to go after Mitch no matter the cost to himself, and protecting my grandmother on my behalf would only be an added push.

"Listen, I need to ensure my grandmother's safety but Keiran can't know about it or why."

"How are you going to explain this to your aunt and keep it from Keiran?"

"I don't know, but there's got to be a way. There's no other rehab center in the entire state. Any other move would be too big. He'd question it."

"I don't know, Lake. Are you sure you want to risk lying to him? I think you should tell him."

"Sheldon, if I tell Keiran where Mitch is, there is no amount of reasoning that will keep him from killing him. He'll be caught and I'll lose him forever."

* * *

ALMOST TWO WEEKS had passed since I learned where John had been keeping Mitch. I had been uneasy and unable to concentrate entirely on my upcoming finals or duties as maid of honor, but somehow, I managed to fool everyone including my volatile boyfriend.

For two weeks, I planned and prayed for a solution that would keep everyone safe and rid the world of Mitch Masters forever, but I was only ever able to come to one dangerous solution.

"What are you thinking about so hard?"

The sudden gruff sound of Keiran's sexy morning voice startled me and stirred a rush of new guilt. I had been so deep in my thoughts I hadn't noticed him awake and watching me. I quickly schooled my features into seductive, playful girlfriend.

"Well..." I left him anticipating my next words as I

slid my hand down his bare chest and into his basketball shorts. “I was trying to make the hard decision of whether to taste you...” It was unnoticeable to the untrained eyes, but I witnessed him suck in air at the feeling of my hand wrapping around his cock. “...or ride you.”

“That’s easy. Do both.”

I shivered at the animalistic sound of his voice indicating the change in his body from slumbering to ready-to-fuck. I forced myself to take my eyes from his cock for a quick look at the clock resting behind his head. It showed only thirty minutes until I had to be out of the shower and dressed for class.

“We don’t have time.”

He groaned and shifted his hips. “Don’t do that to me, baby.”

“Do what?” I blinked innocently while giving his hardened cock a tug. I felt it twitch under my palm and smiled.

“Make me want you so fucking bad and then tell me I can’t have you the way I need you.”

“How do you want me?”

He didn’t bother to respond. Instead, he dislodged my hand and rolled me onto my back. He settled in between my thighs and pushed up his shirt I’d worn to bed at the same time I pushed his shorts from his hips.

“Are you ready?”

“Mhmm... how do you mean?” I decided to torture him a little while longer. I leaned up to run my tongue down his throat and listened for that little intake of breath followed by a groan.

“I mean...” He entered me slowly so I could feel every inch of him. “Is your pussy wet for me?” He stopped once the head of his cock had entered my eager pussy, leaving me the one gasping for more this time.

"Please." It was all I could manage when the feeling of being filled took over.

"I love when you beg for my dick, baby." He gave me another intoxicating inch of him. "It makes me want to fuck you hard."

"Fuck me hard."

We both seemed to break away from our torturous teasing simultaneously. He pulled back and in one motion, served me his entire length. I was sent gasping and teetering over the edge immediately. The rhythm and pace he set was hard and just what I needed to take my mind away from my troubles. I could do nothing but hold on as he rained love bites all over my neck and breasts while he took me hard and unapologetic.

"Lake... Fuck... Baby." I couldn't take the sound of his passionate voice and the sound of our bodies coming together and not come.

I came so fucking hard.

Once I came down from orgasmic bliss, I noticed Keiran had slowed down to a hard grind, now preferring to worship my body. His hands and mouth moved all over me just before he flipped me over on my stomach.

"I can't let you leave me today and not feel your ass against my dick."

Oh, my fuck.

His larger body completely covered me until I could feel every muscle and inch of hot flesh against mine. Just the feel of his sweat dripping on me made me want to come again.

"Come with me. I want your pussy squeezing my dick." A firm slap on my ass followed his order. I felt his fingers run through my hair and make a fist as his pace picked up once more. I threw my ass back, craving the sound of our skin slapping which brought forth a deep growl from him that vibrated down my spine.

Because he couldn't stop there, his fingers made their way to my throbbing clit, making his plea a reality. I came around him at the very moment he came inside me.

We both collapsed amongst the sheets out of breath. I could feel his breath shudder against my heated skin, and I wanted him again. I looked at the clock hopeful and groaned when I realized I should have been dressed five minutes ago.

I felt his weight shift from me to his side of our bed. He was still silent, so I chanced a look at his face to see him watching me, but it wasn't a look I would expect after sex. His gaze was hard and suspicious.

"I know I wasn't what was on your mind. I know when you want me, Lake. Your skin gets so hot and flushed, you nearly take me up in flames with you." I wanted to argue, but no words smart enough to convince him came to mind. "But do you really want to know why I'm on to you?"

Stupid me, I nodded.

"Because if you were really thinking about your lips around my dick, you would have done it the second you wanted it."

"I see you have me figured out completely." There was a bite in my tone even I recognized. Keiran's eyes narrowed.

"Yeah, I do. We'll talk about this when you get home."

He dismissed me, and I wasted no time escaping. But when I reached the entrance to our bathroom, I heard him call my name.

"Yes?"

"We don't lie to each other. Ever."

***

I HAD BEEN on edge all day, dreading going home. Keiran was pissed. It was evident in the way he spoke to me this morning. He didn't even call or text me in between classes per our usual routine. I felt guilty and spent all day brainstorming how to make it up to him and to avoid the interrogation awaiting me.

I stalled as long as I could after classes were over, but when Keiran did send me a text with a single question mark, I knew it was time to pay the piper. I parked at the curb in front of the modest three bedroom home we rented from a middle-aged couple who decided to live life on the road. It was cheaper than we could have found anywhere else within a reasonable distance of school and Keiran's office. An added bonus was the guarantee of the place for the next year at least.

"Don't bitch out. It's just Keiran." My attempt at self-confidence fell flat when I remembered that at the moment, he was a pissed off Keiran. He hated being lied to—I had crossed an invisible line and gotten caught.

When I closed the front door, I was greeted with silence. I was sad to admit I expected to be greeted with rage.

Would I ever get over the little slice of fear I still held for him? It had been four years since we've been together, and he'd never given me a reason to fear him any longer. How could I admit four years of love didn't seem long enough to battle ten years of torment? The thought alone was heartbreaking, but to voice it felt like a betrayal.

I heard his footsteps pounding down the stairs, and then he appeared dressed in a plain white long sleeve shirt and dark jeans. I noticed a duffle bag slung over his shoulder and my heart skipped a beat.

He wouldn't leave me because I told a little white lie, would he?

"Wh—where are you going?"

"Jesse and I have a meeting with a potential client in Texas. They want to meet us face to face and see up front what we're offering."

"How long will you be gone? The wedding—"

"I'll be back in time," he answered before I could finish. He stood on the bottom step, staring and assessing. I refused to fidget like a scolded child, so I met his stare.

He saw right through me and dropped his duffle. The loud thud rang out, but I refused to give in to my inner coward. When he closed in on me with sure steps, I never faltered even if my common sense was telling me to run. The faster, the better.

"If you want to test me, you better be sure you're ready for the consequences."

"Don't threaten me, Keiran. I'm not your plaything anymore."

"You should know better by now. I'm going to ask you this once, so think about your answer. Are you hiding something?"

"What makes you think I'm hiding something?"

"You've been off. Do I need to be worried?"

I wasn't about to tell him the truth, so I stuck with a version of it. "I'm worried about finals and my grandmother settling into a new place."

He searched my face for the longest time, but I was sure he would find nothing. He seemed to realize it too because the next instant, his hands were on my face and his lips took hold of mine. We were moving backward, and then my back was against the wall. His hips moved against me, and I couldn't help but voice my pleasure for the way he commanded my body.

Sometimes I was sure I hated him as much as I craved him.

"I need to protect you," he mumbled against my lips. "Can you understand that?"

The only answer I could muster was to whimper. He swallowed it and me whole. I wanted to be consumed by him.

"Pay attention."

"I can't. You're kissing me."

I shouldn't have said that. He pulled away from my lips but kept the length of his hard body against mine. Without the drug of his kiss, I was forced to face the raw emotion consuming the gray of his eyes. "I need to trust you."

"You can."

"Can I?" I was hurt by the doubt in his gaze but then reminded myself I deserved it.

My nod came slowly as I fought the lump in my throat. What did he want me to do? I needed to protect him as much as he needed to protect me. If our roles were reversed, I had no doubt he would fill my shoes the very way I did.

"Forever, Lake. I'll love you."

"Forever," I whispered back, ignoring the guilt that ate at me for what I planned to do.

When he left, I breathed a little easier because if he had stayed a second longer, he would have broken me. I stood against the wall contemplating if the road I took tomorrow would doom me forever.

Get a grip, Monroe.

How hard could killing one man be?

***

I SENT EMAILS to my professors bright and early, excusing my absence, and arrived at the rehabilitation center later that morning. Little sleep and a long drive had done nothing to settle my rattled nerves. All night, I had battled my conscience and the nagging thought that this wouldn't end well.

Keeping my head low, I made my way to the back exit I'd noticed employees use for a smoke break during my grandmother's intake. Unfortunately, it was locked from the outside.

Checking to make sure the coast was clear, I ducked behind the dumpster close by and waited. It wasn't long—twenty-three minutes to be exact—when the first employee burst through the door with a lit cigarette already in hand. He had his phone to his ear cursing whoever was on the line and didn't see me as I stealthily caught the heavy door and slipped inside.

The smell of the center was similar to Red Rock, so at least, my grandmother had that. I resisted the strong urge to visit her. Her Alzheimer had progressed over the years making her less lucid and less my grandmother each time she saw me. Pictures and other memorabilia no longer helped. It seemed we were destined to lose her one way or another. The part of my heart she held had already broken and was ready to let her go. I only wished I knew which part was selfish.

Brushing off thoughts of my grandmother, I took a deep breath and followed the direction Sheldon reluctantly had given me. When she questioned why I needed to know his room number, I hadn't known myself, but I stored the information anyway. I only told her it was to keep a safe distance. Over two weeks, I slowly let the idea of what I had to do take root until I couldn't see any other solution.

Mitch had to die.

Since I entered from a back exit, it wasn't as easy to find his room, but eventually, I stood in front of room 216. The center was a pretty large one-level building with the dying tucked far away from recovering survivors. This corner was left deserted except for the residents confined to die alone in their rooms. On the other side of the building, I knew nurses and family members roamed.

Here, no one cared.

Those dying were left for dead.

It was only because of the fear of death and the need to avoid it I was able to slip into his room undetected. The room was lit only by a slither of sunlight to keep the room from being completely shadowed by darkness. There were no pictures or memorabilia to overburden the small room. Nothing to testify that the form lying still on the bed meant something to the world. Mitch Masters would leave nothing behind but a legacy of nightmares and greed.

"I knew you would come back for me."

The voice that traveled from the other side of the room was a far cry from the man who kidnapped and held me for ransom four years ago. He didn't look capable of killing anyone, much less his son.

"Hello, Mitch." His head turned to face me, and I knew he was searching my voice out in the dark. I imagined his eyes would be wild with fear and uncertainty.

"Who's there?" He tried to sound unfazed, but it lacked the luster from four years ago. All I heard was desperation to know who had intruded.

"Or is it Mr. Martin? You favor false identity if I remember correctly." If I weren't so alert to my surroundings, I would have missed the way his breath caught.

"Impossible."

"Oh?"

"Why are you here and not my son? He got you doing his dirty work for him now? Didn't think he had it him," he answered before I could. I detected a hint of pride among the malicious intent of his taunt.

"He doesn't know I'm here." It was hard to catch, but a smile slowly spread across his withering face.

"Bad mistake, little girl. I admit, I don't know my son well, but a blind fool could tell he likes control—most of all, of you. You lied to him."

"I did."

"I'm flattered." His voice was bitter when he spoke again. "To what do I owe the pleasure of your company?"

"My presence will be anything but pleasurable for you."

"My, my, how you've grown." He was smiling again. "He has sunk his claws into you, hasn't he?"

"This isn't about me, Mitch." I felt the pain from my teeth grinding and bit down harder, doing anything to keep him from making me run.

"On the contrary, pet. It has everything to do with you. You're here, and he doesn't know it. You snuck away to see me. Do you think my son will give a damn what your purpose is?"

"He won't find out."

"He will. I've kept eyes on him long enough to know where his obsession lies. I wouldn't be surprised if he has eyes on you right now. Come here, girl. I'll make this worth the pain you'll feel when he finds out you betrayed him."

But it wasn't betrayal. I was here to protect him. If not me, it would be Keiran standing in this room. Mitch would already be dead, and Keiran would face the rest of his life in prison if he were caught.

I inched closer to the bed watching Mitch warily. His bloodshot eyes came into clear view as he watched me, too. His skin was pale and too weathered for even his age. He was no longer the strikingly handsome man he once was.

"I hear my brother died."

"Yes. I'm sure you had something to do with that." I blinked away tears for John. Tears that Keiran failed to shed for his uncle. I shifted from one foot and then quickly shifted to the other. Each minute that passed, I drew closer to getting caught. I should have already been gone.

"I won't deny it," he smugly drawled. I sucked in a breath and hated that he noticed. "Though I regret to inform you my involvement was... indirect."

"What are you talking about?"

"The man who I'm sure killed John was hired by me for a different job."

"What job?" He didn't need to answer, though. I realized the answer as soon as I voiced it and felt rage transform my body. I welcomed it and channeled it to my mind. I needed to go through with this.

"My grandniece." His eyes sparkled with a sick sense of pride over what he'd done.

"Or your grandchild," I corrected. Just as quickly, the light in his eyes was extinguished, and he was glaring back at me with the same disdain I showered on him.

"So I've heard."

"You're pathetic," I blurted.

"I never asked for him. He is worthless to me! I already had my meal ticket until his whore mother stole it from me."

"He's a person. Your son. He's not the answer to your sick perversion of happiness."

"You think money is a perversion? Have you ever had millions upon millions, little girl? Anyone would have done what I did if given the chance."

"Keep telling yourself that. But where has it gotten you? You're dying, and there's no amount of money that can change it. Chances are, if you had succeeded, you would have gambled it all away by now, and you'd still be dying."

"I no longer find the fight you found from dating my son endearing. I'd tread carefully."

"How did you do it?"

"Do what?"

"Hire three men to kidnap an innocent child with no money?"

"Who says I don't have money?"

"The string of bad debts trailing you."

"You shouldn't listen to gossip, girl. I have money. What I don't have is enough of it. I don't have enough to pay all my loans with interest."

"And you still want to use your son." I shook my head with barely constrained disgust. "Where did you find those men?"

"As it turns out, there are people who owe me." His voice took a harder edge despite his frailty.

"Who are they?" The last thing I expected to hear was that there were more people out there who wanted to hurt Keiran.

"That would be telling but not to worry, pet. They aren't interested in my son. I merely fed their guilt and collected."

"These people paid you money to hire those men?"

"Not quite."

"I'm sick of riddles."

"Then ask the right questions. Did you really think I'd make it easy for you?"

"It doesn't matter. I didn't come here for answers. I came for your life."

"Oh?" Rather than appearing frightened, his lips twisted with amusement. He and I both knew I wasn't a killer, but I was desperate. I was tired of waiting and wondering when I'd lose Keiran to the grave or prison. "You think I'd let you kill me, girl?"

"You're weak. You can't protect yourself and there is no one here to protect you."

"Or you," he countered.

"Your henchmen? Vick and Freddy?" I felt my lips curl with disdain as I delivered the blow. "They're dead. You have no one," I reiterated slowly.

"And the third? I believe my son hospitalized him, but he isn't dead. Where is he?" I faltered because what else could I do? Greg was the missing link to John's death that hadn't been obvious until now. "Do you know why I am able to die so easily, girl? Because I'll die knowing my son will eventually lose. He's got more enemies than men twice his age."

The truth behind his words caused the well holding my emotions to overflow. "It's all your fault," I gritted. I tasted my tears. They ran freely over my lips and down my chin, escaping into my mouth.

"Maybe." He shrugged his thin shoulders. "But his temper doesn't exactly help, does it?"

No, it does not.

"You know what fuels my son's rage, dear girl?" I didn't answer, but I didn't need to because he smiled a deathly smile. "Guilt."

"He's got a lot to be guilty for. That's hardly news."

"But only one in particular that keeps him awake at night."

I hated him. I hated the smug look on his face. I hated that he wasn't already dead. I forced air into my lungs and promised myself I would rectify that soon. But first, I needed to let Mitch inject whatever poison he could into me. The hatred only made this easier.

"You know something."

"I know that my son isn't as fucked up as he thinks he is, but I must say, thinking you killed your own mother would do that to you."

I felt my body shudder violently and didn't hear anything he might have said after that. Something like a waterfall, or maybe the blood rushing from my veins to my brain had drowned everything out.

"Wait—"

"I haven't said anything more, my dear."

"But you did say Keiran thinks he killed his mother. What does that mean?"

"He was only eight and they had already bred him into a killer. Like any slave, Gabriel was willing to do anything to gain his freedom—until that bitch opened her mouth."

"What did she say?"

"She told him she loved him."

And to a little boy who'd never experienced a tender touch or loving word...

"I knew the moment he couldn't do it so..." He shrugged his frail shoulders.

"You killed her."

A coughing fit prevented him from answering, but I saw it in the sick pleasure in his eyes. He was barely alive and still able to torment anyone in his presence.

"I was standing behind him where he couldn't see," he said when his coughing ended. I was disappointed that he hadn't choked to death sparing me the trouble. "I'm sure he's questioned it as he got older—wondered if he pulled the trigger. It's been fifteen years now. A child's memories are unreliable, and I'm sure with his amount of self-hate, he's convinced himself he's guilty."

"Only because you and those sick fucks did this to him!" I hadn't realized I had shouted until my voice bounced off the walls and echoed around the room. Mitch lifted a shriveled finger to pale lips mockingly. I didn't feel my tears anymore, but I knew they were there. For once, I didn't begrudge them but let them fall freely. I needed the pain.

He took in my face and cackled. "You'll lose him. It's only a matter of time."

I didn't hear my cry. I didn't feel my feet move. The knife I had hidden under my shirt dug into the skin of my fist when I gripped the handle, ready to make my move.

CHAPTER THREE

PRESENT

KEIRAN

"WHAT THE FUCK just happened?" Sheldon whisper-yelled as she descended the stairs from putting Kennedy back to bed. She had become hysterical after seeing Lake hauled away and guns pointed at me. I felt guilty for allowing her to see. She was only four, and she'd already seen too much.

"Say, you can't just black out like that. You have too many strikes against you," Dash scolded. I bit back a sarcastic retort, knowing now wasn't the time to fight. It was normal for him to hold me accountable, but we weren't kids anymore, and this was different. This was my woman in trouble. As soon as I got her out of this shit, I would wring her neck until I had answers.

"Kennedy saw that. You're going to have to answer to her in the morning," Keenan added.

I sucked as much air as I could into my lungs and

then released it all in one spell without tearing my gaze from the window. A part of me was hoping she'd appear safe and this had all been a bad joke.

"I'll talk to her in the morning," I reassured. I looked over at Willow, who was now seated and looking nauseous. "You okay?" I let the apology in my tone speak for itself. She simply nodded and turned to Dash, who placed his hand on her cheek.

"I'll get the lawyer on the phone. We'll need to get ahead of this and get her out before they start interrogating her. If she did do it—"

"What do you mean *if*?" Willow demanded. It was the first time she had spoken since Lake was driven away. "She didn't do it."

"We need to be prepared in case she did."

"She doesn't kill people," Sheldon argued.

"You'd be amazed what someone is willing to do for love," Di murmured. She had been sitting back quiet and a little too calm.

"You saying you know something I don't?" I was stalking her position on the recliner and promising retribution if she lied before anyone could anticipate my move.

"Keiran, calm down."

I gritted my teeth, sick of Dash trying to handle me, and kept my glare fixed on her.

"Well," I prompted when she kept her mouth closed. Her mouth twitched as if she were fighting back a grin, and I swore to fuck if she lost that battle, nothing would keep me from knocking her teeth down her throat. Lake would never forgive me for even considering such a dick move, but I found nothing about this shit funny.

"Only what you failed to see."

"Explain," Keenan demanded. His eyes flashed

with irritation, mirroring my own.

"You made a monster out of her." She sat up and let a ghost of a smile fall across her lips. "Think about it. Someone like you and someone like her should never have crossed paths much less be together. She'd have no choice but to adapt just to survive you and keep you."

I felt myself flinch but ignored it. "I haven't hurt her. I wouldn't."

"But someone wants to hurt you, and every time you knock one down, another pops up. You're no stranger to danger, mister. You embrace it even with so many strikes against you like the dumb male you are."

"What does that have to do with Lake killing Mitch?" Dash asked before I could.

She sighed as if exasperated. "You've got too many eyes on you. Your enemies, the law,"—she ticked off on her fingers—"and as soon as someone breaks a fingernail because of you, even if they are trying to kill you, you're going down. You can't watch your back and keep your freedom. She figured that out."

"She wanted to protect him," Willow whispered.

I couldn't process this—Lake believing she needed to or could protect me. I'd never given her a reason, but she would give me answers. First, I needed to get my hands on her.

"Fuck this. How do we get her out?" I glanced at my best friend, knowing the answer before it was spoken.

"We need my dad," Dash replied with gritted teeth.

* * *

I FOLLOWED BEHIND Dash, feeling uneasy for the first time when entering the overstated extravagance of his childhood home.

Cale Chambers was a ruthless man.

It was fitting that he had one of the most cutthroat legal team known in the free world. It was also known that he was hell-bent on extricating me from Dash's life. I had become a liability issue to his family's name. His legal team had kept me from answering for many violent and damaging offenses. There had only been one slip-thru with my stint in juvie seven years ago, but I would have been slapped with a much larger sentence if it weren't for Cale's lawyers—and he never let me forget it.

I had believed then that Lake set me up, only to find out it had been a jealous team member and an ex-jumpoff. I felt the muscle in my jaw twitch at the reminder of all I had done to her because—simply put—I was a tool. If they had succeeded, not only would Lake not have been mine, but also I would have hurt her.

"Dash, what a pleasant surprise," the haughty voice of his mother greeted him followed by the click of her heels. She appeared looking very much like the well-kept trophy wife she was. Her gaze passed over me briefly and just as quickly, dismissed me as insignificant. She may not have despised me as much as her husband, but she never did little more than tolerate me.

Dash brushed his lips against her cheek and took a step back, too distracted to show proper affection. "Where's my dad?"

"He's in his study, as usual." Her back stiffened as her now cold gaze flickered back to me. "What's this about?" she asked with unmistakable exasperation in her tone.

"Lake's in trouble." He missed her surprised reaction because he had already taken off for the back of the house.

"I knew you'd corrupt that girl," she hissed when he

was gone.

"Yeah?" I kept my emotions in check. Dash would never tolerate me tossing his mother over my shoulder and then on her ass. "You should have stopped me then."

It was a reminder that I didn't like to be challenged. She huffed and stomped off, no doubt after Dash.

I ran through the mental checklist Lake taught me after one too many jealous rages over the course of our relationship.

1. Take a deep breath.

2. Think about the person in front of you. Are they worth it?

3. Think about yourself. Is it worth your freedom?

4. Think about what you have. Is it worth losing those important to you?

5. If any of the answers are no then release and move on.

I still didn't get it, but at least it was better than counting to one hundred as some dipshit counselor advised when the university ordered me to take anger management classes.

I followed behind and found them all tense in Cale's study. Dash must have already relayed why we were here. Cale took one look at me and instantly froze over the Arctic.

"No."

Dash shook his head and calmer than I knew he was feeling inside, he stated, "That's not an option."

"It's the only option. I'm not cleaning up his mess anymore," he shouted while pointing a finger at me in the doorway. I was having a harder time remembering Lake's checklist more by the minute.

"An innocent girl will go to jail, pops."

"She probably isn't innocent. Have you thought

about that?"

"What the fuck? Lake's not a murderer. You don't even know her."

"But I do know they couldn't make a legal arrest without some kind of evidence connecting her. Guilty by a little or guilty by a lot, you're still guilty."

"Fine. I'll hire him myself."

"I've been his client—his biggest client—for over twenty years. He won't take you on without my say so. Now get the fuck out of my house." I stood up straighter at the hateful glare he imperiled on his son.

"I'll liquidate."

"Excuse me?"

"Get your man on board, or I'll liquidate the entire goddamn company."

"Bullshit. You have a board to answer to, son. They'll never agree."

"Money talks, right? Especially when you're losing it." Cale narrowed his eyes, but Dash pretended not to notice. "What if the company makes some bad decisions? A tanked investment here and there. What if I sold off its assets one by one until there was nothing left to keep them interested. The board will do my dirty work for me, won't they, pops?"

Cale lunged across the table in an attempt to grab Dash's neck. I got to him in time to pull him out of reach. Dash didn't even flinch.

I fought back my surprise at Dash's threat. What he was talking was anarchy against his father.

"Cale, do something," his mother shrieked.

The lengths he was willing to go humbled me. He'd be a pariah to his parents if he weren't already.

"I should have never given the company to you," he said with a sneer. "You aren't worthy of such greatness, you ungrateful shit. Now get out of my house!"

Dash walked away without another word, and I followed behind feeling numb. His back was tense the entire walk to the car with his fists clenched at his side. He moved to open the driver's door, but I couldn't endure the ride back without understanding what just happened.

"Fuck man. What was that?"

"Insurance."

"That didn't sound like insurance."

"He'll come around." He looked away as soon as the words escaped not believing them any more than I did.

"And if he doesn't?"

"Then my father can consider his legacy extinct."

* * *

"HOW DID IT go?" I heard as I stepped inside my brother's home, followed by Dash. Willow must have been waiting by the door. Dash shed his coat and then pulled her as close as he could with her belly between them.

"How do you feel about being poor again?" he asked.

She shrugged and bit her lip. "It's suited me for years. I'd be worried about you, though. How would you feel without your silver spoon to keep you warm at night?"

"Who needs a spoon when I've got you to put in my mouth?"

"Ew," Sheldon groaned as she walked by eating a bowl of cereal. "Guys, I'm right here and your niece could hear."

"Shouldn't she be asleep?"

"She is. But I'm saying, hypothetically, what if she

did hear your nastiness?"

"It wouldn't be any more traumatizing than witnessing the actual act." Dash visibly shuddered, and Willow hid her face in his chest as her shoulders shook.

"You're welcome for the pointers," Keenan shouted from somewhere.

"Guys," I interrupted. "My girlfriend."

"Right." Sheldon flopped on the large recliner and took another bite of her cereal. "So what do we do now without Dad on our side?"

"I don't know, but we need to get a lawyer on this first thing. Has anyone called her aunt and Jackson?"

"I tried calling them, but they are vacationing in the Bahamas. I couldn't get through," Willow answered.

"Fine time to vacation in the Bahamas," Keenan griped as he walked into the living room. His hair was wet and his chest was bare.

"Dude, put some clothes on," Dash growled and actually covered Willow's eyes.

"My house," he mumbled back. "It's not my problem if your woman sees something she likes." Willow took that time to snatch Dash's hand away, and Keenan took the opportunity to wink in her direction.

"Now is not the fucking time." My voice rose with each word until it felt like the world shook around me. They each looked contrite enough for me to actually feel my blood flow again.

"Sorry. It's just hard to believe Lake did this. What if the police are just trying it to screw with you?"

"Are you asking if I did this?"

Willow met my stare squarely and said, "Did you?"

"I did not kill Mitch," I admitted slowly. I looked around the room, meeting everyone's eyes. They all nodded, but I could sense their doubt. "Do you think I would let them take her from me if I were guilty?" I knew the moment realization dawned.

"Well, we aren't going to know anything until we get Lake out of there. Dash, what about the company's lawyers?"

"They're corporate. Their expertise is business so they won't be much help."

Willow's eyes lit up as she lifted her head from Dash's chest. "I think my dad can help. He's just as powerful as your dad is. I think I can convince him to put his legal team on this."

"Shit." He snapped his fingers and kissed Willow's lips. "I'll make the call," he offered, perking up. "But I want you in bed. Keenan, can we use your spare room?" Hearing that was still strange. It was a little surreal knowing that my little brother had a family and my room had become a spare in my late uncle's home.

"Yeah, man. You know where it is."

Dash lifted Willow, who looked barely awake, in his arms and started for the stairs. "Guys," Sheldon started, looking pained. "What are we going to do if she did it?"

They all turned to face me for an answer, but all I felt was an overbearing constriction in my chest.

What *was* I going to do?

CHAPTER FOUR

SEVEN MONTHS AGO

LAKE

I WANTED THIS motherfucker dead. I gripped the wooden handle until my hand ached and willed my feet forward.

He watched me with a taunting leer as I approached his bedside. It wasn't until I was near him that I raised the knife from under my shirt.

Quick and clean and it would be over.

His eyes lost the mocking glint at the sight of the knife.

I felt powerful and doomed all at once. Powerful for doing what needed to be done and doomed because the cost would be my soul.

Once I took his life, there would be no turning back, but it had to be done. I had a love to protect.

"Think about what you'll be giving up." He sneered.

"No, Mitch. I'm thinking about what I intend to

keep."

I blinked hard to clear my vision of tears and lifted the knife to strike. I aimed for his heart and struck, but I didn't hear his cry of pain or see his blood escape.

My knife never even pierced his flesh.

Mitch didn't die.

"Lake, what the fuck, girl?"

Shit. Shit. Shit!

I quickly recovered and snatched my arm out of Q's grip and faced him.

"What the hell are you doing here?"

This was bad. Real bad. He would tell Keiran I was here and what I almost did.

"I could ask you the same, so I will. What the hell did I just catch you doing? You're a killer now?"

"I learned from the best."

"You learned nothing, and the fact that you're this stupid place tells me you don't even have a clue."

"Then tell me, Q. What am I not getting?" I had almost forgotten Mitch was in the room, but I could feel him watching us.

"Keiran is fucked up. I'm fucked up. Do you want to be fucked up, too?"

"It's just one man, and Keiran isn't fucked up. Not anymore."

"If you really believed that then why are you here?"

"Because if I don't kill him, I'll lose Keiran forever." I choked before I could complete the admission, but it didn't matter because I felt the threat of it all the same.

Q's eyes flashed with sympathy as he swept a stray hair behind my ear. If Keiran were here, he'd probably break his hand despite the innocence of the act.

"This was stupid, girl. Keiran has killed, but he's no professional. It would be hard for even him to pull this off and you're about to kill a man in broad daylight with more than enough people in this facility to catch you."

I felt the weight of his words on my shoulders and slumped against him. "What am I supposed to do? He can't live."

"I agree."

I felt a chill run down my spine at the change in his tone and looked up. I had expected him to argue but in his eyes, I only saw murder. But then he blinked and the haze cleared. He pulled me across the room until I was standing in the far corner.

"But this isn't your kill."

My stomach turned at the thought of leaving Mitch alive. I couldn't accept this. Q pulled his shirt over his head and wrapped it around his hand. His thin undershirt had lifted, uncovering his stomach when he stretched. I tried not to gawk at the brief glimpse of his physique, but Q was seriously cut into sharp, hard planes. I didn't feel lust, but I did feel girlish admiration for his male form.

"I need to get rid of any prints."

"If I may interject—" Mitch spoke for the first time since Q had shown up.

"You don't have an opinion, bitch. You're dead." The room felt like I had climbed twenty-nine thousand feet up to the death zone. I couldn't breathe, but the sound of my name brought me back to life again.

"Lake," Q growled. He gripped me by my arms and shook me. "You need to get out of here. Now," he added when I didn't move.

"Me? What about you?"

"I'll take care of everything."

"What about Keiran?" It was a struggle to maintain eye contact, but I managed. His stare was invasive and cold.

"What about him?"

"Are you going to tell him a—about this?"

I could see the internal struggle as his eyes shifted. I was asking him to lie to his best friend. It wouldn't be easy to convince him but he had to know Keiran finding out about this would be bad for everyone.

"I'm an accomplice to your lie now. The last thing I want to do is make an enemy out of him. He saved my life."

God, I felt like such an asshole. I had tainted their friendship and created an invisible rift between them.

"You need to go. Don't make me say it again."

He nudged me to the door, but I couldn't convince my feet to move. I took one last look at Mitch, who stared right back and winked.

"Okay," I whispered.

* * *

PRESENT

I ASKED TO make a phone call, knowing I needed a lawyer and fast, but was answered with an angry glare. That had been twelve hours ago and still no phone call. Today was Sunday so I knew I wouldn't be before a court until tomorrow, which meant another night in this place. I had already been interrogated twice. The second round had been a string of angry threats and accusations.

They knew I was there when Mitch was killed.

I was a murderer.

I'd spend the rest of my life in jail.

They'd even gone as far as to taunt me with the possibility of Keiran breaking up with me over the loss of his father. It took everything I had not to snort at that one. He would be angry that I lied and put myself at risk, but he wouldn't mourn a single second over the loss of his father.

"Monroe." Hearing my name called with hostility brought me back to a time when I was afraid of my own shadow. I reminded myself that girl was gone and met the officer's stare. "Your lawyer is here. You're free to go."

"My lawyer? Are you sure?"

He didn't bother to answer and placed the cuffs around my wrist through the space built into the bars before releasing me from my bacteria infested confines. For the hours I spent caged inside, I had more than enough time to conjure up all manner of grime that likely infiltrated my skin by now.

My heart rate accelerated with each step. The guard released me from my cuffs, and I collected my clothes in a clear ziplock bag, changed, and was signed out in less than fifteen minutes. I remained stunned and silent through it all.

"Fourteen minutes and thirty-eight seconds. Good job, boys. You get to keep your jobs after all."

A large man with salt and pepper hair and an exceptionally white smile hurried to my side. When he extended a hand, the cuff of his jacket pushed back, revealing a large Rolex. This man was money, which meant he meant business.

"Hello, Miss Monroe. I hope you are well."

"How—who are you?" I looked around waiting for the punch line.

"Thompson of Thompson & Bain. I'll be taking your case."

"Who hired you?"

"Keiran Masters. I'm a friend of a friend of a friend."

"Meaning?"

"I represent Richard Simon's legal matters."

My shoulders relaxed. Willow must have called her dad. "Where is everyone?"

"Outside. They thought it would be best to wait outside. Just in case things didn't go as planned," he added at my look of confusion. I knew what he wasn't saying. We all knew it was better to keep Keiran as far away from police as possible.

Take a deep breath.

Release.

Before leaving the precinct, Thompson instructed me to appear in court by nine sharp and not to leave town. It was a condition of my unusual release.

"Ok. Let's go." I was eager to get this over with. I wasn't going to run away from Keiran this time.

I stuck my hand in my pockets to keep them from shaking and pushed the door open with my hip. I'd forgotten I hadn't seen daylight for almost twenty-four hours and immediately, used one of my hands to shield my eyes from the sun.

"Damn, man. That was quick."

I heard Dash speak from my right. My eyes were still adjusting, but my body had already sensed Keiran. I felt him move closer. The heat of his body scorched me faster than the sun.

When my eyes were finally adjusted, I witnessed the emotionless set of his face. His eyes were the exact opposite. I was completely enthralled by the storm raging inside.

"Come with me," he growled.

He didn't give me a chance to speak as he took my arm, leading me to his car parked nearby. I attempted to gauge his mood, but he avoided meeting my gaze, so I was left wondering as he got in and drove off. My phone buzzed shortly after with a text from Willow.

I glanced at Keiran in the driver's seat. The muscle in his jaw clenched, and his knuckles were nearly white as he gripped the steering wheel. The engine of the car raced as he pushed it faster than the speed limit allowed.

Don't go home with him, Willow's text said.

He won't hurt me, I texted back and immediately silenced my phone. I knew who Keiran once was just as I know him now. He wouldn't hurt me, and I wouldn't let him if he tried.

We pulled into Keenan and Sheldon's driveway and he cut the engine. We listened to the car settle in silence as the rain began to lightly fall.

"How was I released so early? Shouldn't I have been brought before a judge before making bail?"

"There was never a warrant for your arrest."

"Come again?"

"They never had probable cause that you were the one to murder Mitch so a warrant was never issued. You were taken under false pretenses. It was a set-up."

"But how can that be? I—" I stopped when I realized the hole I was digging was just getting deeper with each word spoken.

Keiran's eyes dilated until he was seething with anger. "You what? Are you about to tell me you killed my father?" When I stared ahead, he punched out at the steering wheel causing the horn to blare. My guilt was written in my silence. "Damn it, Lake!"

"Calm down." I refused to cower no matter how intimidating he could be.

"Don't fucking say that. Don't tell me to calm down."

"I'm not fighting with you in the car, Keiran." I snatched his keys from the ignition and yanked open the door. Storming to the door, I left him to follow or sulk alone in the rain.

"Get back here!"

The rain was pounding down hard now, drowning out his roar. I ignored him and threw open the front door. I guessed everyone decided to leave Keiran and me to sort out our shit since we were completely alone.

"Lake." I could hear his footsteps pounding the floor after me.

"I told you, Keiran. Calm down and we'll talk."

"We talk now."

"I spent a night in jail for the first time. I need aspirin and a hot bath—and in that order."

I took the first step when I left his hand on my upper arm. "Don't walk away from me. Look at me." His voice was rough with grit and desperation and I couldn't bring myself to deny him. I met his eyes and saw the pain in them. He dropped his hand from my arm and wrapped his hands around my waist, tugging me closer. "What's happening?"

"I don't know." But I wish I did.

"Did I do this to you?"

"What do you think you did?"

My voice and heart were pleading because I didn't understand the look in his eyes. He looked confused, heartbroken, and ready to bolt.

"Did my being with you turn you into this? I don't even know you."

"What is there to know, Keiran? Everyone always says how weak I am. How you'll destroy me. How I can't handle you. I just wanted to prove them wrong, and I wanted to protect you."

"You killed my father, Lake."

"I did it for you."

"Yeah? What would make you think I would ever be okay with this?" he asked forcefully.

FEARLESS

When I couldn't find the answer, he turned and walked away from me, and I felt my world crumble right before my eyes.

Chapter Five

KEIRAN

SHE WANTED TO protect me? Why did it sound as if she couldn't trust me?

She lied to me and emasculated me with one blow, but worst of all, she put herself at risk. I let her go because maybe she was right. I needed to calm down before I did something I'd regret. I heard her ascend the stairs as I took a seat in the living room.

I listened to the water run and cursed my mind when it ventured to thoughts of her naked. I even pictured her covered in suds, wet, and wanting.

My dick stretched the material of my jeans, and I suddenly felt hot all over. I had to sleep without her last night, and the reminder refueled my anger until I was on my feet, shedding my shirt dampened by the rain. The water had already shut off, and I pictured her waiting for me in the steaming water.

Up the stairs and across the landing, I shed jeans and shoes until I was naked and standing in front of the bathroom door.

When I didn't hear a sound, I pushed open the door and found her head back as she slept. She was completely encased in bubbles, her body hidden by the soapy water. I wanted in.

She must have sensed me because her eyes popped open. Recognition replaced fatigue and she sat up, watching me carefully.

"What are you doing?" Her eyes flew to my cock, and I could see her throat work as she swallowed. When her lips parted, she let out a little sound I wasn't sure she had heard. The top of her breasts were visible now and when she moved, the water parted, granting me a glimpse of her pink nipples as they hardened.

"I want what I was denied last night, and you're not going to deny me now."

"I wasn't going to."

Thank fuck. I wouldn't have forced her if she had, but we didn't need any more strain on our relationship than we had now. I wasn't sure it would hold under the added pressure.

"Then move back." It was a challenge, and she knew it judging the way her eyes blazed with defiance and lust. She scooted back until her back hit the wall of the tub, and I entered the space but didn't sit. My dick was level with her lips and I wasn't about to miss the opportunity to feel her soft lips wrapped around me.

"You know what to do."

I smirked.

She glared.

Too much time passed, and my dick only got harder. When I grew bored with our silent battle, I gripped the back of her neck and brought her closer. "Don't make me ask again."

"I don't recall you asking at all," she snapped.

Fine. If she wanted to play this game, I'd play it better. "Suck me off, baby. Please?"

"Now you're just being coy."

"And you're pissing me off." It took everything not to shove my dick down her throat, but I wasn't that guy anymore, and she didn't deserve him.

"Maybe I don't want you to be gentle with me."

"No?"

"Gentle is not what I need right now," she reassured.

"Open." I could hear the roughness of my voice and feel her skin as my fingers gripped her tighter. When she opened her mouth just a fraction, I plunged inside, forcing past her teeth and feeling them graze my skin. The pain couldn't stop me or make me care. She gagged when my entire length invaded her mouth, and I groaned from the pleasure of her submission. I wanted—no, I needed—to fuck that sweet, smart mouth of hers.

I pulled back and watched her draw in large gulps of air. Spittle dripped down her chin and tears streaked her reddened face.

"Brace." It was her only warning before I plunged inside her mouth again. "Control your breathing," I demanded. I wouldn't take it easy on her—not after she had asked for this. I'd take her to the very edge until she felt as if she was falling and then I'd bring her back.

I fucked with her and she submitted.

This was the game we played.

Until I came down her throat at least.

I slapped my hands against the tile and fought to catch my breath. Only when I finished coming did I slip my cock from her mouth. She mewled and licked at my still hard cock.

"Fuck. You're perfect."

She didn't respond when she let me go and sat back, letting her eyes fall closed again. I stood staring down at her for long moments. I could tell she sensed me because her body was held stiffly, a far cry from when I entered. When it became apparent I was being ignored, I left the bathroom, ignoring the need to assert my dominance.

Fucking wasn't on the menu. Our little moment in the bathroom wasn't supposed to happen. I was supposed to be pissed not lusting after her. I needed to stay focused to protect her.

My father was dead, but she could still go to prison. Her arrest was to scare her and pump information out of her. Thompson was working on learning what evidence they had against her to build a concrete defense.

Thirty minutes had passed when a door slammed, switching my focus to the stairs and the footsteps that were descending them. I felt my stomach tense and told myself not to fuck this up.

"Keiran?" She stood in front of me now, just between my legs. Her voice was soft, and the nervous flutter I hadn't heard in a long time was back. I pulled her down onto my lap and wrapped an arm around her waist to keep her there. The way she stiffened rather than melted told me my intentions weren't missed. "I'm not going to run."

"We'll see." It was all I could say without starting an argument that would take us off course. "Tell me what happened." I had to wait while she wrung her hands and chewed her lip. Her eyes were wide as she looked anywhere but at me. "If you're thinking of lying—"

"I don't think there's much to say. You already know most of it. I killed Mitch because he needed to die."

"Why do you think that fell on your shoulders?" I fought against myself to keep my voice even. What she did was stupid and she'd gotten caught. She had no idea what she was walking into.

She had no idea how to kill and remain detached.

Did I?

"I wanted to protect you."

"I can take care of myself and *I* take care of us."

"Had I told you where Mitch was, you wouldn't have thought it out. You would have gone and killed him and gotten caught. You have too many strikes."

"And did you think it out? Because you did get caught and murder is murder." My voice was no longer level and rose with each word. She shook against me. "You could get twenty-five to life for that piece of shit!"

Her body stiffened more against me if it were even possible. "It's done," she stated coldly.

I used my arm to crush her against me, enjoying the harsh gasp that escaped her lips. A part of me relished the thought of hurting her even just a little. It's how she affected me. She made me want to hurt her and protect her all at once.

"How did you find out where he was?"

"My grandmother is at the same rehabilitation center John kept Mitch."

She flinched when I swore. "How did you find out?"

Her eyes shifted and she didn't answer for some time. "I saw h—his name when I went to visit my grandmother. It was in a folder at the nurse's station."

I felt my own eyes narrow on the wildly beating pulse at her throat.

"And you just happened to see it?"

"Yes." She wouldn't meet my eyes.

"Why didn't you tell me you were going to visit her?"

"Because you would have made a big deal about me going alone and while you were away."

"You fucking think?"

"What do you want me to say?"

"I want you to tell the fucking truth!"

"Keiran, let it go."

CHAPTER SIX

LAKE

THE AIR BETWEEN us that had been charged with heat had just frozen over with four little words.

"What did you just say?"

"You're yelling and it's getting us nowhere. Besides, I'm hungry." His grip had slackened so I used the opportunity to get away. I was lying just as I lied to him all those months ago, and he knew it. But if he found out Q was there and he was the one to kill Mitch, he would kill him.

I tripped over my feet to get to the kitchen and only a hand on the banister stopped my fall. I knew he had followed me. I could feel the heat of his stare on my back.

"Lake. I'm trying—I'm really trying not to hurt you." His voice sounded strained. I spun around to face him. He stood in the doorway, gripping the sides. His impressive chest moved as he took a deep breath.

"Are you going through the checklist?"

"Yes."

"Is the person in front of you worth your anger?"

His eyebrows drew in, turning his visage harsh. "I don't know."

"Is it worth your freedom?"

"I don't know."

"Is it worth losing me?"

"No."

"Then can I eat now?"

He stared for long moments, and I held my breath waiting for his response. When he finally nodded, I moved to turn away. "But I have one more question first."

My heart skipped and my throat ached. I should have known it wouldn't be so easy. "Yes?"

"Do you have any idea what being mine means?" His voice was full of possession.

He still thought he could own me.

Control me.

If I rolled my eyes, Keiran might kill me. He was just that mad but holding my irritation and my own anger at bay was proving a challenge.

"It's been five years. I'm aware." I kept my tone as bland as possible instead of lashing out like I wanted.

"Wanna bet? Cause I say you don't anymore."

"Well, then, enlighten me, Keiran."

"Being mine means you don't think, you don't plan, and you damn fucking sure don't make a move without my permission."

"Excuse me?"

He stalked forward, invading my space. "Piss me off, Lake. I fucking dare you."

"Step back." I issued my own warning. "I'm not taking this shit from you again."

His eyes flickered with what might have been regret, but it was gone in a blink.

"I won't hurt you, baby." He paused to run his finger down my cheek. It slipped from my face roughly, indicating the force of his next words. "But I will punish you."

* * *

SEVEN MONTHS AGO

I STORMED FROM the center, but when I reached my car, I couldn't bring myself to leave. I came here with the intention of killing Mitch, and I wasn't leaving until he was dead.

I drove my car out of sight knowing Q would check to make sure I had actually left and waited, keeping watch on the door. I didn't have to wait long. Q slowly exited the building and crept away all too calmly with his outer shirt folded in his hand.

I decided to follow after him to make sure he left the city and when he did, I turned back for the center.

I waited once again for another employee to take a smoke break and slipped back inside. It didn't occur to me until I was pushing through his room door once again that I no longer had my knife, but it didn't matter.

Mitch was already dead.

The gaping hole in his throat where blood had gushed, staining his gown and sheets, was proof that Mitch had finally met his deserved ending.

With each step toward his bedside, my relief over his death grew.

Keiran was safe.

I felt a sick pleasure witnessing Mitch's lifeless stare. He deserved to suffer more than he did, but I would take what I could get. I hadn't been the one to deliver the deathblow, but my hand in his death was as rewarding as it was damning. I had repaid him for all the evil he had done and the pain he had caused.

Keiran was finally free though a part of me died with Mitch—the innocence that had made me the perfect victim.

"I hope you suffer in hell, Mitch Masters."

He couldn't hear me, and I wished he could. I needed him to know he had paid his debts and that he didn't win. I heard the sudden splatter of his blood on the wall and looked away, fighting the urge to gag. I shrunk back at the gruesome sight of the red lettering on the wall.

For John.

Why could Q write that? It was damning evidence that could come back to haunt us.

Suddenly, I had the feeling that coming back was a mistake. I ran from the room without looking back, and in my frantic need to escape, I stumbled down the wrong hallway and bumped into a nurse.

"Oh!"

"Sorry!" I forced the apology past my aching throat and attempted to get away when she shouted for me to stop. My instinct was to run but with a dead body that would soon be found it wouldn't have been my smartest move.

"Now where are you off to in such a rush?"

"I was just looking for my grams room. I was hoping to visit her before she took her nap." I was amazed at how easy the lies rolled off my tongue.

"What room is she in?"

"408."

"You're in the wrong wing. Take a left down this corridor and make a right at the end."

"Thanks." I tried once again to leave.

"Wait a second."

Fuck. Fuck. Fuck.

She eyed me suspiciously while taking in my appearance. "You're not wearing a visitor's badge. Did you sign in before roaming these halls?"

I felt the first rivulet of sweat on my top lip. I licked it away nervously and stilled my shaking hands. "Um. I'm sorry. I must have missed it."

"Well, come on. I'll walk you to the nurse's station. You're not allowed back here without signing in and wearing a visitor's badge," she berated unnecessarily.

I followed her to the desk where she handed me a clipboard and pen. Q's wasn't on the log, which meant he came in the same way I had. I scribbled my name and looked around at the busy nurses whose eyes were busy pouring over charts.

The coast was clear so I bolted through the front doors.

* * *

KEIRAN HAD DISAPPEARED after delivering his promise, and Keenan and Sheldon came home with a sleepy Ken a few hours later. Keenan disappeared upstairs to put Kennedy down, and Sheldon pulled me into the living room to grill me.

"How was it?" Sheldon asked with a nervous flutter of her hands. I didn't miss the way she looked me over for signs of abuse, and I couldn't say it was completely unwarranted given our history and how angry he was when we left them.

"I'm fine if that's what you're really asking."

"What happened?" she repeated.

I ran down everything, excluding the blowjob, but I did tell her about his threat before he left. The heat in his eyes promised things I wasn't sure I could handle. He was taking my deception better than expected, but something told me not to be fooled by the calm. It was only a prelude to the storm that always followed.

"What do you think he'll do?"

"I wish I knew. He's taking this better than I expected."

"I wouldn't trust it. We all know how—crazy— he can get. He's distracted now, but what happens later when we clear your name? I mean—you didn't do it. Thompson said the arrest was a fluke to uncover a lead, which is illegal by the way."

I didn't hear much of what she said after that. Guilt chomped away at my consciousness. None of them believed I could kill a man much less be responsible. "Sheldon..." I started but nothing came after.

"Jesus Christ." We both swung and faced the entrance. Neither of us noticed Keenan watching us. The knowing look in his eyes and frazzled stare made me feel like I'd swallowed my tongue. He ran a hand down his face, but his expression was frozen in place. "You did it, didn't you?"

"What? Of course, she didn't do it," Sheldon interrupted, saving me from answering. "It's Lake. She doesn't kill people. You should ask your brother what he's hiding."

He turned his cold gaze to his fiancée and if looks could kill... "I think the only one hiding something is standing right here."

"She didn't do it!"

"Why don't we let Lake answer for herself ?" He turned his black gaze back on me. I felt so exposed. "Lake?"

"Leave it alone."

He continued to berate me anyway, and I just stood

there taking it all in. It wasn't easy admitting you were a murderer. "You do know they're after my brother, don't you? What were you thinking?"

"You're not helping, Keenan. You're scaring her."

No. I shook my head, denying Sheldon's claim, but they didn't seem to notice as they began to argue. I wasn't afraid. I refused to be afraid. I spent my life giving in to fear.

"I killed him," I blurted, stealing their attention again. Wide eyes turned on me, but I didn't see them anymore. I only saw Mitch's blood that poured from the open hole in his throat. "I dug the knife deep in that sick son of bitch's throat, and I'd do it again. He deserved to die. He needed to die."

I sounded monstrous even to my own ears, but my emotions were running too wild to care. Keenan swore and ran his hands through his hair. "Does Keiran know?"

"He knows."

"All of it?" His grilling made my palms sweat. I ran them down my jeans and nodded. Keiran knew as much as I could safely tell him. I didn't expect Keenan to grab and pull me into his side. He looked as much at war with his emotions as I was. "I'm sorry I'm being an asshole. I don't want to see you hurt, and I don't want my brother to lose you. What would Ken do without her Auntie Lake?"

His gentle words affected me more than his cold accusations. "What am I going to do, Keenan? I have to fix this."

"Let your man handle this and accept the consequences when it's time."

"I'm not going to lie down and cower because he throws a tantrum. We're not those people anymore."

"It might be better for you. Safer."

"No."

Rather than argue, the beginnings of a smile broke his pensive expression. "Atta girl." He shrugged and released me. "You always have plan B."

"What's plan B?"

"I kick his ass for you if he gets out of hand."

Sheldon snorted, earning a glare from Keenan. "Careful, woman. I still have tonight." Sheldon shifted and paled as I looked between them.

"What happens tonight?"

"I know she told you where Mitch was."

"How?"

"She told me."

"So you think you'll punish her for it?"

He tore his gaze away from Sheldon and smiled a cocky smile. "I know I will."

"Well, maybe I'll have Keiran kick *your* ass."

"You could try, but I've grown a full inch." He comically poked his chest out with his words. "I won't be so easy to beat now."

"Want to bet?" Keiran's deep voice rumbled from the door. His challenging smirk was far too sexy under the circumstances, and a violent shiver shook my body. As if he sensed my desire, his gaze shot to mine and darkened.

"Damn... You two look ready to hump each other right here. It's like watching a mating dance."

I managed to hear Sheldon giggle at her fiancé over the blood rushing to all my pleasure points. Keiran ignored them and ate up the distance between us to take my hand and lead me upstairs.

"Where have you been?" I asked as soon as his old bedroom door was shut.

"Thompson had some information. I met with him to go over your case."

"Don't you think I needed to be there?"

"So you can tell more lies?"

"This is my problem. You had no right."

"I could say the same to you but get this... I have every right. It was my father you killed. It was *my* right you took, and you're mine. *Mine*," he repeated with force. "But don't worry," he whispered, calm again. "You'll have the opportunity to dig a deeper hole for yourself tomorrow morning."

"Whatever you're going to do, just do it already. I'm sick of your threats. I'm sick of you treating me like I'm weak."

"Aren't you?" he spat venomously.

I didn't know I would slap him, but it felt good when I did. I moved to repeat the hurt, but he caught my wrist and yanked me to him. "You're going to regret that." His voice was too level for the anger I knew brewed inside him. I didn't have time to analyze it because I was tossed face down over the side of the bed. I wasn't given time to recover. His fingers pinched my skin as he ripped the button of my jeans apart and stepped between my legs, forcing them open.

"Your niece is in the next room," I reminded. I was grasping at straws.

"Don't worry. I'm not going to fuck you. Consider this a preview."

He leaned down so I felt his breath on my neck. It was ragged and deep, and I knew he was warning me how close he was to losing it—how dangerous it would be for him to let go and was I willing to let us risk it?

The answer escaped me just like my common sense.

"I'm worried about us."

"You should be." He shoved his hand down the front of my jeans and cupped me through my soaked panties. “You did this.”

He flicked my clit, and I moaned against the bed sheets. “But I swear to fuck, Lake. I’m going to fix us.” He plunged inside me, feeding my hunger. I felt his other hand as his fingers threaded my hair and pulled my head back. “When you’re ready, I’m going to take your ass.”

It was more than just a heated threat. It was a promise that excited me as much as if terrified me.

CHAPTER SEVEN

KEIRAN

SHE STARTED TO protest, but I shut her up by nipping the corner of her mouth. I felt her pussy clench hard around my fingers and somehow, I felt the same sensation around my dick.

"When you're ready," I assured. She nodded looking far too relieved, so I hooked my fingers inside her to catch her attention and felt her gasp against the skin of my throat. "But you will be ready."

It was a warning and a threat. Two things she didn't deserve from me. She should have pushed me away and ordered me out, but fuck me, why did her pussy flood my fingers instead?

Even under the worst of circumstances, I could never get enough of how she still managed to come apart at my command.

"Hey, man. I need to you stop whatever freakiness is going on in there. Q just pulled up."

I listened as Keenan's footsteps retreated at the

same time Lake stiffened. I watched her for a beat, but she didn't move. It looked as if she had stopped breathing altogether so I pulled her up and fixed her clothes, but she continued to look spooked.

"Lake," I repeated her name, but it wasn't until I snapped my fingers that she became aware of me again. "What's up with you?"

"What do you mean?"

"Q shows up and you go catatonic on me."

She avoided my gaze and talked to the floor. "Let's just see what he wants."

"What makes you think he wants something?"

"Seriously?"

This back and forth was getting us nowhere so I took her hand and led her downstairs. Dash, Keenan, and Q were in a corner talking too low to hear. "What's up?"

"Hey, man. I heard they bagged Lake. I came to see what I can do."

"It was a bogus arrest. Those pigs must have gotten desperate because they were fishing."

"Are you sure they were only fishing?"

I felt a nervous twitch at the threat of doom. Or maybe I was just being dramatic. Either way, it didn't stop me from being suspicious. I'd never seen Q nervous, but he looked ready to buckle now.

"Why? Do you know something I don't?" Rather than answer, he turned to address my girlfriend. "Tell him, Lake. I'm giving you one chance or I will."

"Quentin, don't do this."

"Tell me what?" My voice had risen to an ear-shattering level, but Q continued to stare down Lake, who stood with her feet braced and her fists clenched. She looked ready to do battle. I was used to her running.

Q finally met my stare and steeled his jaw. "Lake didn't kill Mitch. I did."

Out of the corner of my eye, I noticed Dash inch closer to me. Keenan pushed Lake and Sheldon behind him and braced, but I hadn't moved.

"The fuck did you just say?"

"Kennedy is upstairs," Keenan cautioned. I ignored him and grilled Q with only my gaze. It didn't take him long to start talking when it became apparent Lake wouldn't.

"The day you left with Fitzgerald to secure a deal, the hold on my leave was pushed through. I figured it was too late to call so I just dropped by. You were already gone, but I caught Lake leaving. She looked...off." He cast a quick glance her way and rubbed a hand across his nape. "I followed her to campus and waited. She didn't stay long, but she headed out of town right after so I followed her to Summit. I hung back at first and called you to give you a report, but I couldn't get through to you."

Fuck, I remembered the missed call that day. When I called him back later, he said nothing about Summit. He'd fucking lied to me.

"She snuck in the back. I followed. It took me a while to track her, but I got there just in time. She—she was going to kill him, man. I stopped her. Whatever he'd been feeding her had pissed her off enough to kill him."

He was wrong. She had gone there *to* kill him. Whatever she learned while there was just an added bonus.

I focused on Lake now who stared back at me with unapologetic eyes. She knew I knew, and she didn't seem to care. I counted the lies and promised to pay her back for every one of them.

"He's who you were protecting all this time? He's why you keep lying to me?" I hadn't realized I was closing in on her until Keenan stepped in my path, completely blocking her from me. "Move."

"You're out of line."

"I won't ask you again."

"Then I'll put you down."

I struggled over my next move because I could tell he was serious. The last thing Keenan and I needed was another reason to fight, but I wouldn't let anyone keep me from her.

"No one's fighting," Dash ordered. He came to stand in front of me, blocking Keenan and Lake from my direct line of vision. "You need to talk this out, but only if Lake is willing." He held my gaze until I nodded and then he turned. "Lake, do you want to go with him?"

"Yes." Her voice was small and hesitant. I could tell she was grasping for strength, but her true nature was to submit and she would. I'd see to it if only to keep her safe.

Dash nodded and Keenan moved, also hesitantly. Lake was acting on her own, and my brother was taking orders from Dash now. I began to realize none of them trusted me to do the right thing—to stay rational and act in everyone's best interest.

Did I even trust me?

Five years had passed, but my past was still very much a part of my present. Maybe it always would be. Maybe I was fighting a losing battle, I thought as Lake came to stand by my side.

She looked up at me with wary eyes, and I stared back down at her wondering what I would do to her before taking her hand and leading her to the stairs.

Before I disappeared with my secretive girlfriend, I

met Q's watchful gaze. I managed to refrain from killing him, but I wasn't through with him. I knew when I was outnumbered, and Kennedy didn't deserve another traumatic experience. She loved the lying motherfucker.

I dragged Lake back upstairs because I didn't know what else to do. Once we were safely inside, I slammed the door and trapped her against it.

"What—"

I gripped her lips a little too roughly. Her skin would bruise, and I relished the idea of seeing her soft skin affected by me. "No more lies. I'm losing control." It sounded like a plea because only she could keep me together, but if I broke... I wasn't sure I could be pieced back together.

"You know it all."

"Do I?"

She nodded and squealed when I slammed my forearms on the door on either side of her head. "You led me—you led everyone—to believe Mitch was still out there, all to feed your lie. I don't even know who the fuck you are!" I breathed her in and stole her ragged breath. Her chest heaved against my own. I needed to get closer. I wanted to intimidate her. To make her yield so I wouldn't feel as if I was losing her.

"I had to. What else could I do?"

I ignored her question and turned away to pace. I felt caged. I needed to release, but that would destroy us. "What else did he tell you, huh?"

"He told me who killed John."

The blood in my veins hardened to ice. My skin prickled and the hair on the back of neck rose. "Who?"

"Greg."

The face of the private investigator I had hospitalized the day I found out Kennedy was kidnapped formed, and I gritted my teeth to keep from spewing as much venom and hate as I could muster. I should have killed him. If I had, John would be alive. It was the first time I expressed regret over his death. It was still hard for me to admit love for the man who saved me.

"There's more." I didn't bother to respond, but I didn't have to. "He was hired by your father to kidnap Kennedy."

"Mitch didn't have any money." Any money he did have couldn't have been enough to hire three men to kidnap someone.

"He said someone owed him."

"Who?"

"He didn't say."

The room descended into silence, but I was too in tune with her not to notice she had more to say. I could sense her inner struggle.

"Talk, Lake."

"I won't apologize for protecting you. You don't want to lose me, but I refuse to lose you." That wasn't what I was expecting her to say. I inched closer despite the voice in my head telling me to stay away. "Tell me you can forgive me."

"Do you think now is the time to ask for forgiveness? You're still lying to me."

"Protecting you!"

"I don't need your fucking protection."

"I don't think you're in the right place to hear what else I have to say."

"So help me—"

"Uncle Keke?" We both froze at the tiny voice infiltrating the door.

Lake flung open the door and found Ken standing on the other side clutching a one-armed doll.

"Ken, baby, what's wrong?"

"I broke my doll." She lifted the doll up for Lake to

inspect with fat tears in her eyes. Lake took the doll while I scooped her up. I met Lake's eyes over her head, and we silently called a truce.

"Where's the arm, sweetie?" Ken dug the arm from the pocket of what Sheldon called her day pajamas. I traded Ken for the doll, and she immediately hid her face on my baby's shoulder while I inspected the doll. It looked like a simple fix. I popped the arm back in the doll and tested it out. Chances were it would break again, but to a four-year-old, it would be a miracle.

"What's her name, Ken?"

"Lulu," she answered without lifting her head.

"Well, I think Lulu is all better and ready for you to play with her." Her head lifted then, and when she noticed her doll looking good as new, her eyes grew as wide as saucers. Her girlish squeal threatened to blow my eardrums as she scrambled from Lake's arms and snatched the doll from my lap.

"Thank you, Uncle Keke. She scrambled up my lap and choked me with a hug for which she made up for with the sweetest kiss to my cheek. Lake watched with tears in her eyes, and I restrained from rolling my eyes.

Women.

I pulled her to my lap when Ken jumped down to run screaming for her dad.

"That was real sweet of you, Uncle Keke." She smiled, but I could only stare back at her. Her smile fell, and worry replaced the temporary escape Kennedy had brought with her broken doll. "What is it?" Her voice shook, and I felt it in my chest.

"I don't think I can forgive you."

* * *

I SHOULDN'T HAVE said it. For the rest of the night, I

had to pretend not to notice her fight not to cry and then to finally give in and cry all night. Like a bastard, I ignored her turmoil and offered her no comfort. I knew what went through her head as she cried.

Did I still love her?

Would I leave her?

I knew, and I didn't do shit about it.

Every night she spent in my bed, I always held her in my arms, safe from the monsters that threatened to break us apart. She counted on that connection just as I did, but we were both denied it tonight because of her lies and my pride.

When I couldn't trust myself anymore not to give in, I left her alone for the solitude the couch provided.

In five years, Lake had taught me how to love, but she hadn't taught me how to forgive. Until now, I had no idea it was something that still eluded me. Effortlessly, she had become my reason, so while I knew I could never let her go, a part of me feared we would never be the same. I couldn't bring myself to trust her. I only felt the need to control her for purely selfish reasons. I couldn't be without her. I refused.

"Hey, man." Q's greeting broke the silence I had settled into and already, I could feel my jaw harden and set. He appeared from the kitchen, holding a beer and dropped into the recliner adjacent to the couch I took over. "We need to talk."

You don't fucking say.

I sat up abruptly and caught that his body was tense and ready for battle.

"What the fuck were you doing there with her?" I whispered as loud as I could without breaking the quiet peace in the house.

"Protecting her like you told me to," he answered just as harshly. "I couldn't get in contact with you to tell you my leave had been approved and she had fled town, so what the fuck was I supposed to do, huh?"

"And after you killed my father? What then?"

"We both know you don't give a shit about him, and we both know what would have happened if I'd told you what she'd done."

"I don't give a shit. She's mine."

"She won't stay that way if you keep being a dick. She's yours yet you keep finding the need to enforce it. The only thing threatening your hold on her is you."

He might have been right. Fuck... I *knew* he was right. It didn't stop me from destroying everything that was good for me.

"Look, it's done. Mitch is dead. I know you wanted to get to him first, but..." He took a swig of his beer and then picked at the label as his frown deepened.

"Why?" I had to know how Lake convinced him to kill Mitch so recklessly.

"John."

"Come again?"

"Your uncle. He didn't deserve to die the way he did and I owed him.

"How the fuck so?"

"He saved my life, and he didn't even know it."

"That's because he didn't care."

He shook his head and regarded me with pity. "The saddest part about this is you really believe your uncle didn't care about you."

"Ten years of absence will make a person think so."

"He saved your life! He saved my life." His voice echoed around us but neither of us seemed to notice.

"Do you really believe that?"

"You really don't?" When I didn't respond, he huffed in frustration and shook his head. "You cannot be that blind."

"John was a coward."

"And you? Are you any better?"

"What the hell are you getting at?"

"You're going to lose that girl because you're afraid she'll break you, but maybe it's what you need, man. You can't be invincible forever."

"Isn't that why one would *be* invincible?"

"Fuck, man. You might be right." He cracked a smile, and I found myself grinning back at him. Why was my relationship with my childhood friend unbendable when my relationship with Lake had cracked right down the middle? Could it have been because she affected me more than anyone else did? I trusted her with a part of me that no one had been able to touch before her.

I groaned and leaned back, covering my eyes with my hands. How the fuck would I get us past this? Ensuring Lake never had the chance to deceive me again was high on my list of priorities.

"How did they bag her?"

I released a humorless laugh. "She signed in. They have her signature on file the day of the murder."

He was already shaking his head before I finished speaking. "That's impossible. She snuck in the back. I saw her."

My chest threatened to break open from the harsh pounding of my heart. She was still lying to me. "Did you see her leave?"

"She left before I did a sweep of the room."

"What about her car?"

"I was a little preoccupied with not getting caught with blood on my hands. Besides, why would she stick around?."

"She told me her grandmother is living at the facility. It's the only reason they aren't able to pin the murder on her yet. She has a valid excuse for being there. The father of her boyfriend also residing there was just a coincidence." It was the story Thompson was able to spin. It was a rocky defense but the best we had. He was also planning to exploit the illegal arrest in court and obliterate their credibility. Whatever idiot made that call would regret it for the rest of his life. I'd make sure of it.

"It sounds like you need to talk to her." He must have anticipated my intent because he added, "But not tonight. It's been a long day. Sleep it off. You need a clear head because your girl's got it in her head that you need to be protected. She won't give in if you push her."

I wanted to argue the point that Lake had been my toy for years, and I knew exactly how to break her when I realized that breaking her was the last thing I wanted. I wanted Lake strong, but I didn't want her fighting my battles. Hell, I didn't even want her fighting her own.

While I struggled, Q stood and announced he was crashing in the basement. I laid my head back against the couch cushions and stared at the ceiling as if the answer to how to deal with my girlfriend was in the paint.

The next morning, after I'd showered, I found her sitting on the side of the bed staring down at her phone. "What's up?" It was meant to sound casual. The way she'd jumped and her eyes widened, I knew I sounded anything but.

"Do you think we can reschedule our court appointment? I'm due for my birth control shot." She looked down at my morning wood tenting my jeans. "It's not something I should miss," she admitted with flushed cheeks.

"We can't reschedule. It's too late. It was also a condition of your release, warrant or not." I didn't add that I was eager to get this handled so I could get her home alone where there would be nowhere for her to run and no one to interfere.

I expected her to argue but she simply nodded, grabbed her toiletry bag, and walked past me to leave the bedroom. She stopped in the threshold and said, "You can't touch me." She slammed the door, leaving me alone to stare after her. I could tell by her demeanor that I had fucked up royally last night, and if we ever got past this, I'd be paying for it for a long time.

I took her spot on the edge of the bed and waited until she finished her shower. When she returned, her eyes avoided me as she moved about the room, clutching the towel closely around her. She was hiding herself from me and it pissed me off more than her silence.

"Lake."

She stiffened before giving me her full attention. "Yes?"

"Why did you go back?"

CHAPTER EIGHT

LAKE

"WHY DID YOU go back?" I was beginning to expect the unexpected so when he asked me a question that seemed out of the blue, I wasn't really surprised, but I was confused. "Q said you slipped into the facility through the back entrance. You must have gone back because how else did your signature get on the logs?"

There was murder in his eyes, and I wasn't sure if the truth would only provoke his bred nature to the surface. "I never left."

"Explain," he growled. I felt the single word like an ache in my bones.

"I waited until Q left and then went back."

"Why?"

"I don't know."

"You don't know?"

"It's what I said, Keiran." God, I felt so exposed. Without clothes, I was even more vulnerable and he looked ready to either fuck me or murder me.

"What happened?"

"I got spooked. Q... he left a message on the wall that said 'For John'—in blood." The veiny throb I'd come to identify as an indicator of Keiran's breaking point made its first appearance, and I wondered if I'd just made things worse. "I suppose he didn't tell you."

He didn't bother to answer and continued to grill me. "And?"

"I ran down the wrong hallway. A nurse caught me. She knew I hadn't signed in because I wasn't wearing a visitor's pass."

"Why didn't you run?"

"With a dead body down the hall? I would have been implicated months ago." And maybe I would have if it hadn't been for the company's lack of foresight on effective filing. Months of logs were missing altogether or stored in the wrong places. If it hadn't been for the investigation, the issue might never have been brought to light.

"Continue," he ordered.

"There's nothing else. I signed in, and when the coast was clear, I left."

"It never occurred to you that the log would implicate you? That it was all one big fuck-up from the get go?"

"Every day since then, but he's dead now. That's all that matters."

"Until you're in prison and I—I—" He made a noise that terrified me and then shot up from the bed to pace.

"You what?"

"Forget it. So Quentin killed him, and you're his accomplice. Where do we go from here, Lake?"

"You're asking me?"

"You seem to think you've got the murder game all figured out. You tell me."

"I never claimed this would be easy. I never wanted to lie to you, but if you want me to say it, then no, I couldn't trust you. You're violent, reckless, and unpredictable."

I held my breath and waited for the explosion that never came. The only sign that he'd heard was his darkened pupils. Wordlessly, he disappeared only to reappear minutes later.

I was doubly confused when he shed his shirt and reached past me to toss it and grab a bottle I hadn't noticed he had laid on the bed. I tried to get a better look, but he captured my chin between his fingers and held my head. Time seemed to stretch as he silently studied me. I knew him well enough to know he was challenging me without uttering a single word. I lifted my chin and matched his gaze. I wouldn't back down. Whatever game he played, I'd play it harder.

"You told me I can't touch you," he said slowly.

"My birth control—"

"Kneel."

"Excuse me?"

Instead of repeating, he anchored his hands around my arms and faced me away from him. He then flattened his hand on my spine and forced me down. I struggled but he restrained me until I couldn't struggle anymore.

"Shhh. Don't speak. I can't control myself if you speak."

"This is control?"

"No, Lake. This is me taking control." The towel—my only shield—was peeled away from my body effortlessly. I couldn't see anything but the sheets trapped under my body. I listened to the sound of his harsh breathing as the smell of his freshly washed skin infiltrated all of my senses.

"Remember what I promised you?"

"You'll have to be more specific." I sensed his smile as he ran a hand down my spine to my bare ass. He stopped there and I tensed.

"I told you I would take you here..." he slipped a finger between my legs to tease forbidden areas, "when you were ready."

"Yes." Was I consenting or acknowledging his promise? God, I wished I knew, because he slid his knee, forcing my legs wider.

"I can't wait that long," he whispered.

Oh, fuck. Did he mean—

I wasn't able to finish piecing it together because he kissed me. A harsh, possessive kiss that promised danger and retribution.

"If I can't have your pussy... I'll have to settle for the next best thing." The ice in his voice froze the blood in my veins until I felt as if I would shatter.

"Keiran—"

"Shh..." His lips trailed the side of my forehead, down to the corner of my lips. After pressing a little peck, he shifted me, bringing my hips higher in the air. "I promise to make you want it."

Could I want this?

I panted and writhed on top of the sheets as his hands freely roamed my body. Unexpectedly, I felt a hot, wet trail of desire escape me and run down the inside of my thigh. I was both mortified and hungry for something I wasn't even sure I wanted.

"Goddamn," he moaned and trailed a fingertip over the thigh that exposed my arousal. "You're dripping, baby. Don't tell me you don't want this, or I might have to fuck you harder."

He reached for the bottle that lay near my head and popped the top. He took a single pass over the heated skin of my ass before spreading me for his teasing. I groaned and gripped the sheets between my teeth when the first wet finger entered me. I sucked in a breath a little too harshly until I was left gasping.

"Easy," he cautioned and slipped his finger deeper. I exhaled and my body accepted more of his invasion. I heard him shift and then his tongue was between my legs, devouring and delivering me to heights I'd never reached, all the while his finger never stopped fucking my ass.

"There's no part of you I can't have," he promised after I fell apart in his mouth.

Stop this!

"Yes." Apparently, my brain and body were at war. I turned my head in time to see him tear open his jeans with a savagery unlike men of our time. A moan escaped my lips as I braced myself for his invasion. The anticipation alone almost killed me, and when his cock pressed against me, ready to take, my heart stopped beating. He used my hair as a noose and brought his face closer.

"Keiran? Lake?" Sheldon's voice on the other side of the door was a like a bucket of cold water, resuscitating and drowning me simultaneously.

"Yes?" The hostility in Keiran's tone was unmistakable.

"Your niece is wondering if you two are coming to have pancakes with her before your court appearance."

And just like a mother, Sheldon had expertly scolded us by reminding us that Kennedy could hear us, and we had somewhere to be. Another moment passed, Sheldon had already retreated back downstairs, and Keiran had still not moved away. He gripped my hair tighter in his fist and brought his lips to my ear.

"Later," he promised, causing me to shudder violently.

* * *

I WAS SENSITIVE to the touch, but Keiran insisted on keeping me in his clutch. A hand on my back, my neck, my thigh. He imprisoned me with a single touch. Several times, I attempted to move away only to be dragged closer. We were standing outside the courthouse when I decided to say something. "I don't want you to touch me if it's because you don't trust me."

"My hands are on you because I want to touch you. Is that a problem?" His brow lifted and the blank look in his eyes told me he wouldn't care if it were.

I wanted to say something cool, snarky, and witty, but nothing came to mind. I was getting tired of the back and forth. One minute we were cold, then hot, and then cold again. I chose to ignore him while we waited to see the judge. Thompson was already waiting when we arrived so we didn't have to wait long.

It was a while into the hearing after muddling through so much legal jargon I even began to understand what was happening.

"Your honor, my client's rights per the Fourth Amendment to the U.S. Constitution was violated the night of June 13th when an arrest was made without a warrant or probable cause."

"Yes, I was made aware of the disgrace Detective Bennett and Detective Fulson made of the entire justice system. What is your point?"

"I request that the two detectives be dismissed from the case, and my client should be let go without bail due to charges not being brought against her to date."

"Your honor, we do have evidence placing Lake

Monroe at the scene, as well as probable cause that she murdered Mitch Masters given their history."

"Then you should have used it to obtain a warrant." The judge dismissed the DA with a glance and regarded Thompson with an equally cold look. Counselor, I am granting your appeal. The detectives responsible will be dismissed and replaced. Lake Monroe is free to go without bail."

The hearing lasted less than fifteen minutes. I was still in disbelief an hour later when we were sitting on one of Dash's many conference rooms at the request of Thompson.

"I'll cut right to the chase. That was only the initial hurdle. The investigation into Mitch Master's murder is ongoing, and because of this small victory, they'll come at you harder, and we have to be ready."

"How will we accomplish that?"

His gaze flicked to Keiran. Something had passed between them before he returned his gaze to me. "The chances of you being indicted increases with each secret you keep. It's not my job to implicate you, but it is my job to acquit you." I could feel Keiran staring as if he could exam my very soul as the lawyer spoke. "As of now, there haven't been any charges officially brought against you, but that could change at any time. You need to be ready for that. You both do. Your grandmother's residency at the center is a strong alibi, but if there is a witness or evidence that can place you any closer to the scene than necessary, it could destroy our entire defense." He clasped his hand together and leaned forward. "Is there such a person?"

I saw Keiran tense, and his fists clenched over the polished oak. We were both thinking of the nurse who had now become a threat. With those simple words spoken, her life had just started to count down.

I met Keiran's gaze and pleaded with my eyes, and when I didn't seem to get through to him, I panicked and silently mouthed, "No."

"Good." Oh no. I'd spoken the word out loud unintentionally. "This means we have a better chance of beating this case before it even starts."

Yes, but only because Keiran would ensure the nurse never had the chance to testify. Thompson left, and Keiran and I continued to stare at each other long after the door had closed.

"No."

"You didn't leave me much choice, did you baby?" The calm tone of his voice belied his malicious intent.

"I don't want anyone dying for me."

His eyes narrowed and his lips curled. "You can't say that after you helped kill my father." He then stood up seemingly to dismiss the conversation.

"I don't want anyone *innocent* dying for me. I said no."

He shoulders tensed as he gripped the door handle. "It's not your decision. Besides... you didn't give *me* a chance to say no."

Chapter Nine

KEIRAN

I PRACTICALLY RAN from the conference room to keep from doing something that would make our situation worse. How the fuck could she ask me not to protect her and at the same time, assume the worse about me? It seemed as if Mitch's murder was bringing to light everything that remained unresolved between us.

She still didn't trust me.

I didn't think Lake would ever lie to me, but with each secret, I felt the pressing need to protect myself from her—to distance myself from her and the ache she was causing in my chest. Her fearless chase was breaking us.

"Why are you walking away?" I heard her call out once we were in the dark parking garage.

"I'm not. I'm running away from doing something we'll both regret. Don't push me right now."

"When are we going to stop running away from each other? I fucked up, but I'm not your enemy so stop treating me like I am."

What? She thought I was treating *her* like the enemy?

I pivoted on my heel and ate up the distance between us. One quick glance around showed we were alone. I grabbed her and forced her against my chest. She refused to submit. I could see it in her eyes, but she wasn't fighting me, either because her mind still cautioned her that a part of me was still dangerous.

"I used to think that no one or nothing could make me turn back because there was nothing worth losing you over. I never counted on you being the one."

Her gaze narrowed with suspicion clouding the blue-green coloring of her eyes. "What does that mean?"

It means I'd give anything—sacrifice anyone—to save her.

"It means get in the car. I'm taking you home."

I released her and waited for her to obey. For her sake and mine, she stepped around me and got in. I didn't move until I heard the door close. When I got in, I turned up the volume and let the heavy guitar of Meg Meyer's Desire fill the tension between us.

Every dark desire she confessed to I wanted with Lake, and when I got her alone, there was nothing that would stop me from seeing it through. She had forgotten my claim on her mind and body. It would be my pleasure reminding her.

For eleven hours, the anticipation built, and she became more nervous with each passing hour. I could almost tell what she was thinking in the way she'd wring her hands or tap her foot. The nervous glances she didn't think I caught were a dead giveaway.

She was scared and trying hard not to feel it. She nearly jumped out of her skin when I slid my hand across the console and gripped her bare thigh. The tight skirt she wore was modestly sexy and left me hard all day. I couldn't stop thinking about the feel of her thighs wrapped around me as I took what I wanted.

It was late when I pulled into the driveway and night had fallen hours ago. I was dead tired, and I could see the same in her eyes when she glanced at me nervously as I shut off the engine. Silently, I gathered our bags and we entered our rented house. The door shutting was like the closing of a bad chapter in our life, and I wondered how much worse I would have to make it before it got better.

"I'm going to pack a bag and stay with a friend." She spoke so timidly that the finality of her words was almost missed.

"Come again?"

She lifted her chin and said, "I think we should spend a night apart."

"You think so, do you?" She slowly nodded but suddenly, looked unsure of her answer. "What makes you think I'm letting you go anywhere?"

"How are you going to keep me here?"

I laughed at her counter but felt none of the humor. It was as if she didn't know me at all. "How?" I repeated. Her face wrinkled in confusion, but then she must have seen it in my eyes because at the very next moment, she ran.

She fucking ran.

And just like the monster I was, I chased.

She had no idea what had reawakened in me due to her lies.

When I caught her in the kitchen and turned her around to witness the fear in her eyes, I felt the painful feeling of regret that quickly disappeared when I reminded myself this was all because of her lies.

As hard as I tried to be, I couldn't take the look in her eyes so I forced her around and bent her over the nearest flat surface, which happened to be the table. With a forceful kick, I sent one of the chairs flying across the room to bounce off the wall and stepped behind her.

"What you think is no longer a concern, and frankly, I don't give a shit."

"Let me go now, or I swear you'll be sorry when you do."

"Is that a promise?"

"It's a guarantee."

I froze. The ice in her voice did that. It should have deterred me, but it only convinced me that only the old me—the monster—could stop her from being reckless. I needed her to fear me again.

"The only guarantee is when I'm through that you won't be able to walk." My fingers scratched her skin, causing her to cry out when I forced her skirt around her waist and tore away her panties until they were bunched around her thighs. I snatched open my jeans and released the painful erection I managed to conceal all day. One pass of my fingers over her heated pussy revealed she was wet and eager.

Without hesitation, I entered her with everything I had and stole her cry with my hand over her mouth. The force of my entrance drove her to the tips of her toes. Her body shook with the pleasure she didn't want to feel. I gripped her neck with the hand that covered her mouth, pushed her flat, and used my own weight to keep her there as I gave it to her in a way she'd never forget and would eventually crave.

I let *him* take over and hoped that one day she would forgive me.

"Do you remember me?" I forced myself deeper inside her, wanting to hear that little breathless sound she made when it hurt so good. "Is he who you wanted?"

"I want you," she moaned. "I don't want this."

I didn't want this either...

"I wish I could believe you." I tortured her clit with my fingers until she came on my cock with a scream that only made my dick harder. She writhed against the table as if seeking more, unaware that I was about to give her more than she could handle.

I brushed her lips with my fingers. "Suck."

She obeyed and took the digits inside her hot mouth. I left her body and surveyed my dick, which was sufficiently coated with her juices, as she eagerly tasted my fingers as if it were my dick. That all came to a halt when I began to enter her. My fingers fell from her mouth when she let out a startled cry.

"Keiran," she whimpered. "What are you—"

"I intend to fuck you again. I'm going to take your ass. Make you submit. Don't fight it," I cooed when she struggled. "Breathe."

I was half way inside her when she finally began to give up the fight. I pressed a kiss on her spine as a reward and slid the rest of the way home. A violent shudder passed through me when I was fully seated, and I was pretty sure Lake had stopped breathing altogether.

"Breathe, baby. I need you to breathe." I waited for the first breath and moved on the exhale. "Good girl." I didn't prepare her for what came next. I simply took.

Hard and unrelenting, I fucked her, demanding her submission while fighting not to give in myself. She owned me, and she didn't even know it.

Her breathless cries filled with pain and pleasure was a shock to my system, driving my hips into her harder. She sucked me in. The need to come built with each stroke until I couldn't fight it anymore.

Chapter Ten

LAKE

THE NEED TO run had been present—screaming even—since leaving Nevada. Touching me, fucking me, taking me was the boy I had fallen in love with, but not the man who made me feel safe and loved. He moved inside me with a relentless power I hadn't felt since he blackmailed me five years ago. Even more surprising was the excitement I felt remembering a much darker Keiran and the way he would fuck me unapologetically.

A strange, foreign part of me didn't want to be taken. I wanted to conquer him the same way he sought to conquer me. With a secret smile he couldn't see, I took a less submissive stand and braced my hands closer to my body, transferring my weight to my hands.

"Lake," he grunted.

His fingers dug into the skin of my hips, and I could feel him watching me. I took a peek over my shoulder and found his eyes staring seductively at half-mast but watching me just as intently.

"What are you—" I held his gaze as I made my next move and lifted my right leg, placing it on the edge of the table. "Oh, baby," he moaned.

Confident that he held me securely, I hooked my right arm around his neck, twisting my upper body and bringing our faces close together. His eyes widened with wariness and surprise.

"If my big, bad wolf wants to conquer me, he'll have to do better."

Challenge replaced surprise when his eyes narrowed. I could feel his chest rumble as he growled and fucked me impossibly harder. He lost the struggle with his conscience and forced me back against the tabletop. When his thrusts turned desperate, his fingers found my pussy and stroked me until I trembled and came apart under him.

When I didn't think our fucking could turn anymore animalistic, he ripped my shirt up the back, pulled from my ass with a savage growl, and spurted his come on my back. I collapsed against the table, both sated and outraged. My legs couldn't hold me up for long, so I collapsed but was caught in his arms and carried toward the stairs.

"In case you didn't catch that, you can't leave."

I didn't have the strength to argue so I let him carry me to the shower. I even let him wash my hair and bathe me, and when he put me to bed, I didn't argue. Almost immediately, he fell into a deep sleep with me anchored to him by an arm tight around my waist. After ten minutes of careful maneuvering, I managed to escape our bed. I quietly dug out the handcuffs he liked to use during our frisky days and handcuffed his hands together. It wouldn't restrain him for long, but it would slow him down.

I dressed, put the key in the bathroom sink, and

sent him a text with the location. He'd wake before morning, and I knew when he did, he would tear the house apart looking for me before he'd think to free himself.

I didn't stop to pack a bag or even have second thoughts. I escaped the apartment, his anger, and ultimately, the doom of our relationship.

I was mentally and physically exhausted so I relished the short drive. The apartments were pretty nice and also ridiculously expensive. I made my way up to the top floor, knocked and waited. My spine was slowly giving out with each second I stood outside the apartment door. The need to run and beg for forgiveness clawed its way inside and threatened to rip out my newfound spine. After I felt as if I'd been bathed in sweat, the door finally opened.

Jesse stood in the entrance, shirtless with sleep-tussled hair. His eyebrow lifted and his mouth quirked as he gripped the door. With his brown, curly hair and surfer's body, he was every girl's—or guy's—heartthrob. His sexual preference was still in question and was a subject neither of us ever felt the need to bring up. Keiran had reluctantly told me about the kiss with Q after I remarked on the noticeable tension between them. I'd never suspected Jesse might be gay, but once I knew, it somehow started to make sense.

"Don't you think he's going to look for you here?" he greeted.

I took that as an invitation and ducked under his arm. "I'm not trying to hide from him. I'm just trying to get away from him."

"It's Keiran. You'd need to hide to get away. You know he's coming after you."

"You'll protect me."

He snorted and disappeared down the hall. "So

what happened?" he yelled from what I assumed was his bedroom.

"Oh, Keiran being Keiran and me trying not to be intimidated by him."

"You think he still wants to intimidate you?"

"He thinks he's protecting me by making me afraid of him again."

He didn't respond right away, but then I heard a hesitant, "Are you?"

"No." And surprisingly, it was true. Keiran was trying to hold us together the only way he knew how, and it only made me sad for what I did to us.

"Then why are you here?"

"Because I know my wolf," I whispered wistfully. Here I was, running from him and lusting after him at the same time. God, I needed therapy.

I didn't think he'd hear me, but then he said, "All right, Red." He emerged from his bedroom and tossed a wad of clothes at me. "I'm assuming you don't have anything to sleep in. Shower's free if you need it."

Keiran had meticulously washed away his release from my back, and I wondered if it was out of guilt for degrading me the way he had. I used Jesse's spare bedroom to change into his t-shirt and flannel, then I walked into the kitchen in time to see and hear Jesse end a call and open the refrigerator while trying too hard to look unassuming.

He avoided my gaze and I grew suspicious. "Who was that?"

"What?"

"Who were you on the phone with?"

"Seriously?"

"Seriously."

He hesitated and then pulled out a carton of milk. "Your man."

I ignored the flutter in my stomach and watched Jesse disappear inside the spacious pantry to grab a box of cereal. How did he find me so fast?

"He called you?"

"No. I called him."

I felt my eyes narrow, but it didn't matter. Jesse had yet to look at me. "I'm beginning to question whose friend you really are."

"He's my partner, Lake. What did you expect?"

"You're *my friend*! God—" I yelled. I immediately turned on my heel and stormed from the kitchen. I could hear him chasing after me, and I sped up.

"Lake wait."

"Go fuck yourself."

"You can't leave. He knows you're here, but I convinced him to stay away for the night. If you leave, he'll drag you back home and that's the last thing you two need right now. He told me what you did to him. I have to say... I'm impressed." He sounded amused and proud.

"I'm not looking for compliments, asshole. You sold me out." I ran for the spare bedroom and snatched up my clothes. Screw the both of them and their men code. I heard Jesse's knock but ignored it as I ripped off his shirt and replaced it with my own. I hated putting on worn clothing after showering, but there was no way I was staying with Keiran's guard dog all night. It was as if he was still winning—still in control. Fuck that.

Jesse did everything he could, minus physical restraint, to stop me from leaving. I flipped him off and fled the apartment.

Keiran was the ass, and yet I was roaming the city in the middle of the night. At that moment, it was hard for me to believe that much had changed about us. Exhausted, I spent the night in a hotel where I should have gone in the first place. By morning, I wasn't any more prepared to face Keiran so I shopped for toiletries and a change of clothes. I then drove five and half hours to the only ally that I had left.

"Whoa, girly. What are you doing here?" Di answered the door, appearing wide awake and wearing a crop top and sweatpants. "Keiran lets you out to play this far?"

"I need a distraction, and I need you to keep your mouth closed about it."

"Don't tell me there's trouble in paradise."

"Di..."

"Fine. Come in." She moved away and let me inside. I followed her into the living room where she plopped down on the couch. "But I want to know what turned you into such a raging bitch."

"I'm not raging."

"But you are acting like a bitch. So spill."

"Mitch is dead," I blurted.

"I heard."

"And it's because of me," I finished solemnly.

"No fucking way," she grinned. I shook my head at her misplaced enthusiasm.

"I didn't kill him."

"But you wanted to."

I so fucking wanted to.

"Have you met his father?"

"No, but I've heard he's a real catch."

"Where are you getting your information from?"

"My bestie," she sighed and lay back against the cushions and threw her left leg over the top. "How is he adapting to daddyhood, anyway?"

"Keenan? He rules with an iron fist," I said sarcastically.

"So, what did you have to do with Mitch's murder

and kudos to you, bitch. He needed to be put down a long time ago."

"I went there to kill him, but Q stopped me."

Di stiffened and her eyes dulled as she stared at me in disbelief. "Q—Quentin was there?"

"He followed me out there the day Keiran went away for business. Apparently, he was assigned to be my watchdog."

"Ever the obedient little slave," she whispered absentmindedly. She stared off, appearing lost. Her body trembled ever so slightly.

"Di?" It took three tries of calling her name to bring her back from wherever she had been trapped.

"Yeah?"

"Where did you go?"

"Somewhere I have no intention of sharing with you or anyone, girly."

"Maybe you should talk about it," I mumbled.

"What?" Her tone was angry, but her green eyes were wide as vulnerability burst from their depths. Di had always been a puzzle, but right now, she looked like a frightened girl.

"You don't talk about your past, but it's clear your past is what haunts you. Therapy might—"

Her eyes narrowed into angry slits, and it shut me up. "Do you want to be kicked out of my apartment?"

"Ok, I won't go there, but can I just say one thing?"

She clenched her teeth and shifted. "What?"

"Fuck being afraid."

I could tell she tried to fight it, but she finally cracked a smile and gained back that sarcastic twinkle in her eye. "You kill a man and you grow a pair of balls."

"I think it's the other way around."

She snorted and said, "Not for you it isn't. Want to get a mani?"

We spent the day getting pampered and spent the night drinking away our issues. I expected Keiran to be lurking around every corner, but as it turned out, I didn't see or hear from him for two days.

CHAPTER ELEVEN

KEIRAN

IT WAS HARD leaving Lake behind, but I had a pretty good idea of where she hid. The need to conquer and control was overwhelming, but I managed to curb those urges in order to protect her. It was why I was stalking the dilapidated house in the middle of the night while she hid from me.

For two days, I watched the home and the family that lived inside. On the third day, when I memorized their routine, I decided to move in. I knew at this time, the woman who lived inside would be getting ready to take her night shift while her husband gave into a drunken night of sleep and the two young girls slept.

When her back was turned, I muffled the scream that would come and whispered, “I’m going to move my hand. Don’t scream and don’t run.” I felt her nod and ignored the guilt at the tremble of her thin frame.

“Wh–who are you.” She fumbled over her words as she retreated. She cast a nervous glance over her shoulder toward the house.

"That's not important."

"I think it is," she countered, keeping her voice low as if she were the intruder. "You're creeping around my yard in the middle of the night, young man."

If this weren't such a high-risk situation, I would have laughed at her need to scold an intruder. "A few months ago, you saw a girl at the facility you work for."

"I see many young girls. You'll have to be more specific."

"A resident was murdered that same day, and you're going to testify against this girl in the murder case."

The grave recognition in her eyes was telling. "Y—yes. I remember. I saw her there the day he was murdered. I'm only giving my recount."

"No, you're not."

"I'm sorry?"

"You're not going to testify." Confusion twisted her expression that quickly turned to fear.

"Are you threatening me?"

"No." I could tell by her deepening frown that I only added to her confusion.

"Are you here to kill me?"

"I won't kill you."

"Then I don't understand."

"I'm here to make you an offer."

"And if I refuse?"

I was growing tired of this chain of questioning. "You won't."

"I'm sorry, but I won't lie to the police for a perfect stranger."

"What about for your life and that of your two little girls tucked inside? They aren't safe."

"Don't touch my little girls."

"I have no intention of hurting them or you, but can your husband say the same?"

"What do you mean?"

Instead of answering, I lifted her arm, ignoring her flinch, to push up her shirtsleeve and reveal the bruising on her arm. "He beats you, and you let him."

"I don't let him."

"You haven't left either."

"It's not that simple. He's only like this because he lost his job and hasn't been able to get another one. He used to be so kind and loving."

"The day you get a clue might be the day it's too late."

"Young man, I won't explain my life to a stranger."

"So let the priest who barely knew you tell your story at your funeral."

She gasped and shrunk back and suppressed the temptation to roll my eyes. "You're very cruel for one so young."

"You have no idea about cruelty. I do. Cruelty would be reporting you and your husband to Child Protective Services so they can find the bruises he leaves on them and take your daughters away for child endangerment."

She grabbed onto my shirt. "Don't. Please."

"And just when you think your nightmare couldn't go on, I'd kill your alcoholic, abusive husband in his sleep and leave you to find him in the morning when you return from the job that feeds his habit."

Her pleas turned into deep sobs as she sunk to the ground. I wouldn't kill her, and I meant it, but I would take everything from her to keep Lake. I helped the emotional woman to her feet and held her against my chest to keep her stable and waited until she calmed.

She hiccupped and looked up to meet my hard

gaze. “What is your offer?”

I shrugged to mask unwanted sympathy and said, “A new life.”

“How can I escape his one?” Her frightened eyes shifted toward the house, and I felt my jaw harden. She was terrified of the man who victimized her instead of protected her. Maybe my anger was because when I looked at her, I didn’t see the abused wife and mother of two, but the scared, innocent I did everything I could to hurt.

“I’ll handle him.”

“I—I don’t want you to kill him,” she pleaded. I felt my lip curl with disgust at the thought of her protecting him.

“Does he hit your girls, too?” She blinked away tears and looked away. “Lie to me and this won’t end in your favor. Has. He. Hit. Them?”

She finally nodded once. It was so quick that if I blinked, I would have missed it. She then released a sound similar to that of a wonder animal. “H—he doesn’t beat them like he beats me, but he can be so rough with Maddie. She’s only four and doesn’t understand sometimes—”

She stopped short at the colorful words that escaped me into the night air. She shrunk back completely, allowing me to catch my reflection of rage in the car window behind her.

Her youngest was only four?

Fuck. Ken.

She was Ken’s age.

Fuck...

He was going to die whether she liked it or not.

“You and your kids are out of here *tonight*.”

* * *

JOHN HAD INVESTED a large portion of his capital into a housing development for leasing. Keenan oversees it while I chose to remain detached from anything that had belonged to John. My name was listed as fifty percent beneficiary, but I never kidded myself into believing I was entitled to any of it. If Lake hadn't unknowingly pushed me into a corner, I would have never made use of it.

"So what do you like to do for fun?"

I suppressed a groan, ignored the tiny voice, and continued to install the security system. I didn't like this shit. Turns out, Laurie's older daughter was ten and not as impartial to boys as I would have assumed. She had been following me around for two days with wide eyes and a girlish blush.

She was the one hitting on me, yet I felt like the pedophile.

"Go away."

"Why? I'm pretty, aren't I?" She batted her eyelashes and I felt sick to my stomach.

"I'm not answering that."

"It's okay. You don't have to. Ryan Holder already told me I was ugly when he cut my hair last week. It's why my mom had to cut bangs."

When I finally stopped working to look at her, I caught her peeking up at her bangs and huff.

Fuck.

"Hey." What was I doing? She was already walking away with her shoulders slumped. My mind drew a blank, but it didn't matter because she stopped and turned to face me with a dejected look.

"Yes, Keiran?"

You're not supposed to care.

Walk away.

"Run that by me again?" I demanded against my better judgment.

She looked confused until I impatiently gestured toward her bangs. "There's this boy…" She frowned and eyed me as if wondering if she should trust me. I gritted my teeth and attempted to find patience. "He's mean and always pushing me around."

"Why?"

She shrugged her little shoulders and stared down at her feet. "I don't know."

"You know," I insisted. She answered with a rough shake of her head. "Are you lying?"

"No," she whispered. Her eyes remained downcast and it took her too long to respond, and by the time she did, I had my answer.

"Cassandra." I had only called her by Cassie as her mom and sister did, but I'd heard her mother use her full name when she meant business so I figured it would work for me. When her chin finally left her chest and her wide eyes stared back at me, I knew I had succeeded.

"He said he hates me—" She hesitated again as a tear escaped and hung onto her bottom lash. "B—because my dad hits his mom."

Fuck.

The son of a bitch wasn't just an alcoholic, abusive husband. He was an alcoholic, abusive, and cheating husband. I stared down into the wide brown eyes of this innocent girl and couldn't accept that her father wasn't dead.

"Does your mom know?"

She nodded, and if possible, her shoulders slumped even more. "I told her but she made me promise not to talk about it anymore."

"Why?" I asked more forcefully than necessary

when dealing with a ten-year-old.

"Because she didn't want my dad to find out. She's scared of him, Keiran. He yells and hits her and he's so mean to Maddie."

"Has he ever hurt you or Maddie?"

"Sometimes he grabs and shakes Maddie when she cries too much."

I managed to keep my voice level despite the rage rising safely beneath the surface. "And you?"

"No. I don't talk to him when he drinks."

Smart kid. "Tell me about the kid who cut your hair."

"Ryan?" I didn't miss how her breathing stopped for just a moment or the increased fear in her eyes at the thought of talking about Ryan. I wondered at the possibility that she might have been more afraid of him than she was of her father.

"Yes. Ryan," I answered slowly to keep my temper in check. I didn't know this girl or her family, but I felt the unwanted desire to protect them when it wasn't my right or my responsibility. "What else has he done to you?"

"He said I was a good for nothing whore like my mother, and it's why she can't keep my father home where he belongs."

I did a poor job of concealing my surprise. "He said that?" She nodded and looked down at her feet again.

That little shit.

"Protect yourself. He won't let anyone else protect you from him."

"But he's bigger than me."

"He may be bigger than you, but you're stronger." I could tell she didn't understand. Even now, her shoulders shook with overpowering fright. If I couldn't make her understand, I knew someone who could.

First, I needed to have a talk with her mother.

I found Maddie and led them both outside. Then from the trunk of my car, I dug out the basketball I felt the need to keep close. I spent twenty minutes showing them how to dribble and even how to dribble between their legs. It took Cassie a few tries while Maddie watched since her legs were too small to perform the trick. Once they were thoroughly distracted with dribbling, I slid back into the modest house and found their mother in the bedroom pointed out by the girls.

"We need to talk." My voice was gruff with impatience simply because I had none. She was completely skittish thanks to her abusive husband and jumped at the sound of my voice. When she cowered in the corner with one glance at my expression, I forced myself to school my features into passivity, enough for her to calm. "We need to talk," I repeated.

"What about?"

"Cassie. Did you know she is being bullied?" The regret in her eyes just before they shifted to fixate on the floor was answer enough. "Why are you allowing this to happen?"

"What did she tell you?"

"Probably more than she ever got to tell you because you're a coward."

"I told you. I don't have to explain myself to you."

"You do if you want to keep them," I threatened without mercy. Failing to protect them was just as much abuse as if she had hit them herself.

"Don't threaten me with my kids. You have no right to judge me," she screamed.

"You think I don't?" I could hear the malice in my voice. It matched the darkness of my heart.

"How could you possibly understand?"

"My father sold me for gambling money and expensive alcohol simply because he hated my mother." I ignored the horror filled gasp that echoed around the room and the frail hand that trembled over her lips. "He not only hated my mother, but he also hated me for everything I didn't provide him."

"What was that?"

"Wealth." She stared at me in disbelief, and I found myself looking away. I needed control over my emotions. This wasn't about me. This was about Cassie and Maddie—two little girls who needed me to make their mother understand where her choices were leading them. "He was heir to a substantial fortune if he were able to marry and produce an heir."

"But if he made a son, didn't he inherit? Why would he sell you because of your mother?"

"Because he also needed to marry, and she refused to marry for anything less than love."

Her frown deepened when she picked up on the tone of my voice. "Is that so wrong?" she asked defensively. I could tell she thought herself in love with Robert, her husband.

I held her stare and admitted something I never thought I ever would. "I blamed my mother for being selfish until the very moment I had what she couldn't find with Mitch."

She stared at me with disbelief. "You?" I didn't react. I only stared. "Sorry," she mumbled.

"Believe me. Falling in love was not something I wanted." My lips twitched with the urge to smile. "She was very persuasive."

"She's a beautiful girl," she said wistfully. "I suppose it makes sense given why you're here and doing so much for perfect strangers. You are willing to kill for her?"

"No. I'm willing to not kill for her. She'd forbid it."

"And you're used to killing?" she questioned nervously.

"Yes. I might have even been born for it."

"Money and death. That's no reason to live."

"Yes. Well, it's a good thing I was saved before I figured that out for myself."

"Oh, but I didn't mean—"

"It doesn't matter. I'm still here. The question is—do you want to be?"

"Of course."

"Why?"

"Why?"

"I plan to kill your husband, Laurie. I need to know why it's worth breaking my vow to her."

For the second time.

I'd never admit that I was afraid to kill again—that I feared each time I took a life that I lost a piece of my humanity all over again.

"Please don't. I—"

I shook my head slowly, indicating I was uninterested in what she had to say for him. I turned away, heading for the door. The sooner I got this over with, the less chance I would have to back out.

"Stop," she shouted, surprising me. The force behind her order was far more than I expected from the tiny slip of a woman. I forced myself to face her again and met stormy eyes in a sea of blue.

So much like Lake when she was upset.

In this case, she was furious.

"I asked you not to, but now I'm telling you. You're not going to kill him."

I charged forward, but she held her ground. I gritted my teeth to keep from shouting and spewing threats and obscenities.

"Why are you protecting him?"

"I'm not protecting him."

"Bullshit."

"Maybe at first, but now I'm protecting you."

My vision of her narrowed as suspicion took over my instincts.

"Why?"

"I don't know. Maybe the same reason you're hell bent on protecting us?" She turned away to pace. "I don't know why, but I do know he's not worth it. I don't know you very well, young man, but something tells me you've overcome a lot and fought a hell of a lot of demons to do it. Don't give that up for someone like Robert. Do you think your lady deserves that?"

No.

Fuck no.

But killing was the only way I knew how to make problems go away. It was all I knew.

Wasn't it?

"You didn't kill me two nights ago," she reminded, and I wondered what she was getting at. She didn't leave me guessing for long. "Think about why."

I knew why, or at least, I thought I did.

"You're not a killer anymore," she continued.

"You don't know me."

"I don't have to. If you were still a killer, you would have killed me and made your job much easier by two days and fifty thousand dollars."

When I had convinced Laurie to leave her home and husband with her daughters, I promised them a new life and fifty grand to get her started, along with a house far away from Robert. After only a split hesitation, she accepted my offer and quietly stole away in the middle of the night with her girls.

"You may not see it yet, but you have a future. Robert stole mine. I won't let him take yours, too."

I didn't move or speak for some time. Every dark part of me leftover from my past wanted to ignore her plea.

"Fine." She looked relieved, and I hated it. I wanted him dead. A part of me felt as if killing Robert would restore the balance between the stolen revenge against my own. I ignored that part and focused on the present. "But I won't always be around. If he comes after you—if he kills you— I want you to remember the decision you made to let him live."

* * *

IT WAS A dick move but necessary. She may not have changed her mind about her husband living, but at least, she would be on guard. I just hoped that if the need arrived, she would find the courage to protect herself and her daughters.

I finished installing the security system and made sure they had everything they needed with the promise to return and hauled ass back to California.

I had an infuriating girlfriend to find, and I think I knew just where to look.

I didn't make it back until two in the morning. Exhausted, I climbed into our bed alone, which seemed bigger and colder without her. I resisted the urge to pout and slid my hand in underneath the sheets instead, finding the hardness beneath. I gripped my dick and reached for my phone with my other hand.

I needed her.

I was determined to get her any way I could at this point.

I clicked on the icon of her naked form as she slept one morning after a night of fucking, engaged the speaker, and laid the phone on my lower stomach just above my cock. I waited—anticipating the moment I would hear her melodic voice.

"Yes, Keiran," she answered sounding sleepy and defiant.

Such a handful.

"Where are you?" I demanded even as my hand began to stroke.

I heard her sigh and imagined the feel of her breath on my dick. It hardened in response.

"It's almost three in the morning. Besides, I told you before. We need time apart to think."

"And I told you that you belong here." *With me.*

"So you can try to scare me?"

Fuck. Why did the thought of feeling her tremble beneath me in fear cause me to lift my hips with need?

"Oh, wait." She laughed but it was filled with sarcasm rather than humor. "You want me back so you can protect me."

"No, baby. I want to control you."

The hitch in her breath had conveyed her true feelings before she said, "What?"

"I crave your fear, and I want you safe. But I *need* to control you." I bit my lip to keep from giving myself away and gave in to the demand for pleasure. My hand stroked faster.

"Is this always how it will be?" When I didn't respond, she called my name. "Keiran?"

"Yeah, baby?" I tried to keep my voice neutral, but the soft moan I'm sure she didn't mean to release gave her away.

"Keiran... are you—are you touching yourself?"

"I need you." I didn't bother to conceal my pleasure.

"What are you doing to me?" she asked, but I could tell it was rhetorical. She was silent, and I wondered if she was listening to me until I heard her breathing quicken. I decided to poke the sensual beast coming awake inside her.

"Just because you aren't home with me where you belong, doesn't mean you can leave me hard and wanting." And I was damn hard. "If you were home, you'd be in our bed. I'd lay you on your back and kiss your soft skin until you were hot enough to set us both on fire. Then I'd spread your legs..." I heard the sound of sheets rustling and knew she obeyed my hidden command. "I'd nibble on your thighs so you'd hurt so good. You like when I make it hurt, don't you?"

"Yes."

My cock released a little drop of pleasure at the sound of her moan. I pictured her thighs flushed with heat and my mark of possession. "I'd touch your clit, baby."

"Ok," she agreed, and I smiled knowing she was doing just that.

"You'd want me to stroke you fast so you can find release, but you wouldn't do that, would you? You're a good girl."

"Damn you, Keiran."

"Slow—I'd savor it—how wet you are and how hot your pussy feels. Savor it."

"I want to come."

"I know you do, but I'm still not inside you."

I'd never grow tired of the sound of her begging. I was a slave to her need. My own cock, straining against my hand as the physical need to release escaped and traveled down the length, proved that. I used the added lubrication to glide my hand up and down easier.

"If you were here," I continued the game, "I would use my fingers to fill you."

"Yes."

"You'd beg for my mouth."

"I want it."

"My tongue would come next so I could taste you."

"Please."

"You'd move against me, sending my fingers deeper inside you. You'd use me, baby and I'd let you."

God, I was so close.

"You'd be right on the edge and just when you're begging to be fucked—"

"Oh, God," she cried. I knew she was much too close to stop now.

"I'd take you, Lake. I'd fuck you so goddamn hard."

My hips tensed with the need to drive into her and give her everything I had promised, and I came.

I fucking came.

Involuntarily, I released a hoarse shout that mirrored her cry on the other end of the line. My name on her lips was all I could hear. Nothing else mattered.

The line became quiet as we settled into the silence of the aftermath.

When seconds turned into long minutes, I picked the phone up, ignoring the sweat and leftover release and disengaged the speaker. I started to speak, but only when I hesitated did I realize how nervous I had become at the possibility of rejection.

"Keiran?" she called, sounding just as nervous as I felt.

"Come home, Lake."

"I—" Silence returned and then she quickly said, "I can't."

The line disconnected, leaving me with a soft cock, a mess, and even more pissed off than I was before.

CHAPTER TWELVE

LAKE

I SILENCED MY phone, shoving it under the pillow—as if it could protect me from giving in and running home, just as he had demanded.

What the hell had I done?

I told myself I was done taking orders, but when I heard his voice and shared his release, I wanted nothing more than to obey.

I rolled onto my stomach and groaned into the pillow. The only thing keeping me sane was to know he was in no better shape than I was.

The sound of movement traveling from the front of the apartment had me shooting upright. Had Keiran found me after all?

Just as quickly, I shook my head, realizing how silly that idea was.

When I heard stumbling, I figured Di must have just come in from another night of drinking. A male groan followed by a giggle and I knew she must have brought someone home with her. My head stopped mid shake when I remembered I wasn't going to judge. I knew Di was screwed up, and the extent became clearer with each encounter. Keiran had told me a summarized account of what had happened to her starting as a young girl thanks to her father.

Actually, it was all because of her father.

I still couldn't believe Mario prostituted his own daughter.

And then to have never met her mother... Although, from what Willow and Keiran had told me about Esmerelda, I considered her fortunate. She disappeared after her attempt to kill Keiran had failed, but knowing she was still out there didn't make me feel any safer.

She'd try again.

It was only a matter of when.

Being with Keiran didn't eliminate the constant fight for survival. I'd learned how to survive him and now I was learning how to survive *with* him.

The unmistakable sound of sex began to drift underneath the door and my eyes widened when I realized they were doing it right in the hall!

I stormed from the bed and yanked open the door. I didn't stop to think about it. I should have stopped to think.

The sight of a tall, muscular man with dark hair—who still wore all his clothes while Di was naked from the waist down—greeted me. His dark jeans were lowered, showing off his muscular ass that flexed with each hard, upward thrust. Di whimpered while her head rested against the wall. A tortured expression marred her features even as her nails dug into his shoulders.

"Harder. Please harder."

Her fingers dropped from his shoulders to grip his powerful ass, encouraging him to take her the way she pleaded. He obliged and powered forward with impossible force. I watched as his head turned ever so slightly to take her lips.

And that's when recognition hit me hard.

I was stuck. Stumped. Stupefied.

Say something!

"Q?"

What followed was like watching a fifty-car pile-up on the freeway—except they froze. Di's eyes popped open and stared back at me. She didn't look surprised or sorry. Her eyes were empty of emotion.

"Oh, shit," the guy, who I quickly realized was not Q but looked a lot like him, swore. He dropped Di's legs from around his waist and quickly yanked up his jeans. Di took her time lowering her dress, unbothered by her nakedness. Her thong lay at their feet, forgotten.

"Sorry, girly. Forgot you were here." She giggled but forgot to add humor. Her guest finally turned, giving me a full picture. He had the short, dark hair and matching eyes, and even the stature that screamed Q. The only thing he lacked was the quiet reserve.

"She's fucking hot. Can she join?" he asked with a lustful stare that would have unnerved me much like Keiran's did. The only flaw was, he wasn't Keiran so it did nothing for me.

"If you want to keep your balls and your life and in that order, I suggest you never think that thought again," Di answered dryly.

"That's too bad." He took one last pass at me with his eyes and then retreated for the bathroom indicating he'd been here before.

"Boyfriend of yours?" I questioned.

"I like to think of him as a fuck buddy. He's reliable, available, and has a big cock."

"He looks like Q." Shit, I didn't mean to say that.

Her emotionless gaze now burned with disdain and a mocking acknowledgment of my observation. Her expression read, *'Yeah so?'*

"Sorry. I like the taste of my feet."

She chuckled and rolled her eyes before pushing away from the wall. "I'll try not to keep you awake," she promised as she disappeared into the bathroom with her Q lookalike.

I didn't realize I was still standing there staring after her until the bathroom door reopened. I dove back into the safety of her guest bedroom to prevent another awkward situation with the reminder that her sex life was none of my business.

Later, I found that early afternoon pancakes could momentarily cure any awkward situation. Di had trouble getting up due to a hangover—and hard sex, if the sounds coming from her bedroom were anything to go by—and I just needed the escape sleep promised, so I slept in.

Di's friend was gone so it was just the two of us, but I couldn't get the sight of her being fucked out of my head. I kept seeing her face contorted with torture rather than pleasure. The way she clung to him and begged for more said it wasn't physical pain that caused her torment.

"Do you want to talk about it?" I looked up to see her take a sip of her coffee and to stare at me over the rim of her cup. I could tell she found it amusing. Even though I couldn't see her lips, I knew she was smirking.

"I didn't take you for a coffee person," I commented, ignoring her question.

She shrugged and took another sip. "It keeps me from crawling back into bed and staying there. It was either this or alcohol." My mouth suddenly felt dry, so I took a sip of orange juice. Or maybe I just needed a distraction.

“So do you?” she repeated.

“No. I think I saw enough. More than enough,” I added.

“Did you touch yourself?”

I regrettably spit out the second sip of orange juice I had just taken. She looked down in disgust at the mess I had made and then handed me a napkin.

“What?” I coughed.

“I’m just wondering if you were shocked by more than just catching the act. Maybe you were turned on?”

“Oh God, no,” I groaned in horror. She burst into laughter, and I knew it was at my expense. “You’re fucking with me,” I guessed with narrowed eyes.

“Yeah, just a little. Have you never been caught in the act before?”

“Yeah, actually, I have.” I could tell my admission surprised her.

“Really?”

“Keenan.”

An involuntary shiver wracked my body at the memory of Keiran fucking me without mercy over his father’s kitchen table. Keenan had walked in and taunted me about how much I shamefully enjoyed the harsh pounding fuck. Something in his voice told me he may have even known I liked being watched, too.

It was something I’d never admit to Keiran. He was too possessive, so it was a good thing I didn’t have a burning desire or fetish for voyeurism. The possibility of being caught only served as something to tip the edge.

“That doesn’t surprise me. He’s a little shit. He probably walked in on purpose.”

“Yeah, probably,” I agreed absentmindedly. My mind wasn’t on Keenan. I was craving the feel of his older brother taking me.

Maybe I should go home.

"I walked in on Dash and Willow, too," I offered just to dim the heat.

"Now that I'd love to see. Dash is yummy."

"Sorry. Willow's got that locked down with no plans to free him, ever."

"I don't want to claim him. I just want to ride his face and maybe anything else he has to offer."

If I had juice in my mouth that time, I definitely would have made an even bigger mess. "Too much," I protested with a laugh.

"Sorry. I'll keep it in my pants," she sighed.

"Q might get jealous." I was instigating. I needed to know if something was or could be between them, but her eyes only darkened with anger, and maybe shame.

"I'm nothing but a dirty memory to Q. A dirty memory he's already forgotten."

The regret in her voice was heartbreaking, and I wondered once again at the past Q and Di shared. I realized the silence that fell between had stretched too long. Her eyes were downcast, and she was no longer eating. I searched for a way to unfuck this situation and rescue my foot, yet again.

"I shouldn't have said that."

"Maybe I should have had a drink," she murmured. A knock at the door saved me from answering that. The last thing Di needed to do was ignore her problems, but I doubt she'd listen anyway. She disappeared to answer the door, and I put our dishes in the sink.

"What are you doing here and who are you?" I heard her say.

Shit.

"Is she here?" I heard Q question.

Fuck!

"Is who here?"

"Don't fuck with me, Diana."

"Oooh, Diana. So formal considering our history. You do remember you used to fuck my brains out when we were little more than tots, don't you?"

I hurried to the door and turned the corner in time to see Keiran's face twist with disgust. Beside him was an equally pissed off Q and a disturbed Jesse, whose astonishment mirrored my own. I was still sore with him so I couldn't muster any sympathy for him.

Keiran noticed me almost immediately. He pushed past Di and into the apartment. He was crazy mad. It was all there in his storm-gray eyes.

"Are you fucking crazy?"

"Keiran, I told you last night I can't do this with you right now."

"You come here of all places?"

"What's wrong with here?"

"Yeah," Di cosigned. "What's wrong with here?"

Keiran didn't bother to acknowledge her. It was Q who spoke up. "Your mother is looking for you, Diana."

* * *

KEIRAN THREATENED TO handcuff me to the steering wheel if I wouldn't come willingly, and he was mad—and crazy—enough for me to believe him, so I thanked Di for her hospitality, ignored Jesse, who pleaded with his eyes for forgiveness, and said goodbye.

Keiran actually scolded me when we drove away. Q had driven his own car but stayed behind to deal with the aftermath. Jesse sat in the back seat fidgeting, and I secretly enjoyed his discomfort. His loyalty had clearly shifted so as long as Keiran and I were at odds, he was the enemy.

"Lake, I'm sorry—"

"Shut it," Keiran and I ordered simultaneously. I watched Keiran's jaw tighten as he kept his gaze fixed on the road. I managed to keep my expression neutral when he sensed my stare and glanced toward me. In my peripheral, I caught Jesse looking between us as if we'd grown two heads.

"Why did you bring him anyway?"

"He wanted to make sure you and he didn't do anything stupid," Jesse answered sarcastically. I ignored him and faced forward again. Only five more hours of uncomfortable tension to go.

At some point, I'd fallen asleep and slept through Keiran dropping off Jesse and driving us home. It wasn't until I felt his arms around me and he lifted me that I woke up.

"Welcome home," he taunted. I looked up and was blinded by his shit-eating grin and wondered how bad things could get if I slapped it off his face.

"Don't be so smug. I could always handcuff you to the bed again and this time, throw away the key."

The anger in his eyes should have scared me, but it tickled me with delight instead. "Don't ever do that again," he warned.

"You handcuff me all the time. Is there some kind of double standard to foreplay now?"

"Have I ever handcuffed you and ran away?"

"I thought I'd shake things up a bit so our sex life doesn't go stale."

I didn't expect him to drop me on the couch and step back. I expected him to try and overpower me with his male ego. He only stared down at me as if trying to piece together a tough equation. It was then I realized how exhausted he appeared. Stress lines decorated his forehead and the bags underneath his eyes took away from the striking irises.

"I was really okay," I said, giving in. "I just needed to think and... I was scared." I sucked in as much air as I could to hide the alarm that blared within.

When had admitting fear become so hard? Once upon a time, I lived in fear until it was as natural as breathing.

"I'm scaring myself."

He hesitated and then sat down next to me. "You're scaring me, too." I couldn't recall a time when I'd heard him speak so softly. It turns out Mitch's death and my lies were leading to a lot of firsts for us.

Keiran had admitted he was afraid and it was because of me.

"So what do we do about it?"

He shook his head and stared deep into my eyes. "Just answer one question first. Did I do this?"

"I don't understand."

"Did loving me do this to you?"

"I don't know," I answered reluctantly. "I only know I wanted to do anything I could to keep you around even it if meant corrupting myself along the way."

He blew out a harsh breath. "I don't know if I can accept that. I don't want you corrupted. I never wanted that for you."

My heart rate accelerated and my chest grew too tight. I couldn't breathe. I couldn't—

"Ar—are you breaking up with me?" He looked as surprised by his words as I was.

"I probably should..."

No.

He leaned his head back against the sofa and closed his eyes tight. I wanted to scream and demand he open them again. I needed to see his eyes. I needed to know if this was real.

"...but there isn't a muscle in my body strong enough to do what's right when it comes to you."

I stared at him in disbelief. When he opened his eyes a tiny fraction to gaze at me, I launched myself into his lap and buried close.

"Don't," I found myself pleading.

"I won't."

"Don't think about it anymore either."

"I'm not."

"Good." My hand followed its own command and slapped him with all the strength I had left—the only strength he didn't take from me with his brief surrender to his conscience.

He grunted in pain, and I realized I wanted more so I tried again only to be stopped by his hand on my wrist. "You're pushing it."

"Do you have any idea what you just did to me?"

"You had my father killed. I think we're even."

"So breaking up with me was your way of getting back at me?"

He shot me an impatient look. "Not in the least, but it's good to know where you stand with us."

"I'll always stand by us."

"Even if my hairline recedes and I grow a beer gut?"

"You don't drink beer."

"You're welcome," he smugly stated causing me to slap him in the six slabs of concrete under discussion. "I told you about that."

The warning in his eyes was clear. I shrieked and scrambled to escape his lap, but he was much too fast. He locked his arms around my waist and sunk his teeth into my shoulder. "I told you," he growled and pushed his hips up until they met mine.

He may have been too much for most women, but his forcefulness was exactly what drove me wild and kept me crazy about him.

It took a special kind of girl to bring Keiran Masters to his knees.

We made out as if we were teens again when he would drag me out from my house in the middle of the night during the summer and into the backseat of his car.

It didn't take long for his jeans to be around his ankles with me also naked from the waist down and riding him as if my life depended on it.

"Oh, my... Fuck," I cried when I finally came and shook around him. He grunted from the force of his own release as he came inside me and nibbled on my jaw before kissing his way down my neck. My hips moved slowly against him, and with his cock lodged deep inside me, I could have easily come a second time.

"I love you," he whispered.

"Love you," I gasped when he sucked my breast into his mouth, "more."

"I doubt that." He released my nipple and grinned up at me with all his boyish goodness.

My eyebrow lifted at his response. "We could always beat the crap out of each other to settle the score like you do with Dash and Keenan."

"I thought we could go upstairs and make another home video."

For Keiran's birthday this year, I finally gave in to his desire to tape us when we made love so we could capture moments that passed between that were fleeting but powerful.

We made a few dirty ones, too.

I captured his lips. It was my turn to kiss him senseless, so when he closed his eyes and gave in, loosening his grip in the process, I made my move.

"You have to catch me first." His eyes popped open, but it was too late. I was already heading for the stairs. I knew without looking back that he chased.

He always would.

* * *

I PUSHED THE cart through the produce aisle heading for the tomatoes. I decided to get an early start on repairing our relationship and left Keiran at home in bed. I read in some girl magazine while waiting for a dentist appointment that the key to a man's heart was through his stomach or his mother, and since I couldn't exactly call his mother from the other side for advice, an omelet would have to do.

Keiran's lovemaking last night surprised me. In all the years we'd been together, he'd never taken me so tenderly. To be honest, it wasn't something I thought him capable of doing. I was definitely grateful to have gotten it on video.

The only thing we couldn't capture was the love in his eyes when he brought us release—that I'd have to rely on only my memory to keep close.

I reluctantly pushed back memories of last night and made quick work of my grocery list. After ringing up with the cashier, I carried my purchases out into the California heat, ready to get back to my temperamental boyfriend.

"Lake Monroe?"

I turned at the sound of my name and immediately took in the badges and holstered pistols as two men approached. Instinct recognized them as the new detectives assigned to replace the two who tried to send me to jail for the rest of my life for a man who deserved so much worse than he got.

"What are you doing here? This is California."

"We're aware of the jurisdiction, Ms. Monroe. I'm Detective Grayson and this is Detective Roberts."

"Boy, you guys are really going for the record books, aren't you? Let me guess... You're here to arrest me without a warrant *again*. Or maybe you've been following me to see if I've been stalking health centers—"

"We just want to ask you a few questions."

"And you thought I'd answer them without my lawyer present?"

"Why not? Do you have something to hide?"

"If you think I'm answering that, you're just as dumb as the last two."

"You do know that if you aren't guilty, then our investigation will clear your name? You'd have no reason not to answer our questions. We could help you."

"Funny. I don't remember asking for your help. Has it ever occurred to you that I'm glad Mitch is dead? Kudos to whoever did it. Now, if you'll excuse me." I attempted to walk away, giving them my ass to kiss.

"We did some more digging, Miss Monroe. Did you know your boyfriend visited his father the day before he was murdered?"

Wait. What?

I turned back around and approached them with quick steps. Maybe I was falling into another trap but something about their smug looks told me maybe not.

"That's impossible. Keiran had no idea where his father was."

The detective eyed me with mock sympathy. "Is that what he told you?"

I hated his condescending smugness. "It's what I know."

"Well, unfortunately for you and your boyfriend,

when we flashed his mug shot around, one of the nurses recognized him. It seems he was smart enough not to log his visit, and I couldn't help but wonder why. Apparently, one of the young, prettier nurses took a liking to him. She recognized him as one of the only visitors he's had since John Masters died."

Truth or not, thanks to years of Keiran's tormenting, I knew when I was being led into a trap. I needed to get out of there and fast.

"Excuse me, detectives. The Nevada state line is calling you back."

This time, when I turned away, I didn't stop. I threw my grocery bags in the car and let them fall wherever and burned rubber from the parking lot. They stood by watching my display with smug grins until I could no longer see them in my rearview mirror.

It couldn't be true, could it?

Why would he lie about knowing where his father was?

If he had gone to see him, why was he left alive?

I couldn't get home fast enough. I considered leaving the groceries in the car but instead, used it as a chance to get my thoughts together.

It was a trick.

It had to be a trick.

I lugged the groceries inside and found Keiran leaning against the counter, eating an apple, shirtless and dressed in gray basketball shorts. His erection was evident, and I felt my tongue swell in my mouth.

I closed my eyes briefly, fighting the temptation, and when I opened them again, he was grinning at me. The cocky fucker knew the effect he had on me.

"Let me help you with those," he smoothly greeted but frowned when I stepped back and dropped the sacks at my feet. "What the fuck?"

"Did you know where your father was the whole time?"

"Come again?

"Did you know your fucking father was at Summit this entire goddamn time?"

"Watch your mouth," he growled. He didn't even have the decency to look surprised or worried that he'd been found out.

"Answer me!"

"Lower. Your. Damn. Voice," he roared. His voice was as loud as if a bomb had detonated. He was standing toe to toe with me by the time he finished, his chest heaving.

Well, I wasn't about to back down. "You knew he was there, didn't you? All this time?"

He exhaled and took a step back. "Keenan told me a couple of weeks before I went to see him."

"Why?" It was no secret Keenan knew where Mitch was, but we all agreed it was better if it were kept a secret from Keiran. I hadn't even known up until my grandmother was admitted to the facility.

"He said he'd been fucking up a lot and wanted to 'knock some shit off his list.'" He shrugged, appearing as clueless as I felt.

"I don't understand—"

"Why I didn't kill him?" I nodded slowly, still trying to piece together the growing puzzle. "Because of you."

"M—Me?"

"Mitch was already dying, and while it would have given me greater pleasure to end him, I made you a promise that I'd already broken once for my brother. I wasn't willing to lose you."

I couldn't see past the tears clouding my vision. He had given up his right to revenge. I had betrayed him, and I then took the right from him.

Even worse, I hadn't trusted him.

I knew you would come back for me. It's what Mitch had said when he saw me. I hadn't understood then and assumed it was the ramblings of a dying, evil man. He'd thought I was Keiran.

"You lied to me."

"Yes."

There was no remorse in his tone or eyes. He ensured I felt guilt, and all the while, he'd been lying to me, too. "I spoke with the new detectives on the case."

His eyes narrowed with suspicion. "When?"

"Don't look at me like I'm the guilty one. They cornered me at the store this morning."

"Did they follow you?"

"Does it matter? I'm sure they know where we live."

"It matters. If they followed you, it means they'll keep following you."

I wanted to take the focus off me—and quick. His stare was beginning to make me sweat. "They told me you went to see him the day before I did, but you were on a business trip."

He shook his head and tossed his leftover apple stem in the trash. "I didn't need to meet Jesse until the next day."

"Why did you go if not to kill him?"

"Because I did go to kill him. I wanted him to die in the worst way. That would never change. The only thing that did was the decision not to. He wasn't worth it. Or so I thought."

"You did the right thing."

"Did I? You didn't seem to think so when you went to kill him, instead."

"Yes, I went, but I'm not even sure I could have."

"Q said you were ready to stab him when he stopped you."

"I guess we'll never know."

He didn't answer. He bent to pick up the sacks of food I had carelessly dropped and started putting them away, effectively ignoring me. I felt like we were back at square one, and just like that, our night and our truce was broken.

CHAPTER THIRTEEN

SEVEN MONTHS AGO

KEIRAN

LAKE HAD LEFT for class an hour ago, and I decided to work from home not caring for the company of our small staff or business partner. I'd been having nightmares about my mother and when I killed her, which was always sure to put me in a foul mood. I hadn't told Lake about them and had no intention to because she'd try to psychoanalyze me.

When the numbers on the screen began to blur a few hours later, I decided to take a break. I was in the middle of fixing a sandwich when the sound of keys turning the lock stopped me in my tracks. Lake wasn't due to be done with classes for another hour.

I waited, and when Keenan turned the corner, I relaxed, though I was surprised to see he'd traveled all this way unannounced. "Sheldon let you out to play?"

In truth, it was Keenan who rarely tolerated leaving

his family. He could barely stand to be away for more than a day before he found some excuse to go crawling back to them. One time, it was because he heard Kennedy cough when he called to say goodnight.

"She didn't put up much of a fuss. It was Ken I had to convince to let me out without kiddie supervision."

"So why didn't you bring her?" I offered a bottle of water and when he declined, I uncapped it and lifted to take a swig.

"Because we need to talk."

The bottle of water stopped halfway to my lips at his tone. "About?"

"Mitch." He waited for an opening. My silence gave him the OK to continue. "I know where he is."

"I know."

"You know where he is?"

"I know you know. What I didn't know was how long it would take you to tell me."

"I'm telling you now."

"So?"

"He's at a cancer rehabilitation facility called Summit Rehabilitation for Cancer Survivors. It's about a four-hour drive from Six Forks."

Which put him just under halfway between here and home. It was the perfect setup for his execution.

"What are you planning to do with this?"

Kill him.

"Nothing," I lied.

"Nothing?"

I shrugged, chugged the water down and tossed it in the trash. I could tell he didn't accept my answer as he looked at me warily.

"Don't make me regret this," he warned.

I convinced him to stay long enough to shoot hoops since this was the longest we'd bonded alone since before he left four years ago. It was our normal, brutal match. Despite the invisible elephant standing between us, neither of us held back.

He took the winning shot, and I laughed when he did his usual gloating dance even as sweat dripped and stung my eyes.

"I have to get back to my ladies," he said when he was done gloating.

"Before you go—" I hesitated because what was I going to say? Was I the only one who still noticed the tension between us? We never talked about the night he left or Sophia.

"Don't force it," he said, reading my mind when I allowed the silence to stretch too long.

"You don't think we need to talk?"

"I don't." He smirked. "We're not the girls," he added, attempting to cut the tension with humor.

I nodded and expelled a breath, relishing how easy that turned out to be. Heart to hearts weren't my thing—our thing. Keenan might have been the lighthearted replica of me.

"Brothers?" I held out my hand, which was left empty due to his shock. I was just as surprised by my outburst that felt more like instinct. It might have been the first time I accepted who we really were to each other out loud.

"Brothers." He clasped my hand and yanked me forward to envelop me in a manly hug. When he ruffled my hair as if *I* were the younger brother, I shoved his ass away. He chuckled, threw up deuces, and showed himself out.

Once I was alone, the silence descended much too fast, and I was left to think about the information Keenan drove half a day to give me. Did he really come here to clear his conscience or did he come here because he wanted Mitch dead? His family was as much in jeopardy as I was.

I shook thoughts of my father off, ignored work and waited for Lake to come home so I could lose myself in her.

* * *

IT ONLY TOOK me a week to make the decision. A business opportunity out of the blue came up, giving me the perfect alibi. Since I was doing this completely solo, I needed to cover every angle. After shadowing Jesse, I picked up enough hacking skills to break past the facilities firewalls for floor plans and resident room charts.

I had everything in place up until yesterday morning when Lake and I got into an argument. I had awakened to find her staring at the ceiling with tortured eyes. I asked her what was on her mind. I was so determined to know the answer that I knew the exact moment she made the decision to lie to me.

With my business trip in only two days, it was just enough to temporarily knock me off my game. I only had a small window of opportunity and couldn't afford the time to interrogate her properly, so I let it go... up until it was time for me to walk out the door. Seeing her pumped me with the need to remind her of the consequences of lying to me.

I came downstairs in time to see her come home from class. She looked from me to the duffle slung over my shoulder with fear. I stared at her wondering what was going through her head, but just like yesterday, I knew she wouldn't tell me.

"Wh—where are you going?"

I felt like a dick for enjoying the fear that caused her voice to falter.

"Jesse and I have a meeting with a potential client in Texas. They want to meet us face to face and see up front what we're offering."

"How long will you be gone? The wedding—"

The wedding? She was lying to me, yet she's worried about the fucking wedding?

I was losing my touch.

"I'll be back in time for our flight," I answered before she could finish. I stood on the bottom step, daring her to meet my gaze. When her shoulders squared and her eyes met mine, I accepted the challenge, dropped my duffle bag, and closed the gap between us. "If you want to test me, you better be sure you're ready for the consequences."

"Don't threaten me, Keiran. I'm not your plaything anymore."

Oh, you were always so much more than just something to play with.

"You should know better by now, so I'm going to ask you this once—so think about your answer. Are you hiding something?"

"What makes you think I'm hiding something?"

"You've been off. Do I need to be worried?"

"I'm worried about finals and my grandmother settling into a new place."

I searched her eyes for a clue that would tell me what the fuck was going on but found nothing, so I did the next best thing. I grabbed her hot as fuck face between my hands and kissed the fuck out of her. My knees felt as if they would buckle, so I moved us to the nearest wall and pushed my hips against her.

"I need to protect you," I whispered while kissing her. "Can you understand that?"

She whimpered as if it was all she could muster and continued to kiss me back.

"Pay attention," I ordered, turning the tables.

"I can't. You're kissing me."

Damn, why did she have to say that? I stopped kissing her but kept her close, wanting to feel her body. I waited for the haze of lust to clear before I spoke. "I need to trust you."

"You can."

"Can I?"

She nodded slowly but looked like she wanted to protest.

"Forever, Lake. I'll love you." I ignored the guilt that ate at me for what I planned to do.

"Forever," she whispered back.

It was hard, but I managed to pull away, leaving her against the wall and placing my head in the game for what came next.

I ate up the highway until I crossed the Nevada state line. Only then could I manage to slow down to a reasonable speed. My eagerness to see my father dead was disturbing to someone who hadn't walked in my shoes, but I could only think of it as a long overdue chore.

The serenity of the facility grounds and the knowledge that Mitch had spent his last years in undeserved tranquility pissed me off more than the reminder that my own father sold and led me down this path.

I studied the schematics one last time and mentally traced my steps before leaving my car. I quickly found my point of entrance easy enough, and within moments, I was standing in front of Mitch's door. I didn't hesitate to enter the sterilized room that still managed to smell like death and took in the sleeping form not five feet away.

Mitch Masters was a resourceful, evil man, but he looked like neither now. His hair and skin appeared wilted and even his breathing was fragile. He slept but from the way he looked, he might as well have been dead. I'd known he was dying when John admitted to caring for him, but personally seeing it was all the more satisfying.

"I knew you'd come for me."

The voice was delivered on ragged threads as it traveled the room to send a chill down my spine. I hadn't even noticed he had awakened to watch me as I did the same.

"Yet you don't sound afraid. My uncle isn't alive to protect you anymore."

"Yes, I was told of his unfortunate accident."

"He was gunned down at a stop light. It was no accident."

"And you're here to avenge him?"

It was hard to express my feelings for my uncle and his death, and I sure as fuck wasn't about to bare all to my father who'd like nothing more than to carve out my heart if he suspected I had one.

"I'm not going to kill you," I said instead. The dark part of my soul raged at the lost opportunity. It needed Mitch Masters—the man who sired and sold me—to pay with his life.

"Of course, you are. You're a killer. It's all you'll ever be."

"You don't know me well enough to say that, pops." I exaggerated the endearment to act as an insult, but if he caught it, he didn't let on.

"You're my son. I know you better than anyone. I made you who you are long before I ever sold you."

I snorted. "I hope the money was worth it."

"I spent it on crap tables, cheap hookers, and booze." His smile was slow but more disturbing than the evil behind it was the unwanted pain that caused me to flinch. He chuckled when he noticed my involuntary reaction. "Don't be weak, boy. Love is for the weak, and those who carry the Masters name aren't weak."

"You're not dead yet." It was a warning.

"If you're not going to kill me then why are you here?"

"I wanted you to know that you lost."

"What exactly did I lose?"

"The chance to break me."

"I didn't need to break you. I just needed you to believe I did, and you did believe."

"I think the cancer is eating at your brain." He didn't react to the insult. Instead, he eyed me. Calculating.

"How long have you lived your life believing you were a monster? A trained killer? How much normality did you miss out on because of me? I took your entire goddamn past, and if I weren't dying, I'd take your future. Your life is meaningless. You're nothing more than a bad investment. I don't care what that whore of yours makes you feel. She weakens you with lies all for the pleasure of what's in between her thighs."

It should have been enough to send me into a murderous rage. Instead, I saw straight through it as a desperate attempt to break me one last time. I stared down at him until the smug look on his face disappeared.

"I'd stick around," I finally said when the tension grew too thick, "but I have a business to run and a girl to love, not to mention my little brother is getting married next week. See you around, pops. Maybe in hell one day."

CHAPTER FOURTEEN

PRESENT

LAKE

KEIRAN HAD DISAPPEARED inside his office after our fight, leaving me to deal with the newly cracked pieces of our relationship. After pouting and worrying for an hour, I decided to get started on the reading for the start of my summer classes, which were to begin in a couple of days. I tried not to think about how much of my life could have crashed and burned if my arrest had been real.

Even now, it was still a likely possibility. It was only a matter of time before they found the evidence to make a warranted arrest.

I ran my sweaty palms down my bare legs and tried to concentrate on the black and white print. After reading the same sentence fifteen times, I tossed the textbook away and began to pace. I never even noticed when Keiran entered the room until his deep voice broke my trance.

"What are you doing?"

"Pacing."

"I can see that. *Why* are you pacing?"

"Because I'm thinking?"

"The investigation," he guessed correctly. "Don't worry about it."

"How can you say that?" My pacing quickened. "That woman saw me and she's testifying. I don't understand why they haven't even made a real arrest yet."

"Because she's not testifying. I took care of it."

I came to a screeching halt and rushed to get to the side of the room where he stood. "You didn't." I searched his eyes for signs of someone who could kill someone innocent but only saw pain reflected down at me.

"I didn't kill her. I offered her money and a safe place to stay for her and her two daughters."

"A safe place to stay?"

"Her husband was beating her."

I nodded and processed the thought of Keiran playing the knight in shining armor to strangers. Somehow, it wasn't as difficult to picture as I had imagined. "How much money did you offer her?"

"Fifty."

"Grand?" I asked, incredulous.

"Is that a problem?"

I ignored the bite in his tone and continued to stare. It was at this moment that I began to wonder how well I knew his heart. Apparently, I underestimated the depth it was capable of meeting.

Was I so skeptical of him all the time?

"That's very generous," I admitted, concealing my surprise. He shrugged and continued to watch me closely.

"Actually, I wanted to talk to you about them."

"What about?"

"Laurie's oldest is being bullied in school."

"Yeah?"

"I was thinking you could talk to her."

"Mean girls aren't really my forte."

"It's a little boy whose mother is having an affair with her father."

"Are you sure we should be getting involved in this?"

"Are you serious?" I didn't miss the raging storm in his eyes and failed at concealing my surprise. "I thought if anyone might understand, you would."

"You do realize that being in contact with this family is illegal? We could be charged with intimidating a witness."

"They haven't brought charges against you yet, and do you know why? Because the mother of the daughter I'm asking you to talk to will not testify against you. Without her, they have no chance of indicting you."

"What makes you think I can help this girl? I spent most of my life giving in to fear."

"Like you're doing right now?"

"What?"

"A ten-year-old girl needs your help and you're bitching out."

"Did you just call me a bitch?"

"No, but I should have. You're acting like one."

"Since when did you care? You had no qualms about making my life a living hell, and suddenly, you want to fix this little girl's life? Why?"

His nostrils flared, but he remained silent. Two sure signs that I had gone too far. In truth, I had no idea why I was resisting. I wanted to help this girl, but the petty part of me was standing in the way.

Why this girl and not me?

I suffered emotional—and sometimes physical—pain at his hands for ten years. The only time I didn't suffer was the year he went to juvie, and even then, I walked on eggs shells, anticipating the day he returned.

The aftermath had been more dangerous than I gave him credit for.

His eyes slowly shifted around the room, and I knew he was trying to regain his composure, but I could only think of it as the countdown of a bomb.

When his eyes finally settled on me again, what followed wasn't an explosion. His smooth voice washed over me instead.

"I'll never get the chance to make right what I did to you. It haunts me. I—"

"You think helping this little girl will make it right with me?"

"I think helping Cassie will make it right for both of us."

Maybe it was the idea of him wanting to make it up to ten-year-old me, or hearing him say her name as if she were already someone special to him, melted me. "Cassie… Her name is Cassie?" I cooed.

"Should I have started with that?" he grinned, picking up on my sudden acquiesce.

"I shouldn't have freaked out on you. Of course, I want to help her, it's just that a part of me still hurts for the little girl who was afraid of her own shadow because of the possibility that it was actually you standing behind me."

"I'll apologize to you every day for the rest of my life if that's what it will take."

"Or you can just love me."

He stepped up until his chest was pressed against mine as he stared down at me with growing intensity—

"I thought that's what I've been doing"—and sarcasm.

I wrapped my arms around his neck with a coquettish smile. "A girl needs to be reminded every now and then."

"I seem to remember reminding you very thoroughly last night. I even have it on video."

I felt my body grow hot at the reminder of all that occurred last night and decided to change the subject. "So when do I get to meet this Cassie?"

"How about this weekend?"

I nodded. "I still can't believe you corrupted a witness." And was that pride I heard in my voice?

"Believe it, baby. There's nothing I wouldn't do for you."

And I now knew that included giving up his chance at killing the father who sold him and secretly killed his mother.

"Can I ask you something?"

"Sure." His answer was slowed down by wariness.

"What if you didn't kill your mother?"

It was obvious by the way his body jerked that it hadn't been the question he expected.

"Where is this coming from?"

"You want to right so many wrongs about your past, and I know this must haunt you... What if you didn't do it?"

"You're right," he agreed but pulled away. His face twisted with disgust, and I knew this wasn't going to end well. "There are many things about my past I want to undo but killing my mother can never be one of them."

"But—"

"Fuck." He shoved his hands through his hair. His eyes shifting wildly. "I'm not doing this."

He moved for the door, but I couldn't let him leave

like this.

"But you didn't do it!" I shouted too late.

He had already stormed out.

* * *

THE NEXT COUPLE of days, I struggled with telling Keiran the truth about Sophia's death. Mitch had led him to believe he killed his own mother, and while Keiran refused to talk about it, I knew it haunted him.

Would there ever be a right time to tell him? After his episode two days ago, I had begun to think it was better never to tell him.

What would the truth do to him? Would he accept it as the truth or would he believe Mitch was fucking with him even in death?

Keiran hadn't spoken a word to me in the two days since I tested the waters. Though it didn't stop him from turning to me at night or in the morning when we would wake or even in the middle of the day.

And since the first time he took me, I wasn't strong enough to deny him so I let him use my body as an escape. It was the only way to help him while he struggled with his demons.

"Hey," I heard from the doorway as I pulled on jeans. Today was my first day of summer class, and I was reluctant to go. The tension between us only made me want to latch myself to him, afraid he might bolt.

"Hey."

He didn't move from the door. He continued to stare as I pulled on a t-shirt and slid my feet into flip-flops. I grabbed my messenger bag and pulled it over my head and held onto the strap to keep it from latching.

"Class?" he asked stating the obvious. Maybe he

was feeling as insecure as I was.

A girl could only hope.

"Yup. First day. I have two—"

"Come here," he interrupted. I blew my growing bangs out my eyes so I could see how serious he was. The intensity of his stare told me he was very serious. My feet moved before my brain could give the command. When my brain finally did catch up, I stopped and decided to make him meet me the rest of the way.

I should have known better.

He gripped the strap of my bag and tugged me the rest of the way.

In a way, the move defined the scope of our relationship. I challenged him, and he pushed back, obliterating all my defenses.

"Are you talking to me yet?" he pouted.

"Wha— I thought you weren't talking to me?"

"I fucked up," he sighed. "I shouldn't have walked out on you like that."

I mentally tallied in our head the fights we've had in a short amount of time. "Do you realize we've fought more since I was arrested than we have in the five years we've been together?"

"I realize I do a lot of things wrong when it comes to you."

"Don't be so hard on yourself. I did get your father killed."

His eyes darkened, and I prepared myself for another argument when he kissed me instead.

"After you're done with classes there's somewhere I want to take you."

"Where?"

"After class," he said and let me go. He walked past me and disappeared into our master bath. I stared at the closed bathroom door, willing myself to shake off the effect he had on me. I was finally able to move and left for class wondering about his mysterious request.

When I got home a few hours later, I was greeted by the sight of him zipping up a small backpack. He took my bag from me, dropped it by the door, and led me back out. I got the sense he was in a hurry, so I didn't ask questions until he pulled up to a building with a sign that read 'Shooting Sports.'

"What are we doing here?"

He put the car in park and turned in his seat to face me. "I'm not always going to be around. If you're going to protect yourself, you need to know how."

My eyebrows rose to my forehead. "That's very big of you, Keiran Masters."

"My generosity isn't the only thing big about me," he flirted.

I rolled my eyes and grinned back at him. "Yes. Your ego is much bigger."

"If you're good, I'll let you feel how big my ego is all night."

"So, is this going to be like when you taught me to bowl? Because I don't think I have as much constraint. You don't scare me as much, and you're much hotter now than you were then."

It was his turn to look surprised. "Really? How so?"

"Well, for one, you aren't finding ways to make me cry every day. Your muscles are bigger—more defined. Your voice is deeper—smoother." My own lowered seductively as I ticked off reasons why he was so irresistible to me. "I think you might have even grown an inch."

"Inch and a half," he corrected.

"Oh, wow," I gushed, stroking his ego and watching his chest puff. He smirked, seeing past my response.

"What else do you think is sexy about me?"

I leaned over until my lips were touching his. "I also think you have finessed the fine art of fucking." I wanted him to kiss me, but he leaned away and quirked an eyebrow.

"You think?"

"It's been hours," I answered, referring to this morning's session in the shower. "A girl forgets."

"I think you might have hit your head against the tile too many times while we were fucking if you forgot that."

CHAPTER FIFTEEN

KEIRAN

SHE MIGHT HAVE been daring me to drag her from the car and show her how well I mastered the art of fucking over the hood of my car, but we were in too public a place and under enough law enforcing eyes as it was.

My eyes narrowed as I considered my options, and she smirked at me with her glossy, pink lips in return, confirming my suspicions.

"There's always tonight, baby."

It was more than a warning. It was a promise to deliver. Her smirk dropped, and she began to vibrate with anticipation.

Wordlessly, I got out of the car and headed for the entrance, leaving her to follow behind with slow steps. With my back to her, I smiled, relishing the fact that there was never a dull moment with her. I secretly enjoyed her incessant need to challenge me to prove she was no longer afraid.

Tormenting her years ago wasn't always about hating her. A predator enjoyed the chase, and she made a damn good prey.

"Hey, Keiran!" the owner greeted me. I noticed Lake's surprise at his familiarity with me and smiled at the owner, shaking his hand. I never told her I came here often because I knew she'd worry about the reasons why.

I had known one day I would see Mitch again and this time, I had more than one reason to care if he ever came back at all. I needed to be ready, and I had believed a soft heart like hers wouldn't understand. I'd believed she would want me to take the high road.

I was wrong as fuck.

Lake had wanted Mitch dead.

Maybe even more than I did.

I watched her while she curiously looked over the guns in the case and felt my dick harden knowing she was willing to kill—willing to give up her innocent soul—for me.

She deserved than all of me. I just needed to figure out what came next so I could give that to her. First, I had to make sure she was around to accept me.

"I see you like this one, little lady. A revolver is certainly a more suitable gun for you."

He grinned at me but then cleared his throat when he saw my warning look. Bart was old and set in his ways and didn't think much of women with guns, but he was also wise enough to know I wouldn't tolerate his biased views when it came to Lake.

"Sorry, I just like the classic look of it," she corrected a little too sweetly. I knew she picked up on his meaning but hid her irritation with sarcasm. I was usually on the receiving end of it, particularly during the week when she becomes a hormonal bitch. "What I really want to see is this one."

My chest swelled with pride when she pointed at the bigger, more powerful weapon beside it. She looked at me for approval when the owner turned to grab his key, and I nodded. It was impressive and had a helluva kick, but I'd teach her how to handle it.

"Have you ever held a gun?" Bart questioned as he rested the gun on the glass.

"Yes." His furry brows lifted, but he quickly recovered after a quick glance at me.

"Ever shot one?"

"No."

He nodded, seemingly satisfied, and grabbed a box of rounds.

"I just need to run down the safety protocol before you start."

"Ok."

"The first are simple. Don't shoot anyone here and don't shoot yourself. Keep the peacemaking end pointed down range at all times." He rambled off the rest of the rules while I paid the fee and purchased the targets and ammo. When he finished, I grabbed the box of rounds and gun case, then led her to the lanes.

"It's loud in there," she shouted.

I shouldered off my pack and dug out the ear and eye protection. I handed her a brand new set I had picked up for her while she was in class. She gushed over the bright blue buds and clear goggles as if I'd just handed her a diamond ring. I smiled and rolled my eyes while she put them on and then opened the door for her to enter.

When we reached our bay, I sat down our stuff and grabbed the paper targets, staple gun, and cardboard. The hanger for the target was already pulled in so I set up the target and sent it out to the furthest mark.

She looked at me as if I was crazy, and I resisted the urge to laugh.

Instead, I bent low until my lips rested on her ear. "Watch me."

And because I couldn't leave it there, I trailed my lips down the side of her neck, feeling her shiver beneath me. She looked up with a painful expression, begging with her eyes to be fucked. Ignoring her plea, I pushed her safely behind me and shoved the magazine clip into the gun.

I set up to take the first shot and once I had my aim perfectly nested, I didn't hesitate. I emptied the clip into the target and swept the brass off the counter once I was done. Lake came to stand next to me and pulled the target in with narrowed eyes. I braced my hip against the counter and crossed my arms as I watched her study the target.

"You're a good shot."

"Thank you. Your turn." She suddenly looked nervous as I set up the next target and sent it out. This time, I stopped it at the first mark. I loaded the clip, handed her the gun, and waited. I needed to see where her instincts led her.

She maintained a steady grip despite her nervous flush, but her awkward positioning displayed zero control over the weapon. She flipped the switch of the safety, aimed and fired. I searched the target and was relieved that she, at least, hit the target.

I reached out and flipped the safety so she could lower her arm. "First thing you need to know is that you don't fire until you're sure of your shot."

"You didn't hesitate," she quipped.

"I was sure of where I was aiming."

She blew her bangs away and turned to face me. "What makes you think that wasn't where I was aiming?"

"If you shoot, you should shoot to kill."

"I hit it, didn't I?"

"You hit the paper, but you didn't kill your target."

"What's the difference?"

"The silhouette," I pointed out. She studied the target again. Her lips formed a perfect O when she understood. "Try again, but this time, fix your footing." I paused, remembering her comment in the car. "And you were right. It is like bowling."

She immediately fixed her footing and looked to me for approval. I made some minor adjustments and then showed her how to grip the gun properly.

"Now, I want you to aim using the rear and front sights." I pointed them out using my fingers. "Use the rear sight to aim your front sight where you want the bullet to go—in this case, the silhouette. The rest isn't there."

"Okay." She switched to fire, brought the gun up, and aimed, using what I had taught her.

"Good. Now breathe in, and when you're ready, squeeze the trigger slowly and shoot on the exhale. Aim for the center."

She breathed in and began to squeeze the trigger slowly until the metallic click engaged and the round left the chamber. She immediately put the gun on safety and peered at the target. She found her mark hit dead center and released a happy squeal. She once again looked to me for approval. I offered her a nod and sent the target all the way out.

"That's good, baby. Real good. Now hit it again."

* * *

WE STAYED UNTIL the range closed. Lake insisted on

bringing her final target home because she finally managed to get a headshot. I took us to a romantic restaurant despite us being severely underdressed. I wouldn't let the dirty stares we got as we were shown to our table stop me from wining and dining her tonight.

"This is nice." She smiled. "What's the occasion?"

"To my future bodyguard." The waiter came and took our drink orders.

"Not that I don't appreciate this, but I think our clothes are getting us dirty looks."

"So what should we do about that, bodyguard?"

She seemed to consider it for a moment before she turned to the couple at the nearest table diagonal from ours and cheerfully waved at them with her middle finger. They looked on in horror and finally turned back to their meal.

"How's that for inappropriate?"

"God, you're a monster," I accused in a high pitch.

She giggled and peeked at me from under her eyelashes. "Can I be your monster?"

"That depends on you and if you can handle the job. I'm not easily scared."

"I had something else in mind as your monstrous bodyguard."

"Yeah? What?"

"What if we got married?" Her eyes changed from confident and playful to terrified and unsure.

What the fuck just happened?

"Did you just propose to me?"

"No."

Well fuck. Why did her denial of a proposal irritate me?

"I'm a traditional romantic, and I just think it would be nice to know if it's on the table."

The only thing my mind could consider being on

the table right now was her naked body as I fucked her.

"It's definitely on the table."

"Good." Satisfied, she picked up her menu. I closed a hand around it before she could open it.

"But I'd be careful the next time you feel the need to test the waters. I just might accept it."

"Noted."

The waiter returned with our drinks and took our orders. After a peaceful meal, we returned home where I made love to my 'almost' fiancée.

The next morning, I was up before her and thought of the perfect way to bring her back to the world of the living. She was already on her back, so I slid down and spread her legs gently. She moaned and I tensed, waiting for her to wake. When she didn't, I gripped her thighs softly and dove in.

I was salivating by the time my tongue first touched her pussy. The pounding I gave her last night was evident, so I took my time and worshiped her right. I knew the moment she came awake.

"Keep your hands above your head."

"Why do you always do this to me?" she gasped. I flicked my tongue across her clit before answering.

"Do what? Want to know how each taste is better than the last? Bring you pleasure?" I didn't wait for her answer. I tortured her with my mouth until she came, and when her body jerked for the last time, I moved over her and kissed her hard as fuck. When I pulled back, she chased my lips like the greedy bitch she was.

"Turn over."

"Why?"

"Because it's what I want." The heat in her eyes ignited to pure fire. She turned over, giving me the aerial view of her slender back. My gaze traveled the length until I reached what I was after. I bent low and took the plump flesh between my teeth just because I could and smiled when she yelped. "Turn your head and close your eyes."

When she turned her head toward the window, I reached into the nightstand drawer and pulled out the small bottle of lube I'd gotten after I had her ass the first time. I lifted her hips until her back was arched to my liking. She was curious but knew speaking wasn't allowed when I got like this.

I made quick work of the lube and leaned over her again, bringing my hips to rest against her ass with a grip on my cock. Watching her face, I entered her slowly.

She gasped.

I pushed deeper.

She writhed.

I held my breath.

We were both slaves to the feeling of my cock filling her.

Her pain-filled whimper when my cock was fully seated spurred my hips to move, wanting to hear the sound again.

"Keiran, it's deep," she moaned.

"I know, baby." I didn't pull back to offer her relief. I pushed harder simply because I needed to take her to the edge of sanity and have her beg for more so I'd know without a doubt she was mine. "Tell me you love me."

She bit into the pillow when I fucked into her harder. The sound of my hips impacting her ass rang about our bedroom.

"Fucking tell me."

"I love you. So much, baby. Please," she shrieked.

I forced her flat with my weight, gripped her neck, and kissed her mouth hard as hell.

I dominated this girl, yet she owned me.

Completely.

And I wasn't even sorry for it.

I shoved my hand underneath her and stroked her clit with my fingers as I took her ass until she shook beneath me and collapsed.

"Forever, Lake."

Chapter Sixteen

LAKE

THE REST OF the week passed peacefully. Keiran and I managed to jump into our routine again. The only invisible hiccup was Keiran's controlling need to know where I was at all times. In the last few days, he appeared twice, waiting for me outside my classes with a look that dared me to argue. By Friday, I had reached my breaking point when I wanted to go running, and he insisted on coming with me.

It would have been okay if he wasn't in the middle of a business call with Jesse, which he cut short to follow me around for four miles. More than once, I made up my mind to make him stop, but then I remembered how exhausting fighting with him could be, so I decided to ride it out and see how long it'd last.

Saturday morning came and I was feeling restless, so I hunted down Keiran in the basement doing sit-ups.

"Hey," I greeted. He paused long enough to take me in with his hot gaze before pumping out his last set.

"How about we play one-on-one?"

Over the years, he taught me about the game. I still couldn't beat him, but I was able to score on him and make him work for the win.

He flipped onto his hands and began pushing his body up and down. I tried to become fixated on his flexing muscles or his strong back.

"You bored?" he grunted as he continued pushing.

"Kind of. I'm all studied out."

"I was thinking"—push—"we could—"push—"visit Laurie and the girls today."

"Oh. Yeah, sure. I'm sorry I forgot." Watching him, it was amazing I was still able to form a complete thought.

"I noticed." He finally stopped the erotic torture show and stood up to regard me with knowing eyes. "See something you want?"

"What are you talking about, Masters? I already own you." I flashed him a cocky grin.

"Yeah?" The change in his voice was my only warning. He pushed me, none too gently, against the wall, causing the shelves to rattle and brought his body flush with mine. "Then show me, baby."

I didn't hesitate and did something he'd never expect. I wrapped my hand around his throat and pulled his head down until I could reach his lips. He leaned forward to take my lips so I tightened my grip around his neck.

"You kiss me when I say. Not before."

"Lake." It was a warning not to push this game too far. His molten gaze might have been filled with anger, but the hardness pressed against my stomach told me he was more than interested.

"Shhh. Don't speak. Just feel." I finally gave in because my submissive subconscious demanded it. He tasted like fresh morning, mint, and cool blue Gatorade. I pulled away only when I felt myself losing control and lifted his shirt I'd worn to bed. I shivered from the cool air of the basement and tied a knot to keep it at my waist. He eyed my naked pussy and hips, and I could have sworn he stopped breathing completely. The only sign of life came from his fists clenching at his side. I knew he was struggling with restraint and hid my smile. I never knew it would be this fun to control him.

To reward his good behavior, I reached inside his shorts and watched his eyes darken as I gripped his cock, stroking and teasing.

"I know what you want."

"I doubt that," he countered smoothly despite the pounding beat of his heart vibrating within his impressive chest. I took his flat nipple in my mouth, biting hard and enjoying his wince from the pain.

"You mean you don't want to fuck me?"

"I want to do more than that. I want to consume you completely until you need me just to be." He leaned down until his lips rested against my ear. "Enjoy your power while it lasts, little mouse, because I will consume you." He straightened and challenged me with his gaze to continue our game.

"Lift my leg," I ordered calmly without giving my true feelings away. I prayed he hadn't noticed my shaking body when he wrapped my leg around his waist. I tugged his cock from his shorts and used him to tease my clit.

Up and down, I used the length of his cock to pleasure me.

Pre-cum escaped the head of his cock, mixing with my own arousal. Before long, his hips began to move, adding to my pleasure.

"Fuck," I groaned when the friction became too

much. The leg that touched the floor began to shake uncontrollably signaling my undoing. His grip on me tightened and then I was lifted. He hooked my legs in the crook of his arms and took over our mutual torture using his hips.

"God. I need..."

"Just give the command," he reminded.

"Fu—fuck me, please."

He didn't hesitate to obey, slamming inside of me without mercy—determined to take what we both needed. The force once again rattled the shelves next to us. A knick-knack that didn't belong to us toppled to the floor.

It wasn't enough to stop the frenzy of his powerful hips as he forced me to take everything he promised to give. My cries echoed around us as I desperately clung to him.

I needed more.

I was still in control, wasn't I?

"If you're going to fuck me then fuck me," I challenged. "Don't hold back."

His body jerked, and he stopped moving inside me. He looked at me for only a split second and then he moved.

His hand around my nape surprised me, but I definitely wasn't prepared to be tossed on the floor like garbage. I landed on my hands, and the impact vibrated through my hands and up my arms.

I didn't have time to recover before he was on me.

My hips were lifted in the air.

He forced his way inside me once again.

The impact was enough to steal my breath away, and I loved every second of it.

"Am I holding back now?" he mocked. My answer was a pitiful, high-pitched sound. His dark chuckle shook my core. "Be careful what you ask for."

And like always with Keiran, I had no idea what I was getting myself into whenever I provoked him purposely. I craved his slow careful, loving. But I couldn't deny that sometimes I needed it like this—like he still hated me.

I looked over my shoulder to see his darkened eyes and his teeth clenched in a silent growl, so I leaned forward on my elbows, creating a deeper arch and threw my ass back, matching his force.

"I know exactly what I want, Masters. Do you?"

He forced my cheek against the floor with a strong hand at my nape and pumped hard with his hips three times. "It will always be you," he answered raggedly. I felt him release inside me immediately after, and I came with a silent cry.

He collapsed next to me while I stayed put. I went into this with control and yet I felt used and dirty. I smiled against the carpeting and turned my head to see him with his eyes shut tight and his chest heaving.

I decided I could watch him forever, but then he stood and helped me up, leaving me to wonder if forever was overestimated. He searched my eyes appearing unsure.

"I'm okay," I said, reading his mind.

He pushed away stray hair sticking to my face. "Was I too rough?"

"Yes." He frowned and opened his mouth, ready to apologize. "And I liked it."

"Only liked it?"

"You don't really need me to give praise to your dick, do you?" He only stared back at me expectantly. I suppressed an eyeball and said unenthusiastically, "Oh, Keiran, you're a sex machine—the king. Your dick is the biggest and so awesome. You rocked my world, baby...

How's that?"

His lips quirked—the only sign of his amusement. "Could use some improvement, but I'll take it."

I snorted and leaned against him. My legs were no longer able to hold me up without support. Keiran noticed so he lifted me and headed for the stairs.

"We need to go. It's a long ride."

"Not with your come making a sticky mess between my thighs. I need a shower first." His gaze shot down to the area in question and his face twisted in agony for round two. "Join me?"

* * *

I SIGHED AND shifted for the umpteenth time. I was beginning to think we should live in our car. We didn't reach the housing development until late afternoon, so I was grateful we decided to stay overnight. The houses were in various stages of completion, but most of them were fully completed and functional judging by the kids that played up and down the street.

We pulled into the third driveway belonging to a quaint college style house. Keiran had told me all about the mother and two little girls as well as their abusive father, so I instantly recognized the girl with dark bangs and curly ponytail sitting on the steps and clutching a book.

She looked up as we parked and released a bright smile. "Keiran!" She hugged his waist when he stepped out of the car.

"Hey, Cassie. Where are your mom and sister?"

"Maddie's asleep and mom went to the store." She retook her seat on the steps. Keiran followed her and pulled me down to sit on his lap.

"You're here alone?" I recognized the dangerous

edge in Keiran's tone, though to untrained ears, he appeared calm and merely curious. From what Keiran had told me, they were a little young to be left alone. "How long has she been gone?"

Cassie seemed to pick up on his change of mood. She looked from Keiran to me uncertainly. "An hour. Who is she?"

"She's my girlfriend, and she's here for you."

"Hi, Cassie. I'm Lake."

"Wow, you're really pretty." She reached out and touched my bangs. "And you have bangs."

"So you like bangs, huh?"

"I don't know. My mom had to cut them because a boy at school cut my hair."

"I'm going to go check on Maddie," Keiran interrupted. He tapped my hip so I could stand up, and once he was inside, I sat back down.

"Why do you think he did that?"

"Cause he hates me."

"Why does he hate you?" Unlike me, maybe this little girl would know why she was a target. It took ten years for me to start demanding answers.

"My dad does bad stuff to his mom."

"Like what?" I started to feel as if this could go on all day.

"He hits her, but I don't know why. Do you think my dad is married to his mom, too?"

"No, sweetie. Sometimes adults don't always do the right thing. Let's talk about this boy."

"What about him?"

"Let's start with his name."

"His name is Ryan."

"And are you afraid of this Ryan?" She nodded and in her eyes reflected a girl I hadn't known for a long time. "It feels as if it's very hard to not be afraid, doesn't it?"

"He's bigger than me, and he said if I ever told anyone, I'd be sorry." Her frustration was apparent. The anger in her eyes burned bright, and I knew she hated that he was in control.

"He might be right, but do you know what will make you feel worse?"

"What?"

"Not telling anyone. He's only as powerful as you allow him to be and underneath his tough shell is a scared little boy who probably feels as helpless as you do."

"So what do I do?"

Do I tell her to run like I did or fight back? Neither was a sure thing. "You do what your instincts tell you to do."

"He makes me want to punch him in the nose," she grumbled. "Can I do that?"

"Do you think physical violence will solve your problem?"

She shrugged in that way ten-year-olds do when they know the answer but don't want to admit it.

"It will make me feel better. I'll embarrass him in front of all his friends like he does me."

"Can I ask you something? I want you to think hard about this."

"Okay."

"Has he ever threatened to hurt you?"

Her face twisted hard as she tried to remember. "Do you mean like pull my hair and stuff?"

I took a deep breath and told myself it was necessary. "I mean has he threatened to kill you?"

Her eyes widened as if the prospect of dying never entered her mind. I was relieved, to say the least. At her age, I had already expected to die.

"No. Never. Do you think he will?"

"No, sweetie, I don't, but make a promise, okay?" She nodded her permission to enter the pact. "If he ever does, I want you to tell an adult right away."

"Like my mom?"

Something told me her mother wouldn't come to her daughter's rescue. "Don't wait. Tell a teacher, your principal—and yes, your mom, too."

"She didn't listen to me before," she pouted, confirming my suspicion.

"Then you keep telling her until she does." She seemed to understand, and since I couldn't think of anything else to say, I asked her about the book she was reading. She became completely animated as she filled me in on the adventures of *Harriet the Spy*. I was familiar with the fictional character, but she told it better.

When the sun began to set, I convinced her to come inside and found Keiran in one of the bedrooms with Maddie in his lap, holding a book. I stood back and listened to his melodic, deep voice fill the room as he patiently read to her.

"The cow mooed—"

"Do the moo! You have to do the moo."

"The cow moooooed all the way home." I stifled my laugh with a hand over my lips as he closed the book and set it aside.

"K—Ka..." Her nose wrinkled as she struggled to say his name. She was a light-haired version of Ken.

"You can call me Keke," he begrudgingly offered, and I felt the shock to my heart just as it melted. I had been the one to advise Kennedy to call him by his dubious nickname and to this day, he vowed revenge. Pointing out that she would eventually outgrow the name didn't help. He still despised it, but he would never risk hurting Kennedy's feelings for his male ego.

"Keke, can you read another?"

"That depends... Are you going to make me moo if I don't?"

"No, silly. That's a cow."

"Pick a book." His innocent surrender drew me in until I found myself sitting between his legs with my own crossed and my hands on his shins. I needed to be in his space.

This was Keiran in rare form and something I may never see again after Kennedy grows older and Dash and Willow's son follow.

"This one!" She shoved the book in his hand and crawled back into his lap. When her bright brown eyes rested on me, she slammed her head back against his chest and held my stare as if laying claim. My own narrowed, challenging her, even as I secretly cried a river of amused tears inside.

"Enough, ladies." Keiran smirked but his gaze never even left the front cover. He was always aware of me even when he wasn't watching me. "At least rabbits are quiet."

"Yes, but they make this cute little wiggle with their nose," I snitched.

"Yeah! Like this—" She wriggled her nose and turned her eyes to see. Keiran met my gaze and promised retribution. Maddie looked up with a wide smile, but he only stared back at her. "Try it," she encouraged, unperturbed.

I pulled out my phone and hit record, needing to capture this moment to use as a bargaining tool later when he got me alone.

"No."

"Pleeeeease."

"Yes, pleeeeease. Wriggle your nose like a good little bunny." My hole only got deeper, but it was worth it.

I was hidden behind my phone, but I could see his face perfectly as the video recorded.

"Later," he mouthed and wriggled his nose.

Maddie cackled and wiggled in his lap with glee. She even reached up to squeeze his nose, and I could practically see steam coming from his ears.

"You make a cute angry bunny," I cooed.

His eyes narrowed, and I knew I'd gone too far. "Maddie, will you excuse us?"

Shit.

She jumped down off his lap and skipped out with the book, which had been my only chance for a weapon. As soon as the door was closed, Keiran stepped forward. I countered by taking two steps back.

"Come here." His nostrils flared.

"No." I giggled even though I was scared shitless. When he lunged, I squealed and turned to run. I managed to get the door open, but his hand above me slammed it closed. He smashed me against the door with his hard body and exhaled against my neck.

It wasn't fair to be that pissed and so fucking sexy at the same time.

"The reason—the *only* reason—I don't bend you over and make you scream and cry how sorry you are for pissing me off is because I don't want to traumatize the girls, but don't push too far, Lake. There's always my car."

Like the time he overheard me agreeing with a classmate that one of his teammates was pretty cute. She had a crush on him and wanted me to introduce them. Of course, I never got to explain any of this. He dragged me from the party and managed to stay pissed until we reached our rental. He bent me over the hood of his car right there in the yard for anyone to walk past and see, and pounded me until my cries became hoarse, and I admitted that Brian Hinkley was the ugliest fucker alive.

"Don't make promises you can't keep," I whispered with as much sultriness as I could.

He groaned and turned me around, no longer appearing as pissed as he had been sixty seconds before.

"So what happened with Cassie?"

I was put off by the abrupt change in topic but answered anyway. "Not much. We talked but it occurred to me that she could just solve her daughter's 'Ryan' problem if she moved her to another school. Why doesn't she just do that?"

"She said she didn't want to uproot them too quickly with changing homes and leaving their father."

"And you agreed with her?"

He stared until I began to squirm. "I had other things on my mind."

I immediately knew what he alluded to—me killing his father and going missing in the middle of the night. He opened the bedroom door and led us to the front of the house where the girls were arguing over which cartoon to watch.

"It just seems like Cassie would be better off. Maddie isn't in school yet so she would hardly be affected."

"It's none of our business."

"You made this your business."

"Do you really want to fight about this? They are safe and she won't testify."

I was prevented from arguing with him by the front door opening and the woman I recognized from the facility entering.

CHAPTER SEVENTEEN

KEIRAN

I COULD TELL she wanted to argue so I was relieved when the front door opened and Laurie appeared. I was also thankful to see store bags in her hand, or I would have gone postal.

"Where have you been?" I asked anyway. I didn't have the right to question this woman or what she did with her kids. Not to mention they weren't my responsibility. I felt it anyway.

She held up the grocery bags, but her eyes weren't on me. She stared at Lake who stared back. I did a double take because I couldn't fucking recognize the look in her eyes.

Whatever it was made Laurie pale and lower her gaze. I couldn't let it go on another second. I gripped her elbow hard to catch her attention and pulled her away.

"What the fuck are you doing?"

"What?" she snapped. All she was missing was the

neck roll. I stifled the urge to grab said neck until she remembered who called the shots. I sounded like a chauvinistic prick, but this was what she did to me. No one else.

"What was that?"

"I don't know what she was talking about."

"The car," I reminded her.

She had the good sense to appear afraid. "I don't know," she said again. "I don't trust her. What if she testifies anyway? Do you really trust her?"

"Of course not," I spat. "But she's our only chance of beating the charges."

"You think they'll find something?"

Fuck. Did I lie to her? I was sure they would. I didn't know how closely they were watching, but I knew the grocery incident wasn't the last we'd hear from them.

"I think we should be prepared if they do." I told myself it wasn't a lie.

"Fine. I'll be good."

"You better." I kissed her lips softly and walked her back over to Laurie. She must have sent the girls away because they were nowhere to be found.

"You're supposed to be lying low and why did you leave them alone?" She looked insulted, but I didn't give a shit. "Do you think this is the first time she's had to look after Maddie? Their father is a drunk, young man. I'd come home some days to check on Maddie in the middle of the day and find him passed out drunk on the couch. Sometimes as early as ten."

"Why not leave them with someone who wasn't drunk by ten?" Lake grilled. I shot her look to chill the fuck out.

"He'd find wherever they were and drive them home, drunk or not."

I shook my head but didn't say more. Every time she spoke about her husband, I questioned the decision to let him live.

"Look, we're out of here. You have my number if you need it, but lay low, Laurie. You're in more danger now than you were living with him."

She nodded and waved goodbye from the porch as we drove away.

I drove us to a hotel nearby for the night. It was too long a drive to make tonight. We decided to stay in since Lake had homework to get through. I ordered room service and pulled out my own laptop. We worked in comfortable silence until the food arrived.

I paid for the food and turned around to see her drop the last of her clothing on the way to the bathroom. She paused at the entrance and sent a come-hither look over her shoulder before disappearing behind the door.

The shower came on as I set the food down and stripped as fast as I could.

She teased me all day, and even after I promised retribution, she found the courage to continue. I had to applaud her. Instead, I joined her and ate her pussy against the shower wall until she shook and collapsed to her knees.

"While you're down there," I prompted and fell silent.

I waited to see what she would do. A teasing smile on her lips kept me guessing, but then she gripped me in her small, soft hands. I loved the look in her eyes as she gripped me with bold hands and stroked as she lowered her head ever so slowly. She never severed eye contact, and I loved that so fucking much.

Her tongue touched me with the shy, innocence of someone who had not been sucking me off on a regular basis for the last five years.

I loved that, too.

"I'm sorry I called you a cute, angry bunny," she cooed and sucked me deep until my entire length disappeared down her throat. My head fell back against my will. I wanted to watch her.

I really did. But she was so damn good at this.

My knees nearly buckled when she released me with a loud pop and hungrily wrapped her lips around the tip, but I wasn't going out like that so I counted to ten in my head.

"Keiran?"

"Yeah?"

"I want you to come in my mouth, 'kay?"

Son of a bitch. I should have known she wouldn't play fair. She worked me over with her tongue and mouth. Her cheeks hollowed as she sucked me vigorously until I did come in her mouth. I had to bite my lip to keep from crying out like a bitch when she swallowed my come in one gulp and licked her lips as if it were the tastiest fucking thing she had ever had.

We managed to finish our shower without molesting each other again. I stepped out first and dried off while she washed her hair. By the time I slipped into shorts, she was stepping out, so I grabbed a fresh towel and enveloped her in its warmth. She never liked the chill that came after leaving the steam from a hot shower.

"I'm starving." My lips quirked as I debated the dirty joke that popped in my head. She watched me curiously and then her eyes popped wide.

"Keiran Masters, don't you dare say whatever dirty, dumb joke you're about to tell. That's Keenan's thing."

"I'm starting to think he's the fun brother."

"Don't worry." She wrapped her arms around me

with a flirtatious smile. "You're much more useful to me for things that matter. Like feeding me."

"Come on, my sexy gremlin. I ordered chicken alfredo."

We drove home early the next morning and spent the day playing in bed. I would tickle her until she cried, and she would wrap her lips around me and dare me not to come. We managed to keep it together until Monday night when I received a frantic call from Laurie.

"That was Laurie," I announced, entering the kitchen where Lake was studying and cleaning.

"Oh yeah? How are she and the girls?"

"Not sure. She says Cassie was suspended from school today."

"Oh no," she exclaimed, but it sounded forced. "What happened?" I watched her casually spray and wipe the same spot on the counter with narrowed eyes.

"She punched Ryan Holder in the nose and kicked him between the legs. Do you know anything about that?"

"You asked me to talk to her and I did. What's the big deal? She stood up for herself."

"Or made it worse. We don't know this kid or what he's capable of."

"Should I have told her to just accept the hell he'll make of her childhood like I let you do to me? Would that have been smart?"

"It would have been safe."

"Listen to me, Keiran. Ryan Holder is not you, and Cassie Finch is not me. It may seem like it, but our history is not being repeated. He's a bully with a bad kid complex, nothing more."

"You don't know that."

"But I know fear. I lived in it for ten years. It's not

always the same. She's telling herself she's too afraid to fight, but her eyes didn't lie, Keiran. She wanted to. She just didn't know how. I just wanted to survive you."

"He'll retaliate," I gritted.

"And she'll fight harder."

"You better hope you're right. Laurie is pissed. This might not end well for us."

"If it helps, I didn't tell her to hit him. I told her to trust her instincts. I guess her instinct was to punch him." I shrugged as if it were inconsequential but the ten-year-old me who was too afraid to fight back jumped with joy.

"You better hope this doesn't backfire on you."

"It won't. Do you know how much I regret never fighting back when I had the chance? A part of me wishes I could go back in time and punch *you* in the nose."

I pulled her close and peered into her eyes. "But you were right, Ryan Holder isn't me. He's not a killer. I am. If you had fought back, I would never have been able to fall in love with you."

"That's the most romantic threat I've ever heard," she cried. "Thank you."

"You're welcome."

* * *

WE MANAGED TO find normality once again, and it only took us two weeks to do it. Lake was busy with classes, and Jesse and I had finally secured the two clients we'd been working on for months now. It was Jesse's idea to celebrate, but since Lake had a test to study for, we decided to throw an office happy hour celebration.

I stayed in my office until the last possible moment

before taking a deep breath and entering the festivities. It wasn't long before Jesse's assistant, Samantha, was there to greet me. "Mr. Masters, are you staying for the party?"

"It looks like it," I offered with warmth. I'd been hoping in the months since she'd been hired that she would catch the hint that I wasn't interested, but she believed her looks and fake tits could get her anything she wanted.

Before Lake, it would have gotten her one night in my bed...or at least bent over the trunk of my car.

"Hey, man," Jesse interrupted whatever else she had been about to say. He dismissed her with a look that managed to impress me, and she stomped away. "Good call on Roxboro earlier. You made us a shit ton of money."

"He was an easier sell than he likes to think," I remarked with a dry tone.

"Nevertheless, two clients in twenty-fours is a record for us. Couldn't do it without you."

"Are you always this emotional?" I snarled.

"Are you always this cold?" he countered and chuckled.

"Depends. Do you still want Lake?" We'd had this conversation many times before, but for some reason, I always needed the reassurance that he wouldn't ever be after Lake.

"Ah, man, come on. I knew I shouldn't have told you. It was one harmless crush for like two weeks. Then I discovered Mindy Jacobs. Remember her?"

"I vaguely remember a blow job or two."

"Yeah, she did like blowing. Anyway, my crush on Lake passed when I discovered how easy high school girls were."

"Lake was in high school."

"Yeah, but she wasn't easy and to be frank, man, she wasn't easy for many reasons. It was hard to stay attracted to her when she was afraid of her own shadow. She'd jump at the sound of my voice. I felt like some kind of pervert."

"Maybe you are."

"You have nothing to worry about. Lake wants you, and I want—" He frowned and looked away. "I don't know what I want."

"I'm not worried."

"Then what's with all the hostility?"

"It's fun when you sweat."

"You're an ass, you know that?"

"I know." I clapped him on the back and changed the subject. Samantha eventually snaked her way back over, and that's when I started drinking. I flirted around the edges of the legal driving limits, and when I reached my cap, I decided to call it a night. Without the option to drink, I couldn't tolerate her nauseous flirting for another hour, so I called it a night.

I nodded to Jesse on my way out. He was chatting up an intern he was insisting we hire. I had to admit the kid was a genius. We had already discussed hiring him when he graduated.

Our office was located in the heart of Stanford, about fifteen minutes from our rental. Since it was late, it only took me about ten minutes to make it home. But when I got home, I found Lake's car missing and the house completely dark. She should have been home hours ago.

I checked my phone but didn't find a missed call or message. I called and messaged her, and with each passing minute of no contact, I grew nervous.

I was just about to call her again when a knock at my door interrupted me. I didn't hesitate to answer and ate up the distance to the door.

Maybe she had lost her key. That notion was quickly dismissed when I opened the door to two suits and a yard full of police cruisers.

"Keiran Masters?"

"Yeah?"

"We have a warrant for your arrest."

CHAPTER EIGHTEEN

LAKE

MY PROFESSOR DISMISSED my last class with a painful reminder of our exam the next day. I pretended not to sweat over the first exam of the term, especially when it counted for twenty percent of my final grade. The last two weeks had been peaceful to the naked eye, but I had been consumed with thoughts of going to prison for the rest of my life.

I made my way across campus to Green Library since Cubberley's limited space was already full with other students studying.

Damn, it's hot.

I wanted this test over with.

I wanted school over with.

I wanted this investigation over with so I could go back to wondering about the simple things, such as, if Keiran and I would ever get married and if he'd ever get over his fear of having kids. Two weeks ago, when I asked him if marriage was on the table, it had been my deepest desire to ask about kids.

Having kids wasn't something I always aspired to do but having them with Keiran set my heart on fire. I just needed him to want it, too.

I reached the library and settled in for a few hours of studying. If I could, I would stay put all night, but I knew how anxious Keiran could get when I wasn't in bed and waiting on *him*. I stifled the urge to roll my eyes and flipped open my first chapter.

Three hours and three double espressos later, I was ready to call it quits—at least until I made it home where I would pull an all-nighter. I packed up my bag and entered the cool summer night air. The sun had long since set so I was grateful my car was parked near-by.

I only managed to make it ten feet before I was surrounded for the second time in my life. I recognized the two detectives who cornered me at the grocery store two weeks ago.

"Well, Ms. Monroe. It appears you won't be getting out of this one so easily."

My only thought as I was handcuffed and led away with an audience nearby was that I was grateful Keiran hadn't been around to witness me getting arrested again. Without Dash or Keenan around, it was unlikely he would have kept his composure.

At least, he was safely home by now though I didn't know how long that would last when he realized my absence wasn't due to me losing track of time.

* * *

I COULDN'T DO this again. My leg bounced, my palms were sweating, and my heart beat wild in my chest. This time was real. They had a warrant for my arrest. A new development was all I'd been told before being held in a room with bright lights and a dingy white table.

Despite the late hour, it was at least an hour before I saw anyone. Detective Grayson and Roberts entered with grave expressions meant to unnerve me. I was already a step ahead of them and felt like passing out now would be the sane thing to do. I didn't have a good feeling about this but tried not to let it show.

"Sorry about the wait. When you're catching bad guys, time just gets away from you." He chuckled alone in the quiet room until it became awkward enough for him to get a clue. I watched his jaw harden as he cleared his throat and took a seat. "I'll get right to it. Does the name Laurie Finch ring a bell?"

"Why would it?" Keep it together.

"She was the nurse who identified you at the facility the day your boyfriend's father was murdered."

"What is this about?" I wasn't willing to fall victim to his games. I'd make him tell me everything he knew rather than the other way around. And just as suspected, he didn't pass up the opportunity to gloat.

"It appears your boyfriend intimidated the witness against testifying. Are you saying you know nothing about that?"

"I wasn't aware there were criminal charges. Let's start with that. At the time, he allegedly intimidated this witness, were there criminal charges brought against him or me?"

"You well know of our investigation—"

"You're reaching for the clouds when you can't even see the sky. Was the warrant even real?"

"Oh, it was very real, Miss Monroe. Thanks to your boyfriend, it was the break we needed to convince a judge you're guilty."

"Innocent," I snapped, "until proven guilty."

"We'll see."

"I hope you have something else under your sleeve or else I plan to make a fool out of your so-called justice system once again."

"We have a statement from Mrs. Finch claiming that your boyfriend admitted to the crime and offered a large sum of money to keep her mouth closed."

What?

No.

The cuffs clinked on the table as my hands shook.

"You're no longer prime rib, sweetheart."

God.

Keiran is.

I wasn't aware of what he had said after. I could see his lips moving but everything had gone silent. I only remember the room spinning before I lost my grip on consciousness.

When I came to, there was a nurse standing over me, and I was left with an unwanted sense of déjà vu.

"You're awake."

It was seventeen-year-old me all over again.

I lifted my hand to block the light. My eyes were sensitive as if I hadn't seen daylight in weeks.

"What happened?"

"You lost consciousness and have been out for about a day. Dehydration and stress will do that to you." She dropped the clipboard and effectively dismissed me by leaving the room.

* * *

AS SOON AS I was able, I called the one person I knew who would help Keiran at any cost.

"What's going on? Word on the street is you're a regular 007."

"Dash, I need you."

"What's going on?" His voice was no longer playful. He already sounded as if he might lose it, and I hadn't even told him why.

"Listen. I didn't call Keenan because I can trust you to keep it together. He's as temperamental as his brother is. I was arrested last night."

He swore, and I could already hear him moving in the background.

"Where's Keiran?"

"I don't know. I was at school when they picked me up. I can't say more over the phone, but Keiran may be in trouble."

"I'm on my way."

"I need you to call Thompson."

"Consider it already done."

"Ok," I said slowly. The receiver trembled in my hand as I replaced it. A sense of helplessness assaulted me when my only connection to my life and freedom was gone—at least for the next few hours. As it turns out, the next few hours were the hardest. The detectives were able to harass me one more time with threats and theories before Thompson finally arrived.

"Lake, I apologize for the delay. We couldn't get ahold of Keiran. I'm afraid he was arrested last night, as well."

"Oh, God. Laurie Finch?"

"Yes. It appears she made a statement two days ago pointing Keiran as the confessed murderer of Mitch, and she also confessed to bribery."

"I don't understand. He didn't kill Mitch. How could he have confessed to it?"

"I intend to find out. He says he didn't make a confession."

But what about the money? "Did he say anything

else?"

"He told me what I needed to do my job."

"His words?"

"Yes. Now, we have a bail hearing scheduled for you at the end of the week."

"I can't wait that long."

"Unfortunately, we have to extradite you due to the breach in jurisdiction. Besides, it's too late an hour to get you before a judge, not to mention the hours of travel to get you before the right judge. I had to pull some heavy strings to get you in this week as it is."

"Will Keiran be there?"

"Yes, but I want to warn you with Keiran's priors, it won't be easy. I want you prepared for the possibility that his bail will be denied."

I nodded my understanding and watched him go. When the guards came back in, I hardened myself for the next thirty-six hours. To do that, I momentarily let go of everything that could weaken me.

Two days later, we were extradited to Nevada for the bail hearing. I never got to lay eyes on Keiran until the hearing later that week. I was brought in before him, but when he finally walked in shortly after, the sight of him didn't offer relief. My stomach lurched at the bruises on his face. Other than that, he didn't look any worse for wear, but it was enough to make me feel sick to my stomach.

His eyes immediately found mine and searched me over. Once he was satisfied I hadn't suffered the same fate, he smiled to reassure me. When I didn't smile back, his face dropped and he questioned me with his dark gaze.

"Before we begin," the judge spoke—her hard gaze and ramrod posture told me she wouldn't be easy or sympathetic, "I'd like someone to explain this custody's appearance."

"Yes, well, we had a hard time subduing him during interrogation."

"He was in handcuffs, was he not?"

"Your honor, Keiran Masters was able to assault Detective Roberts." The district attorney gestured to the detective in question who looked like he suffered a broken nose.

"What brought on this attack?"

"We told him his girlfriend, Lake Monroe, was also taken into custody."

Oh, Keiran...

"Are you pursuing additional charges?"

"No need. We'll have enough to put him away for the rest of his life."

"Don't get ahead of yourself, counselor. Not in my court." Maybe she would be reasonable after all. I stood with my future in the balance and wondered how Keiran could be so calm. I looked over and found him watching me, and I knew he was more worried about me than about the hearing.

"Let's proceed."

The hearing took longer than the first had. I went into this with a little hope, but by the end, I was sweating a river and ready to let my tears join the party.

"I'll allow the release of Lake Monroe at fifty thousand dollars. However, Keiran Masters will remain in custody until the trial, which will be set at a later date."

"Your honor—"

"My ruling has been made, counselor. Keiran has proven he is more than capable—and willing, I might add, of violence."

What?

No.

Keiran was good. Why couldn't anyone see just how

good he wanted to be?

I had to endure them taking him away again. He took one last look at me over his shoulder and asked me with his eyes to keep it together. I never felt as alone as I did when the door opened and he disappeared from sight.

“Dash is waiting outside to take you away from this place,” Thompson informed.

“I can’t leave him.”

“You have to. I suspected this would happen, and so did he. I don’t know him well, but something tells me he can take care of himself and able to think better knowing you’re safe and out of here.”

Was he right? Could this be better?

“Go. I have to look after Keiran.”

I nodded and sought the nearest exit. Each step I took toward freedom felt more as if I was abandoning him.

Dash was waiting outside just as Thompson promised. He rushed up the steps just to walk back down with me. I’d never admit it to him and risk inflating his ego, but he was very adept at reading a girl’s emotions. It was probably what got him laid so much in high school.

We reached the bottom of the stairs where he turned to me and looked me over much the same way Keiran had done but without the sense of possession.

“How are you holding up?” he asked as he hugged me.

“It’s a miracle I’m even still standing at all. I don’t think I can feel my legs, but I can feel everything in my stomach and it wants out.”

“Makes sense. You look like you’re about to turn green.”

“I don’t understand why they won’t release him.”

He let me go to shove his hands in his pockets and released a deep breath. "I'm not really surprised. The courts tend to be harder on people with priors and Keiran is far from a saint."

"Not helping," I grumbled. He opened his passenger for me and gestured me inside then got in on his side.

"Your man's a badass, babe. What can I say?"

"Is it wrong to wish he never helped that woman?"

"He didn't do it for her. He did it for you. Everything he does is for you. Every move he makes and doesn't make is all because of what he thinks will make him worthy of you."

"Except doing the right thing backfired on him. I doubt I'll be a factor next time."

"Let's hope there isn't a next time, and even if there were, you should know Keiran isn't so easily moved. He wants you, and he'll do whatever it takes to keep you."

I realized he might have been right and decided not to argue. Besides, my inability to believe in him is what got us into this. Keiran gave up revenge against his father for me. His ability to be good was something I would never question again.

"What do we do now?"

"Thompson says they're after Keiran now, but they'll likely try to get you as an accomplice. We need to work on your defense."

"They said he confessed to Laurie."

"We both know that's bullshit."

"I think I just needed to hear it from someone other than my own head."

"What? You don't believe he's innocent?"

"No, that's not it. I know Q killed Mitch. I was there. I might as well have orchestrated the whole thing. I had no idea Q felt so strongly about Mitch."

"He doesn't, but he owed a debt to John. Otherwise, he'd have been left dead in a dumpster or a ditch."

"We need to find Laurie and get answers."

"Can't. Keiran won't like it.

"Keiran isn't here, and I have to know why she did this to us—to him."

"It's done. Going after her will only look bad. If she calls the police—"

"Take me or I go on my own as soon as your back is turned."

I expected Dash to get angry or make threats. He simply turned his head with his mouth open slightly. I'd surprised him. "That's some pair of balls," he remarked. "Keiran did a real job with you."

"Well?"

"Fine. But it will take some time to find her. She's probably gone by now."

Thoughts of the girls crept into my subconscious, and I began to remember the things Keiran had told me about Laurie's husband.

"She went back home."

Like a moth to a flame.

We had just reached the city. Dash didn't question it. He made a U-turn, heading back toward the highway.

"Are you sure?"

I'd made nothing but mistakes these last few months, but dirty and wearing last week's clothing, I was determined to see it through.

"No, but we're going to find out."

CHAPTER NINETEEN

LAKE

"HOW DID YOU know where she lived?" I asked as Dash picked the lock. No one appeared to be home. The driveway was free of cars and the house was completely dark.

"Keiran gave me the address when he first staked out the house."

"When did he stake out the house?"

"He found the time to save your life while you ran away from him for two days."

"You sure know how to lay on the guilt trip."

"Because there aren't many times Keiran isn't wrong. In fact, I never thought he would ever be right about anything."

"Your point?"

"You shouldn't have run from your problems." The tumblers clicked, and Dash pushed open the door.

Was he talking to Willow or me? I decided not to open that can of worms and said, instead, "Running was the best thing I could have done for the survival of our relationship."

"There you go again."

"What?"

"You keep doubting him."

"You're wrong. It's not just him I don't trust. It's me." He stopped walking and waited for me to explain. "Old habits die hard," I simply said.

We couldn't find any sign of life. Laurie, the girls, and even Robert were gone. "So what do we do now?" Just as I asked, we came to a door that we had missed. Dash pushed me back so he could enter first.

"Looks like the basement."

We followed the old stairs down, and my eyes immediately landed on the form sprawled at the bottom.

"Fuck!" Dash rushed over to her and gently flipped her over. We both cringed at the sight of a needle stuck in her arm. He carefully lifted the needle and looked around for somewhere to dispose of it. After tossing it into a nearby trash bin, he tried to shake her awake."

"She's sweating and her skin is hot. We need to get her under some water to cool her down." He lifted her and rushed up the basement stairs, taking two at a time. I followed behind him until we reached the guest bathroom. He gently placed her in the tub while I yanked on the faucet. The shock of the cold water brought her back to life with a cry of pain. When she looked as if she would pass out again, I hit her with another blast of cold water.

"Robert, no. Please."

"Laurie, it's Lake Monroe. Where are the girls?"

Her eyes popped open at the sound of my voice. Her eyes shifted unfocused before landing on me.

"Lake?"

"What happened to you? Where are the girls?" I repeated. The silence of the house was haunting.

"Oh God. I think he took them. He took my little girls." She shivered, and I wondered if it was just the cold water or the thought of him fleeing with her daughters.

"Why did you go to the police?"

"B—b—because he made me."

"How did he find you?" Dash questioned.

"I went down to Cassie's school to pick up her homework after she was suspended, and he was there, waiting. I never even saw him until it was too late. He made me take him to the girls and after, he beat and drugged me for two weeks until I just wanted to make it stop. He even started beating Cassie until I told him about Keiran and agreed to turn him in. Oh God, I just wanted it to stop. He hit her so hard. She begged for me to help her. What was I supposed to do?" she croaked.

I ignored her question and asked, "How did you end up in the basement unconscious?"

"After he made sure I gave the police enough information to have Keiran arrested, he locked me in the basement. The last thing I remember was him coming down here and shoving a needle in my arm."

Dash met my gaze over her head as we shared the same thought.

This was all so fucked.

We helped her from the tub when she seemed stable, and Dash wrapped a towel around her.

"Did Keiran really confess to Mitch's murder to you?"

"N—no. Greg told me everything I had to say."

I shook my head as my mind filled with bitterness. "The one person who probably could have helped your daughters you put behind bars."

"I'm sorry. I wish I could take it back." She really

looked as if she wished she could take it back.

"You can." I bit the inside of my cheek in order to calm down. I didn't want to traumatize her any more than she already was. I also remembered Keiran's advice that if we wanted this woman to stay on our side, we'd need to finesse her.

"I thought your husband's name was Robert?" Dash questioned before I could continue. "You said Greg told you everything to say."

"Greg is Robert's brother and a private investigator. Robert isn't smart enough to deceive the cops." She laughed humorlessly.

"Tell us about him."

"Robert?"

"His brother," Dash gritted. I knew he must have been drawing the same conclusion as I, but what could the odds have been?

"There's not much to tell. He's sort of a drifter. He used to do PI work with his partners until recently. They were murdered while on a case. Greg himself had been recovering from an attack." She shuddered at the memory. "I don't understand how anyone could want to hurt him. Greg's always so kind and attentive."

Dash and I shared another look as she went on about him.

There was something in her eyes when she talked about him. Each time she said his name, her eyes brightened and her voice softened.

"You're in love with him."

"I think it's the worst kept secret, and I fear even Robert knows. He would never chance us being alone together and kept him away from our home whenever he could. Last week was the first time I'd seen him in a while."

"Is there anything else you're hiding?"

"Yes... Greg is Maddie's father."

* * *

WE TOOK LAURIE to the hospital against her protests. I ran over everything in my head during the drive, and while she was admitted, we came up with only one possible conclusion.

"We're screwed," Dash stated as soon as they wheeled her back. He had voiced my very thought, but a stronger part of me didn't want to give up so easily.

"Not necessarily."

"I don't need to see the motherfucker to know this Greg is the same private investigator Keiran put in the hospital and who killed John." Dash didn't react to the news of John's killer, so I knew Keiran must have already filled him in. "Then we get her to make a statement."

"She's in love with him. He's the father of her youngest daughter. She's not testifying against him. If she finds out Keiran was the one to put her precious lover in the hospital and killed his team, she won't testify for us at all."

"So what do we do."

He sighed, leaned his head against the wall, and squeezed his eyes closed. "I don't know." Just then, my phone rang with a call from Q. I answered and took a seat next to where Dash was standing.

"I'm guessing I don't have to ask if Keiran was bonded since I'm calling you," he griped.

"They said his proven history of violence was too extensive to take the risk."

"I wanted to let you know I can't get leave this time."

"I don't think there's much we can do. They think

they have a confession from Keiran about Mitch's murder, and our one chance at getting him out is a hopeless romantic."

"Wait. What?"

"The PI who killed John is Laurie Finch's brother-in-law and also her lover."

"No, I mean why would Keiran have confessed to the murder?"

"She lied. Greg told her what to say."

I heard him release a deep breath he must have taken and then silence filled the line. "Lake, I have to tell you something, but I need you to remain calm. Is Dash with you?"

"Yes."

"Is he listening?"

I looked up and found Dash was indeed watching me. I wasn't sure if he could hear or not so I said, "He's paying attention."

"I didn't kill Mitch," he blurted.

"What? But I went back—the message—and you said—"

"I only said what I said to protect you. You and I both know how vicious Keiran can get. Mitch was his kill. His sole right to revenge."

"You didn't have to say it. I can handle Keiran."

"I can handle him better."

"He could have killed you."

"He could have tried," he said, and I could swear I heard him snort.

"Do you think he would have wanted to kill me?"

"No, and it only would have pissed him off more. He would have found other ways to punish you. I couldn't let him destroy the one good thing that made him human."

If Q had been standing in front of me, and if my life

weren't crumbling around me, I might have kissed his cheek. It seemed that no one was willing to let our relationship fail.

"So if you didn't kill Mitch, who did?"

I could already feel Dash's stare, but then he shoved from the wall and snatched the phone from my hand. "What the fuck is she talking about?" I heard Dash demand. He started pacing as Q talked. Dash, Q, the hospital—everything disappeared as the puzzle shattered further, and I began to rearrange the pieces.

Suddenly, Dash cursed, bringing me back to reality on a tidal wave, and he ended the call. His jaw hardened as he said, "We need to go. I need to talk to Keiran."

He handed me my phone, and we headed for the elevator. Once inside, he stabbed the button for the parking garage a little too hard. I could feel his anger building and filling the space of the elevator. I could only imagine how Keiran would take the news.

The elevator opened, and I ran to keep up with Dash's strides as his long legs ate up the concrete. I started to call out to him—to tell him to slow down. Neither of us was aware of the danger until it was too late.

When he froze, I slammed into his back and nearly toppled, but placed his hand behind to catch me just in time. He positioned me so his body completely blocked mine, but also prevented me from seeing what made him stop so suddenly.

"The last time we saw each other, it was under different circumstances."

Oh, fuck. I recognized that voice.

"The last time you were wearing a chair."

"Don't get cocky. It's just you, me... and the pretty blonde behind you. Oh... and this gun I have pointed at your head, I suppose."

He had a gun?

I tried to get a look at him, but Dash was too tall. I'd need to stick my head out, and I had a feeling it was exactly what Dash didn't want me to do.

At least Greg couldn't see me...

I could maybe call for help.

My phone was already in my hand, so I quickly pulled up the group message, sent a text, and prayed. Faintly, I heard Dash's own phone vibrate in his pocket. It was my single beacon of hope. I took one more action for insurance and then hid my phone.

"Now that the pleasantries have been exchanged let's get down to business. Move."

The determination in his voice made my own blood run cold.

"We're not going anywhere with you."

His chuckle echoed around the nearly empty level. "I don't want you. I want the girl, and I was only going to ask once." I recognized the sound of the hammer being pulled back.

Dash...

I tried to push him out of the way and give myself up, but he was too heavy, and it was much too late. The sound of the gunshot rang out. Dash crumbled to the ground and I screamed.

I screamed, and I screamed, and I screamed, but none of it did any good so I fell to my knees to try to help him. I moved to turn him over—he was so still—but a painful tug of my hair kept me from reaching him.

"You little cunt," he breathed. "Looks like you got your little friend killed poking your nose where it doesn't belong."

"What do you want?"

"I know you mean something to someone I want dead, and I think you know exactly who he is."

"No," I cried. He yanked me further and further

away from Dash. I just needed to get to him.

"Oh, don't worry, sweetie. I won't touch him. I'll let prison kill him. I bet he'll make someone a nice piece of ass in the meantime."

I decided to ignore that. Keiran was no one's bitch. "What do you want?"

"I want him to confess to the murder of his father."

"But he didn't do it!"

"I know he didn't. I did."

"What?" I stopped, but he only dragged me harder. His fingers dug into my skin causing me to hiss and glare at him.

"The bastard promised me money for killing his brother and didn't deliver so I killed him for his debt."

* * *

For John.

That's what the message on the wall meant.

It all clicked into place. Q had lied to protect me, which meant Greg must have followed us that day. I don't believe it was a mere coincidence. All I had to do was confirm it.

Wherever Greg took me, it wasn't far. When he forced me into his car, he had run his hands down my body—*looking for my phone* is what he said. My skin still crawled from his touch. A bag, shielding my eyes had come next, and then he tied my hands.

"We're here," he singsonged.

"I'm being kidnapped," I reminded dryly. "I don't need a running commentary."

My head kept replaying the sight of Dash lying there so still. The agony of not knowing had consumed me since I was forced to leave him.

"You have a lot of mouth. I wonder how your little

boyfriend shuts you up. I bet he sticks his cock in that pretty little mouth of yours. Keep it up, little girl, and I'll do the same."

The last thing I wanted was for him to touch me again. Unfortunately, he had to in order to get me from the car. He walked me up short steps, and then I heard a door open followed by another. I guessed he took me to a house and I prayed it wasn't his. If I got out of this alive, I'd be scrubbing my skin nonstop for at least a week.

The bag was suddenly snatched from my head, and I immediately looked around for an exit. He had me in a room that was surprisingly clean.

"Sit," he ordered and remembering his threat, I didn't hesitate. "She obeys. He's trained you well."

Trained me? Am I a dog?

I decided to keep the retort to myself and held still as he removed the zip tie. I was surprised he was taking chances. Maybe he wasn't used to kidnapping. Either way, I intended to use my freedom of movement to get away first chance I got. With as much subtlety as I could muster, I looked around for anything that could be used as a weapon.

"Don't think about it, or I'll kill you as soon as I have what I want from your boyfriend."

"Aren't you anyway?"

"Maybe. Or maybe I'd hate to see a pretty thing like you go to waste. I always thought you were sexy. I wanted you in the worst way."

"We've only met once."

"I'm sure your boyfriend knew," he said, ignoring my response. "I'm sure it's the real reason he tried to bash my head in with a chair. He probably couldn't care less about his precious niece."

"That's where you're wrong. He wouldn't kill you

because I wouldn't want him to, but he'd chop your heart into little pieces for her."

"That's touching but enough stalling. We have a job to do."

"He's not going to confess to a murder he didn't do. You won't intimidate him."

"But I can persuade him."

"How could you possibly persuade him to—*Oh*..."

"Yes, little lady. Oh."

CHAPTER TWENTY

KEIRAN

I NEEDED OUT. I thought I'd be okay knowing Lake was out and safe, but now I needed to see for myself that she was okay. She looked off during the hearing and not because she was concerned about me. I needed to know what caused this new fear I sensed.

I never wanted to be back here. Never thought I would be. In a way, Lake had screwed me. I cared for my future and no longer ran from my past. Consequently, I lost what it took to survive this place. Prison would be worse. I'd need to fight—possibly kill—to survive but I'd never get her out of my head. She was a permanent part of me. My cell door opening provided me escape from my inner turmoil.

"You have a visitor."

I smiled at the thought of Lake fulfilling my need to see her. Only a few hours had passed since she'd been released. I gave Dash strict instructions not to let her leave Nevada for any reason, not that she could. I figured she'd be back to tell me how stupid I was for being okay with all this.

I made my way to the visitor room and tried to hide my disappointment at the sight of my brother sitting at the table instead. His hands were fisted, covering the bottom half of his face. His head was down so he didn't see me approach.

"What's going on?"

When his head lifted at the sound of my voice, and I got the first glance at his teary gaze, I nearly lost it. Keenan was known to be overly emotional but there were only two times I remember seeing him like this—the day he found out I killed our mother and the day he almost lost Sheldon in a car crash.

"I—there was—fuck." He stumbled over words even as his eyes filled with more tears.

"Spit. It. Out." His undoing was provoking mine. I knew this was bad, and I wasn't all that sure anymore that I wanted to know.

"Dash, man. He was shot after the hearing."

Every fiber of my being crumbled into a questionable existence. My mind couldn't quite piece together all he was telling me. It was probably why I didn't move or speak for far too long.

Dash had been shot after the hearing.

I didn't need to ask if his injuries were serious. The emotional state of my brother was enough to go on, but then it clicked. Lake had been with Dash. He was supposed to take her somewhere safe, but something happened to him. I could have very well lost my best friend, but my mind was now stuck on one thing.

"Where's Lake?"

"We don't know. We do know she was with him when he was shot. She sent a message to the group just before he was shot."

"What did it say?"

"Summit County Hospital. It's where Dash was found shot in the parking garage."

"That doesn't make sense. Why would she be at the hospital in Summit?" I knew Keenan wouldn't have these answers with Dash injured and Lake missing, but the questions that tormented my mind spilled out anyway.

Guilt was already chipping away at what remained of it. I was given a family to care about with the same in return. I was supposed to keep them safe. Instead, my best friend was probably dying, and the girl who fearlessly chased away my monsters was missing.

I finally realized they were safer when I walked among the monsters, so I stopped running away from the inevitable. I knew what I had to do.

"Find whoever touched them, and I'll kill them. I'll do it. I don't care if I have to destroy my goddamn soul in the process."

There was no turning back. I let the monsters back in.

* * *

KEENAN HAD LOOKED on in disappointment before he silently stood up from the table and left. I waited for the guard to come for me and led me back to my cell. When the bars loudly shut behind me, I embraced the darkness of my heart once again and melded with the shadows of the cell. I leaned my forearms against the concrete wall and hid my face. I willed myself to breathe when all I wanted was to kill.

I was useless behind bars and as helpless as Lake and Dash, but if I had to keep the motherfucker who tried to take them from me on ice for twenty years, I'd welcome the anticipation.

"Inmate!" The nightstick hitting my cell door caught my attention and pulled me back to temporary sanity. "You're popular today. You have another visitor."

I ran through the list of people it could be and came up short. Thompson had to return to Seattle to wrap up a case. I was led back to the visiting room I had left only an hour ago. When I walked inside, I stopped short, taken aback once again.

I might have been staring at a ghost. She sat ramrod straight with her attention on a man sitting next to her. I blinked hard to clear my vision of the reddening haze. I recognized him instantly as the PI behind Kennedy's kidnapping and John's death. I still wasn't sure whether to believe the latter considering the source it had come from.

He looked up at the same time she did. I knew she sensed me. Her body tensed when she found me standing there, but my attention wasn't on her. It was focused on the grinning fucker who also stared back at me. When he reached up to twirl a lock of her hair, I lost it.

I rushed forward, intending to kill him here and now. Turns out, I wouldn't have to wait twenty years after all.

No one saw me make my move. They were all oblivious. It was the perfect window of opportunity. I could practically smell his blood, but then Lake stood up, her chair scraping the floor as it slid backward. The plea held within in her blue-green eyes won me over.

Damn her.

"Why?" I growled at her—or rather, the monsters did. They smelled blood and retribution.

"This isn't you anymore," she reminded.

I snarled at her and watched her shrink back. "You're wrong. It is me. It always has been." She knew what her disappearance had done to me. What if Dash didn't make it?

"I hate to break up this moment, but I'm not here for this shit. Sit."

"Fuck you." I'd be damned if I obeyed and took the commands given to a dog.

"No, I don't think so, but you will sit." He gripped Lake tighter than necessary, and she stifled a cry. I picked up on his subtle threat to use her against me. I gritted my teeth and sat after noticing a nearby guard's attention was focused on our table.

"Let her go." My hands itched to get his hands off her. He had to be six shades of stupid to touch what's mine.

"I will as soon as you give me what I want."

"Which is?"

"I want you to plead guilty to the murder of your father."

"What do you know about his murder?"

"I killed him, son. Isn't it obvious?" he scoffed as if he were truly affronted.

"What's not obvious is why you think I'd plead guilty to his murder?"

He nodded his head at Lake who wisely remained silent the entire time. I knew the shock of my backward slide into darkness was what had her nearly catatonic. "Because I'll make her suffer to the very last moment. I'll fuck her, too. I'm curious to know what kind of treasure lies underneath her tight clothing. She might as well be wearing nothing. She's just as sexy in or out."

"You're not going to touch her."

"I beg to differ. Maybe I'll touch her anyway as a bargaining chip not to kill her."

"You touch her, then you might as well kill her. She'll be useless to me." I heard her intake of breath and willed myself not to look at her. One look would give everything away.

"That's funny you say that. She seemed confident in your love for her just hours ago."

I knew men like Greg. He was going to kill her, and possibly rape her, whether I pled guilty or not. It was in his eyes. As soon as he left here and got her alone, he'd rape and kill her. I hated what I had to do but Lake was alone. I was stuck in here and everyone was preoccupied with Dash's shooting. No one would be able to save her, including me.

"She a fucking chick. I take good care of my toys, and she's a decent fuck. Her virginity was a bonus and kept me around. I'm a killer, motherfucker, not a lover."

I did look at her then and tried to convey the reality of her situation. I just hoped she didn't wait until the last minute to realize just how alone she was. She was going to have to save herself. I held Greg's stare, but my next words were for her. "I'm stuck behind bars. I can't fight, so you do what you have to do. You'll win."

CHAPTER TWENTY-ONE

LAKE

IN THE FACE of fear once more, I battled with the natural instinct to falter and the foreign need to fight. Keiran had sat and watched us go with a grave look in his eyes. When Greg's back was turned, I pushed aside the hurt and took one last look at him. He smiled a sad smile that didn't reach his eyes and mouthed, 'I love you.'

My mouth fell open with the realization that it had all been bullshit.

An act.

I was too wrapped up in the hurtful words he spoke to see the truth. I replayed the conversation between him and Greg and the look he gave me just before Greg snatched me away from the table.

What had he really been trying to say?

Greg ended the visit before he could say more. I knew he was going to kill me, and there was nothing I could do about it.

"I'm stuck behind bars. I can't fight so you do what you have to do. You'll win."

It clicked.

It all fucking clicked.

He wanted me to fight back.

I had to win—for him, me and for what may be our future. I absently slid my hand across my belly, temporarily forgetting the detachment I had forced myself to feel.

"Your boyfriend fucked up bad. Either that was complete bullshit or you are one deluded chick to believe he is in love with you. I almost felt sorry for you." I was brought back to reality by his gruff voice and rough handling as he pulled us across the street.

This was my cue.

My first stand for survival.

"I—I just don't understand. I thought he loved me."

"Chick's always think it's love."

I sniffled to showcase my woe while silently wondering if he knew he was too old to still refer to women as chicks.

"All those years wasted thinking we had something special. I'd never been anything more than his whore."

"Maybe killing you will be doing you a favor," he stated as he pushed me against the car and yanked my hands behind me. With them hidden, he secured the zip tie once more and shoved me inside his musty car, but not before pushing his groin against my ass. I revolted at the feel of him harden.

Keep it together.

Be distraught.

"Please let me go. I'm not important to him. Can't you see I've suffered enough?"

"I'm sorry, darling, but I have to be sure he's not trying to pull the wool over my eyes." He didn't put the bag back over my head and when he started the car and drove off, he pulled out his gun and rested it on his thigh closest to the door. I eyed it and wondered at my chances of getting to it and not killing us both in the process.

He drove us nearly an hour out of town and into the middle of nowhere. I wasn't familiar with the area, but I did recognize the terror pooling in my stomach. He made a sudden right when the blood flow from my veins to my head ceased. After only a short distance, he finally stopped.

"This is the end of the line, girly." He reached for his gun, and I searched my brain for a way out.

"Wait!" I held out my hands to ward him off.

"No stalling," he grinned and pointed the gun at my head.

"He has money!" The hammer clicked.

"You're lying."

"You know who his father is. Their family has money."

"Mitch was broke. He couldn't pay for the hit on his brother so..."

"But their family isn't. Keiran and his brother inherited a large fortune when they turned twenty-one. His brother keeps a safe and I know the code."

"How much are we talking about?"

"A hundred grand." I let the lie roll off my tongue and hoped he believed me.

He whistled and chortled, "That's a lot of cash. Do you think I'm stupid?"

Not only are you stupid but you're greedy, too. "N—no of course not. It's true, and if it's not, you can kill me on the spot." He didn't reply and the silence unnerved me, but when he pulled the gun away, I released the breath I'd been holding.

"If you're lying, I intend to do just that."

* * *

HE DIDN'T DRIVE straight to Six Forks, cutting my victory celebration at not dying sooner than later short. It wasn't until we arrived at a small, white two-story house that I realized why.

A little boy with dark hair was angrily yanking on the chain of his bike with a scowl as Greg pulled me from the car. I watched him curiously. Something about him seemed familiar. He didn't look up, but I knew he was aware of us because he stopped yanking on the chain. He kept his head low but his breathing deepened with short angry breaths.

Greg ignored him completely, pulling me to the front door and knocking. I looked around for neighbors or anyone who could help.

"Don't try anything or I will shoot you on the spot."

The door opened and an older man with a rough looking mustache and bald head answered. He searched my face with disinterest before turning drunken eyes to my kidnapper.

"This her?" he slurred. He was definitely drunk.

"Yeah." He shoved me inside without warning causing me to stumble to the floor. "She says there's money and a shit ton of it."

"How much?"

"Hundred grand. What do you think?"

"She's lying." My heart felt as if it were thrown into overdrive at his answer. I could feel them both watching me. "Laurie says he paid her fifty just to lie in court. I think we can get more."

He must have been Robert, Laurie's husband.

"Shit. You might be right." I didn't have time to

process the new information. I felt a boot on my ribs that he used to shove me off my knees and gain my attention. He looked down at me with clenched teeth when I looked up. "I want everything that's in that safe."

"It's not as if I can stop you," I retorted.

"She's got a mouth on her. Reminds me of Laurie before I beat it out of her." My fists clenched at the hidden threat, but it wasn't only me upset by it. Greg's nostrils flared at the mention of Laurie and the abuse she had suffered. I almost snorted. It wasn't as if he was a crusader against women's abuse.

"Uncle Greg?" The soft, familiar voice of the little girl standing at the bottom of the staircase brought us all out of the moment.

Cassie.

She looked terrified as she faced her father who drunkenly scowled down at her. "I thought I told you to stay in the room."

"I heard voices."

"That's because grown-ups are talking, now get," he ordered too viciously to be speaking to a ten-year-old.

She turned to go, but then her gaze landed on me, sealing her fate. Recognition brought hope, moving her forward while I wished her away.

"Lake? Did you come to take us home now?"

"I said get," her father roared and slapped her. She cried out as she fell to the floor, but she never even looked at him. Her gaze remained fixed on me as she silently pled for help just before she ran to the back.

"What the fuck, brother? She's a kid—*your* kid. You shouldn't be hurting them."

Robert turned angry eyes on his brother. Resentment and distrust burned brightly in his dark brown eyes. "I can do whatever the fuck I want to them.

They're mine." He paused and I could practically see the evil glow through his eyes. "That goes for their mother, too."

"Until you kill her," Greg shot back with equal disdain. The wheels in my head started turning as they prepared for battle.

"Maybe then you'll stop believing she'll ever be yours. She'll never be yours. I'll kill her first. "

"What the fuck are you talking about?"

Robert poked him in his chest and drunkenly swayed. "I'm talking about you believing that Laurie is yours. She doesn't love you, little brother, and she never will. She's mine."

"Really? Have you asked her lately how she feels or have you just been beating her so you can scare her into staying."

That was an opening. I inhaled, released, and decided to take it.

"I think I can answer that." They both redirected their attention to me.

"What do you know about it?"

"It's simple. She's in love with Greg and has been for at least four years." I looked between them, waiting for the blow to settle.

"She said that?" Greg asked.

"You don't know what you're talking about," Robert spat.

I decided to focus on Robert. He would be the one to save my life. "I know that Maddie isn't yours." I turned on the younger brother and challenged him with my stare. "Is she, Greg?"

"You little bitch. I will kill you right here. Money be damn—"

A drunken fist thrown across his jaw stopped him from finishing. The force sent him to the floor with a hard thud. "Is that true?" Robert roared.

"You don't deserve her. She loves me," Greg yelled back. I suppressed the urge to roll my eyes. The scene was like two little boys fighting over a toy. If this played well, neither of them would see her again anyway.

They squared off again, allowing me to rise to my feet unnoticed. Greg still had a surprisingly steady grip on his gun, which he held by his side.

"She's a whore fucking two brothers and you believed she's in love with you?"

"What you and she had died a long time ago when you couldn't consume anything that didn't come in a liquor bottle."

"No. It died the day you shoved your cock inside my wife." They charged again and clashed, toppling the furniture and breaking anything in their path. It was the perfect opening I needed to run, but then I heard the faint sound of crying travel down the stairs and reminded myself that this was for them, too. I couldn't leave them.

Robert sent another blow to Greg's face, surprisingly holding his own in his drunken state. I looked around and realized I was close to the kitchen entrance. The kitchen had knives. A knife meant protection. I inched into the kitchen and tore open every drawer I could reach until I located the jackpot. Finding the biggest one, I snatched it and returned in time to see Robert gain control and snatch the gun from his brother who looked badly beaten.

Yes. I silently pleaded with him to let the rage consume him. When he hesitated too long, I hid the knife under my shirt and searched for the perfect catalyst until the evil thought formulated.

"Robert," I called softly to avoid spooking him. "You need to do it. He'll just take the money, the girls...

Laurie. He'll steal it all and leave you behind. He even gloated about it when I told him about the money."

"She's not going anywhere."

I schooled my face and lowered my voice further until I oozed sympathy. "But she has to." He watched and waited for the answer. After I survived this, I would question how far I'd gone and probably even mourn the lost part of my conscience, but right now, I was in survival mode. "He plans to kill you once you help him get the money. Why do you think he came here instead of straight to the money? I'm one girl. He didn't need help." I may have possessed half their strength making me no match physically, but I had the ability to mind fuck them until they defeated each other.

"That's a lie," Greg shouted.

"When you're dead, they are planning to elope so they can spend the rest of their lives together living with all the riches you ever wanted. Isn't that why you turned to alcohol?" I baited, remembering what Keiran had told me about him. "Laurie told me so when she told me she's pregnant...with *Greg's* baby." I lowered my gaze with sympathy and said, "I'm sorry, Robert, but I'm afraid you're already out of the picture."

Just shoot him already.

"Not if he's dead." He pulled the trigger, sending a bullet into Greg's prone body.

I worked for it, but I hadn't prepared for it.

The shock of what I'd done paralyzed me, but then the girl's scream echoed from the upper level so I made my move.

His back was turned, so I plunged the knife straight down the back of his neck and because I wasn't taking chances, I stabbed him deep a second time. He was dead before he hit the floor. The knife fell from my hands as I took a step back and studied him for signs of life. What disturbed me the most was that I didn't feel any different.

Movement from a few feet away snatched my attention from the guy I *knew* was dead to the guy I *thought* was dead.

"I need a hospital," he groaned while clutching his stomach.

"Why would I do that?"

"You're not a killer," he seethed.

"Your dead brother a few feet away regrettably argues."

"That was a clever move, bitch. Now take me to the hospital."

"I didn't have reason to kill him, but I have more than enough reasons to kill you." I stepped over his dead brother and picked up the gun. Pointing it at him, I cocked my head. "So why wouldn't I?"

"Because I can help your boyfriend."

"How?"

"I'll turn myself in and confess to his father's murder."

"Why would you do that? Do you fear death so much?"

"I won't get life. I can be out in time to see my baby graduate from college." He looked so hopeful. It was too bad really.

"What baby?" I asked coldly. I held his gaze until he visibly began to sweat or maybe it was the stress from his organs shutting down.

"But you said—"

"I said a lot of things. Only some of them were true."

"You bitch!" He moved in a pitiful attempt to lunge for me, so I shot his leg and shoulder. He collapsed back against the floor, staining the carpet further with his new wound. He looked as if he was barely breathing so I ran upstairs to find the girls.

I searched every room until I found them huddled together in the bathtub. My heart ached for them knowing they would suffer later through bad memories and nightmares. Sadly, it wasn't over for them.

Maddie wailed into her sister's shoulder at the sight of the gun, and I cursed my stupidity for not hiding it.

"Lake, what's happening? Where are my daddy and Uncle Greg?" Cassie sobbed.

"Sweetie, everything is going to be okay, but I need you girls to be very brave and come downstairs with me."

"We can't. My daddy will get mad."

"I promise I won't let anything happen to you." I held out the hand that wasn't holding the gun and waited for her to make a decision. I exhaled relief when she finally took my hand and helped her sister up. "Now I want you to close your eyes—both of you—and keep them shut. Hold tight to Maddie's hand and don't let go, okay?"

They both nodded and closed their eyes. I led them out and down the stairs. Greg lay there with his eyes closed, but as we passed, his eyes popped open. "Keep your eyes closed, girls. Almost there." I pointed the gun at his head and silently dared him to move.

I opened the door and led them safely outside. The little boy from before stood on the porch clutching a bat.

"Ar–are you okay?" he asked, but it wasn't directed at me. His gaze was on Cassie. She looked as surprised as I did when she nodded. I was studying his handsome features and mentally calculating all the hearts he would break one day when it suddenly dawned on me... this was Cassie's Ryan. I was further stumped when he took her hand from mine and pulled her close to him. He then looked up at me and hardened his tone. "What happened?"

It took me a few tries to form words. "Ryan, I need you to do me a favor." He quickly recovered from the surprise of me knowing his name. "I need you to look after them. Get them as far away from this house as possible. Is there a neighbor who can look after you?"

He hesitantly nodded and said, "Mrs. Peterson already called the cops. We can wait with her."

"Good." I watched them leave before opening Greg's car door and fishing out my phone. I sent up a prayer before turning on the screen and nearly fell to my knees at the saved voice recording notification.

It worked.

The recording lasted a couple of hours before an incoming call interrupted the recording. There were missed calls from Keenan, Sheldon, Willow, and my aunt. I pushed them to the back of my mind once again and headed for the house once more. I still had to finish this.

I drew the gun again and entered the house. Greg had managed to sit himself up against the wall.

"If you don't help me now, you'll seal his fate. He'll rot and die in prison!"

"I sealed his future before you shot my friend."

I kept the gun trained on him and lifted my phone. I hit record letting our conversation and his confession play out as well as his plan to blackmail Keiran by using me. His angry face contorted with rage as he continued to spew threats.

"See you in hell, Greg."

I left him inside with his dead brother and sat on the porch to wait for the cavalry.

Chapter Twenty-Two

KEIRAN

I HAD BEEN reduced to a rabid, wild animal as I paced my cell. It had been an entire fucking week since Lake walked out of here with her life in the balance. I told her to fight. I told her she'd win. Had I been wrong? In some way, had I caused her death or saved her?

Not one person came by to see me or answered my phone calls. I began to think they were all dead, and just when the possibility became more real, I was given the first sign of life.

"You're lawyer's here," the guard announced. I couldn't let him cuff me fast enough. Once he did, he led me to the rooms used for lawyer visitation. Thompson was sitting there along with the idiot detective. The one whose nose I'd broken was nowhere to be found.

"Masters, today might be a good day for you," the detective greeted. I kept my anger in check because answers were more important to me, and I wouldn't get any if I had to be dragged back to my cell.

“Why am I here?” I directed my question at Thompson and ignored the detective.

“You’re being released.”

“Come again?” I felt the detective’s stare and fought to keep my composure. I told myself if this were a trick, my lawyer wouldn’t be here.

“Your father’s murderer has been apprehended, but you’ll be required to testify at the trial to give your account of what took place here a week ago when Gregory Finch kidnapped Lake Monroe in order to blackmail a false confession from you.”

Lake was alive?

She had to be.

Only she and I knew what took place here other than Greg.

“Is that what happened?” the detective asked. I did look at him then. I wasn’t required to answer him, but I decided not to make this last any longer than necessary.

I nodded and turned my attention back to my attorney. “Is Lake okay? Where is she?”

“She’s waiting for you. We just need to get your statement to start the process. It should only be a matter of hours before you’re released.”

He slid over the papers displayed out in front of him while the detective excused himself. After the paperwork was filed, he stood and collected the papers along with his briefcase. I called out to him before he could leave. Lake once told me a smile and a thank you went a long way after I complained about the plain cheese pizza she brought home one night. Who eats pizza without meat?

“Yes?”

“Thank you.”

He smiled then and laughed as if I told a joke. Had I said it wrong?

"You need to go home, shower, buy some flowers, and figure out a way to thank your girlfriend. She did it."

He left then and I let him go. The guard came in and escorted me back to my cell. I didn't remember the walk back or the clang of the cell door shutting for what I hoped was the last time.

I could only think about her.

She did it.

* * *

THOMPSON MADE GOOD on his promise, and I was released three hours later. I stepped out into the Nevada heat and was greeted by Lake as she sat cross-legged on the hood of my car parked at the curb.

"Hey there, handsome. I was told you may need a ride home and a pretty thing to get you there."

"And you were duped into doing the dastardly deed?" I played along as I descended the short steps. It took everything not to run just to touch her. I finally stood in front of her as she slid down the hood and opened her legs.

"Nope." She grabbed my shirt and kissed me hard. "I volunteered."

"Is everyone okay? Dash?"

"Everyone is fine, and so is Dash." She smiled as she kissed me again. "He handled surgery like a boss."

I didn't need the details to know he was likely shot protecting Lake. Thanking him and seeing for myself that he was okay couldn't wait.

"Take me to see him." She nodded and I gave her room to help her down. "Should I drive?"

"No, I got this," she stated with a cocky undertone. I slid low in my seat and turned so I could watch her.

She handled my car with ease, and I could feel my dick rock up just watching her drive.

"You're really good at that."

She glanced at me with a confused frown. "What?"

"Taking the driver's seat. It's sexy." I used to thrive on her fear but seeing her be so...fearless—for lack of a better word—was even more exciting.

"My driving turns you on?" she asked incredulously.

"It was a metaphor, baby."

"Oh," she simply said, but the blush that colored her cheeks told me she was thinking a lot more than she let on.

"What are you thinking?"

"About your metaphor?"

"My metaphor made you blush?"

"No. I, umm... I just like when you call me baby. I haven't heard it in a couple of weeks. It makes me feel like a virgin all over again."

Yeah... My dick definitely likes that.

But instead of responding to my baser urges, I cleared my throat of the nerves that built up and got serious.

"How did you do it?"

"Do what?"

"Get away from him and get me released."

"I fought like you told me to, and as far as your release, it was nothing more than quick thinking and a stroke of luck." Her answer only spurred more questions rather than answer them.

"Explain. It's a long ride to Summit. You might as well get it out of the way now." She huffed and I knew I had her. I made her start with the morning she left the hearing up until she came to get me. I was torn between pride and anger at the risks she took to get the upper hand but decided not to get hung up on them.

By the time we made it to the hospital, I was completely on edge. I needed to get up there and see my best friend, but first, I had one more thing to do.

I jumped out as soon as she parked so I could open the door for her, and then I took her hand in mine and lifted her out. Once the door was closed, I backed her against it and shoved my fingers in her hair. I rested my forehead on hers and breathed her in as well as the knowledge that she was alive and stronger than ever. I searched for the right words, but only two came to mind.

"Thank you."

"For what?"

"For saving me... again."

"Again?"

"Again," I repeated. I couldn't explain it, but I knew without her, I'd be either in prison or dead by now.

"Well, in that case, you're welcome... again." I smiled because no matter what, she would always be a handful. "Come on. I'm sure Dash is just as anxious to see you. I told him we were coming."

We walked hand in hand as she led me to his room. When we reached his room, I saw Keenan in the corner whispering—likely something dirty—in Sheldon's ear while she giggle and fingered his shirt. Ken sat in one of the chairs, clutching a tablet.

"Did the Ninjas save the day again?"

Her head popped up at the sound of my voice. Keenan and Sheldon also ceased their make out session. "Uncle Keke!" She tossed the tablet in the seat next to her and wiggled her way down to run over to me. I was ready for her and scooped her up. Lake casually disappeared inside Dash's room. "Daddy said you were playing hide and seek. Did you win?"

I looked over her head and raised an eyebrow at my brother. He shrugged as he walked over with his arm around Sheldon. "It's nice to see you walk among the free again." His tone was light, but his searching gaze was heavy with uncertainty given the last time we spoke.

"I'm okay," I offered and set Ken down. He didn't look surprised that I read his mind. He nodded and let go of Sheldon to embrace me. Sheldon took her turn next, and when I let her go, the door to Dash's room opened and Willow came out. She froze when she saw me but then rushed forward and threw her arms around me.

"I thought we lost you again," she whispered.

"Me too."

"So you're not going to turn into crazy, evil douche again, right? Because I'll put you down. I'll do it." I burst out laughing—not because I thought she was joking but because she looked completely serious.

"I promise if I do, you have first dibs."

She offered a satisfied nod. "Dash is awake, but Lake is in there right now."

It was my turn to nod and say, "I'll wait." A few minutes later, Lake emerged deep in thought. I watched her, willing her to look up, but she didn't. She simply walked into a nearby restroom and shut the door. I sat there for another moment debating whether to go after her, but then Willow placed a hand on my shoulder.

"I'll talk to her and see what's up." I hesitated because I knew Willow would talk to her, girls had a code just like we did. Most rarely kept to it, but girls like Lake, Willow, and Sheldon did.

Whatever it is... I'd get it out of her later.

I let Willow go after her and made my way into Dash's room. He was sitting up and fiddling with his phone.

"Were you waiting for an invitation?" he smirked and lowered his phone.

"I had to stave off the welcoming party."

"The girls can get pretty emotional," he agreed. "Keenan included." He laughed but then leaned his head back with a frown as he rubbed his chest.

"Hurts like a bitch, doesn't it?"

"I still can't believe Keenan took six of these." He truly looked bewildered as he breathed deeply in and out, probably willing the pain to pass. "You know... women say nothing beats childbirth on the pain scale, but I can't see how anything could be worse than getting shot."

"Don't let Willow or your sister hear you say that."

"Shit. You're right. Her emotional state these days is... delicate. Borderline psychotic. I sleep with one eye open and one hand over my dick because I have no idea what to expect from one day to the next. Wait until you have your first."

"That's not going to happen." I took a seat to disguise the fact that my legs had turned to jelly from his remark.

"Still afraid to have kids?"

I didn't know what I felt so I chose not to answer. "Do you think it will be a deal breaker for Lake?" I asked instead.

"I think she loves and wants *you*. Anything else is a bonus."

"I'll remember you said that when I ask her to marry me, and she says no."

He sat up too quickly and groaned in pain as he slowly fell back.

"You're asking her to marry you?"

"I need a ring first and to figure out how to ask

her—"

"I'll call my family's jeweler and you only need to say, 'Lake Monroe, will you marry me?'"

"If it's that simple, why haven't you asked Willow yet?"

He smirked and nodded toward his jacket. "Get my bag." I walked over and grabbed his bag and looked back at him. "The inside pocket," he answered. I reached and pulled out a small velvet box.

"Are you serious?" I didn't need to open to know what it was. I opened it anyway and was impressed by the large diamond and two smaller purple stones that flanked it. On the inside of the platinum band read, 'Summer Will Never End.'

"I was going to ask her later that night but that bastard shot me."

"Congrats, man."

"I haven't asked her yet."

"There's only one answer, and I'm pretty sure you know that as well or you wouldn't have gotten the ring." I put the ring back in his bag and sat in the chair next to his bed so I could gather my thoughts. It seemed like yesterday we were seventeen and eighteen and plotting to ruin one girl's life until she crumbled into nothing, and then fast forward six years, we are talking about marriage.

"I know you didn't come in here to stare at me because of how amazingly hot I am." I snorted, but then ran a hand through my hair like a chick would because she was hot and she knew it.

"Why, when I have all this to look forward to, when I get myself alone?"

"You're a true hideous hag."

"Fuck you, man. Chicks dig, tall, dark, and mysterious."

"That's where you got it wrong, my man. No girl can resist a huge dick. Besides, I have all the boyish charm you lack." I laughed when he tried to flip his hair. When the laughter finally died, we were left with heavy silence and everything that still remained unsaid between us.

"You know you don't have to make it a thing," he said.

"What do you mean?"

"Me getting shot. I only did what you would have."

"I just..." Like with Lake, I couldn't think of the right words to say. "I don't know what to say. Thank you."

"You still believe you have to fight the bad guys alone, but you wouldn't be alive without us and vice versa. Taking that bullet for Lake was like me taking it for you, too. I'd die for you any day, precious." I sent him a nasty look when he reached out to touch my cheek, and he dropped his hand."

"I just need you to stay alive. You have too much to live for to go dying for me. When will you be discharged?"

"Should be tomorrow and then six weeks of taking it easy. At least I'll be strong enough to hold my son when he arrives."

I clapped him on the shoulder and stood to leave.

Lake was back in the waiting room, sitting with Kennedy as she toyed with the table again while Sheldon and Willow talked about the baby. I had enough of listening to that when Sheldon was pregnant with Ken. I walked over and lifted Lake from her seat. "So, back to California?"

"Not yet. There are people that want to meet you."

I scrubbed my hand down my face and tried to stifle my aggravation.

"I don't want to meet anyone. I just want to take you home and forget the past two weeks happened."

"And you will, but there are some people you might need to talk to. I think they can answer some questions."

"They. They. They. Why the mystery?"

"Because I think you need to hear it from them." She smiled, but I didn't return the favor.

What the fuck was she trying to do to me?

"Please," she said picking up on my irritation. "Just trust me."

CHAPTER TWENTY-THREE

ONE WEEK AGO

LAKE

AFTER GIVING MY account of the shooting and the kidnapping and the events leading to the death of one man—because Greg just refused to die—I was taken in but not before making sure the girls... and Ryan were all safe. His mother came home and threw a screaming fit about the state of her house but that was all right, too. I had the proof to clear Keiran and me. Greg was read his rights and taken to the hospital by ambulance.

The first rough patch didn't come until Cassie and Maddie were taken into CPS custody while their mother recovered from physical abuse and drug abuse. I was told I wouldn't be allowed to see them.

I then phoned Thompson, who informed me he wouldn't be able to fly in until he wrapped up a high-profile case at the end of the week. To make things worse, he advised me not to contact Keiran.

"We have a real chance of having the charges dropped for good. We wouldn't want to set him off now," was all the reason he'd given when I'd asked why.

Once I left the police station, I called Keenan who had been blowing up my phone nonstop since the kidnapping. After he had calmed down, he barked an order to stay put so he could pick me up. Since Dash had been shot here in Summit's hospital garage, Keenan was able to get to me quickly.

"This is all so fucked," he breathed after I repeated the story to him. He took in my appearance and agreed to take me back to Six Forks where I could shower and rest. He told me Kennedy was staying with a neighbor to watch over her since Sheldon's parents were out of the country. I was thankful I was able to stop Greg before I led him here to look for money that didn't exist. At least not in a safe.

It was late, but once he dropped me off with the order to rest, he picked up Kennedy, thanking the neighbor, and then took the four-hour drive back to Summit, leaving Ken with me. I thought he was crazy, but I knew he wouldn't stay away from Sheldon when she needed him. I put Kennedy to bed and took a long hot shower before finding one of Keiran's old tees and crawling into his old bed. I remembered so many things about this bed—some terrifying and others exhilarating. I drifted off to sleep thinking about my younger, tortured Master.

The next morning, I borrowed a pair of shorts and a t-shirt from Sheldon and then fed Kennedy while answering a million and one questions ranging from the whereabouts of her parents and how long I can hold my breath underwater.

I was finally able to hustle her out the door but was stopped short by an elderly couple on the front porch.

They were looking around as if lost before settling their gazes on me simultaneously.

"Uh, hi. Can I help you?"

"Oh, dear, I think we have the wrong house," the lady spoke up. "I'm Wendy and this is my husband, Daniel. We're just looking for our grandsons. Could you help us?"

"I'll try. What are their names?" I didn't know these people but something about them being here felt strangely eerie.

"Keiran and Keenan Masters."

* * *

PRESENT

KEEPING KEIRAN ON ice for one day was like asking a pot of water not to boil. I had no idea what had him so high strung. For the rest of the day, he watched me as if I had killed his father all over again. Thankfully, he disappeared with Keenan the next morning and didn't return until early afternoon, giving me some time to put a plan into action.

I'd told Willow and Sheldon about Wendy and Daniel the day they appeared, and they agreed it would be better to wait until the dust settled. Since Dash was out of the hospital, I figured now would be the best time to introduce them to their grandparents.

They arrived just before Keiran and Keenan got back, so when they walked in and were greeted by strangers, the tension noticeably grew.

"Shelly? Why are there strangers in our living room?" Keenan's tone wasn't playful or mildly curious, and Keiran was already studying the couple with suspicion.

Sheldon looked like she'd been caught with her hand in the cookie jar so I decided to answer him, but then Daniel spoke up.

"My name is Daniel and this is my wife, Wendy. We have been anxious to meet you two."

"Why?" Keiran asked, ever the suspicious one.

"Because, young man, we're your grandparents." I could tell by Wendy's tone that she didn't appreciate his rudeness, but I warned them when they showed up a week ago it wouldn't be so easy to walk into their lives.

"That doesn't answer his question," Keenan remarked.

"I can see the young lady didn't exaggerate how intense you two could be. You're just like your father when he was your age."

Bad move.

Bad move.

Bad move.

"We're nothing like him," Keiran growled.

"We know all about what Mitch has done, and I can understand why you resent him—" Keenan snorted, interrupting her. "I'm not finished speaking," she snapped and he had enough sense to look contrite. "As I was saying, I understand your resentment, but I wasn't speaking of my youngest son. I was speaking of John. He may not have been either of your father's biologically, but he took you in, provided for you, and loved you whether you choose to believe it or not."

"Are you getting to a point?"

"You will show my wife some respect," Daniel reprimanded this time. "I can see while my oldest son provided for you, he hasn't taught you much in manners."

"He was too busy staying away to care what we did. As I recall, you two were nowhere to be found, so I repeat—why are you here now?"

"Both of our sons are dead. Whether you want it or not, we're here to offer closure. For you and for ourselves."

"He's right," Wendy added. "We never wanted to stay away, but we believed it was safer this way. So did John. When you were old enough to take care of yourselves, he stayed away so if Mitch ever came looking for you, he could throw him off your trail and it worked. It took him *ten years* to find you because of what John sacrificed. He didn't deserve your hatred."

"He said he found us because the money ran out."

"Mitch was never good with money, so we cut him off a long time ago. I don't know what he told you but he's *always* looked for you, and it was because of John that he didn't find you sooner."

"Why should we believe you?"

"We have no right to ask you to trust or accept us, but we will anyway. We've waited so long just to finally be in the same room with you. We started to think it would never be possible. But then Mitch died..."

"Are you happy about that?"

"Of course not. He may have had his issues, but I am still his mother."

"Lady, he had more than issues. He sold his own son and kidnapped my daughter."

"So there is a child." Wendy looked so hopeful that I prayed he wouldn't break her heart. I didn't believe these people were evil or meant them harm, unlike their son.

Keenan scrutinized them, and then his body slowly lost its tension. "Her name is Kennedy and she's four."

"Are there anymore?" Daniel asked. His gaze was trained on Keiran, who visibly paled at the mention of having kids.

"No," he brusquely replied.

He nodded. "Okay then... May we meet her?"

I watched Keenan's eyes flicker with uncertainty and knew he struggled with the curiosity of his newfound grandparents and the need to protect his daughter."

"I guess that will be all right," he answered slowly.

"She should be waking from her nap now," Sheldon offered. Keenan merely lifted his chin and Sheldon took off for the stairs. I couldn't stand the heat, so I followed behind her under the guise of assistance.

"Do you think we made a mistake?"

Kennedy was up and playing with her toys so Sheldon took her into the bathroom to clean her up.

"I don't know," she finally answered. "It's hard to tell. I believe Wendy and Daniel mean well, and it would be nice for Kennedy to have another strong parental influence. My parents can be so cold."

"Mommy, we're going somewhere?" She finished washing her face and hands and tackled her bed hair.

"We're going downstairs so you can meet two very important people."

"Oh... Who?"

Sheldon froze mid brush and turned to me for help. "It's a surprise," I answered. Sheldon nodded her agreement with my answer and resumed fixing her hair. When she was done, she cleaned up the bathroom and gave Kennedy a once over.

"All right, Ken Doll. Let's go get 'em."

"Barbie's suck. Ninjas rule." She took off for the stairs giggling with glee.

"Kennedy Sophia, don't you dare say that word again and don't even *think* about running down those stairs." She halted with one foot over the top step at the sound of her mother's tone.

"But daddy said it," she exclaimed with wide eyes.

"Snitch!" Keenan yelled up the stairs. Kennedy slapped her hands over her mouth and giggled. Sheldon then led her downstairs hand in hand to meet her great grandparents.

* * *

KENNEDY HIT IT off with Wendy and Daniel immediately. She asked endless questions, showed them her ninja turtle action figures, and even demanded her great grandfather show her a trick. He didn't know any so after fumbling, he told her a joke instead that Kennedy alone found hilarious.

Sheldon and I decided to cook spaghetti for dinner when the hour grew late, leaving Keiran and Keenan alone with their grandparents. For the last few hours, Keiran had been sneaking glances and communicating that he'd want answers later. Other than that, he ignored me and answered his grandparent's questions.

"So boys," Daniel began as we sat down to eat, "John told me you two played basketball. What were your positions again?"

"Point guard."

"Power forward."

"And Keiran, you were team captain of your high school and college teams? Impressive." Keiran nodded and shrugged as if it were no big deal.

"He was more than that," Keenan boasted. "He was invited to one of the best training camps in the country. The NBA and NCAA sponsor these camps as a way to get an early look at playing potential."

"It seemed more for showmanship," Keiran remarked with disinterest.

Keenan, however, was more than animated for the two of them. "He even played with Sean Ramers at the camp." Keiran's gaze shot up from his plate while my hand, lifting a fork full of food, froze midway.

"I'm sorry. Did you say Sean Ramers?"

"Yeah. He's a recent NFL draft pick."

"But wasn't this camp for basketball players?"

"He played basketball and football in high school because he couldn't choose between the sports. When he went to Nebraska, he decided on football. It was a real loss to basketball."

"And you said Keiran knew him?"

Keenan, unfortunately, caught on to the shift in the air and promptly clamped his mouth shut. It was too late anyway. I heard what I needed to hear.

"You have *got* to be kidding me." I pushed back my chair and stood up from the table.

Keiran caught my arm, restraining me. "Where are you going?"

"Away from you." I snatched my arm away from him and headed for the front door. He called my name, but I only walked faster while I dug his spare car key from my back pocket. When I opened the front door and noticed the Mercedes blocking in Keiran's car, a growl ripped through me.

"Lake!" The sound of him calling my name with such authority only fueled my anger. I turned back to face him.

"You manipulative bastard! You staged the entire thing, didn't you?"

"It's not what you think. I only did it to keep you safe."

"Oh, that makes everything okay. Should I just bend over for you now?" I stared at him expectantly.

"I didn't want to lie to you, but you being so far away drove me fucking crazy. You were thirteen hundred miles away," he gritted.

"I lost my best friend for four fucking years because you're a selfish, controlling bastard."

"You wanted to leave. You couldn't handle it either."

"I never would have left her if I didn't think it was necessary."

"Exactly," he barked, stalking me as I backed away. "You would have stayed and been miserable and unprotected, and I couldn't allow that to happen."

"It wasn't your decision. I shouldn't have to explain this to you. Even after she ran away, you continued to lie." When he reached for me, I shifted, pissing him off further. "Is this how it will be?"

"What?"

"You manipulating me to get your way. Is that how it will be? What about what I want?"

"I gave you what you wanted."

"Only because it was better for you! I didn't want it like that. I didn't want to hurt Willow. She was gone, Keiran, and if it weren't for that crazy bitch, Esmerelda, she would have never come back."

"You don't know that."

"But I do know you're a fucking liar."

CHAPTER TWENTY-FOUR

KEIRAN

I WAS FUCKING this up. She looked at me as if I disgusted her, and I deserved it. The lie I told to get her close and keep her there had been a thorn in my side for five years. I wanted to come clean every time she looked at me with love and trust, but it never seemed like the right time.

My brother unintentionally brought it to light, and now I'd been backed into a corner. The only thing I could do now was to try to make her understand, but as I said, I was fucking this up.

"It's late and you have nowhere to go."

"Nowhere to go or nowhere you'd let me go," she questioned, seeing right through me.

"Just stay tonight and hear me out in the morning." When she didn't budge or soften, I added, "Please."

"A few hours won't change anything." She sounded sad and wouldn't meet my gaze. She walked past me and into the house. My relief was short lived when I returned to the kitchen just to find her empty seat and five sets of eyes watching me.

"She said goodnight and went upstairs," Sheldon offered. I nodded and stood awkwardly in the doorway. They all watched me closely, but I didn't see them. I was torn between finishing my first dinner with my grandparents and un-fucking-up my relationship once more.

"Well, I think I'm stuffed," Daniel announced and stood. He pulled back Wendy's chair and helped her from her seat.

"Yes, I think we'll go now," Wendy said, taking his cue. They said goodbye to Kennedy and promised to see her again before leaving.

As they passed, Daniel clapped a hand on my shoulder and mumbled, "Do the right thing."

The front door closed behind him, and the momentary silence was broken my Keenan. "You want to tell me what I just walked into?"

"Ditto," Sheldon chimed.

I scrubbed a hand across the back of my neck and forced myself to speak. "I set up the fight with Sean to get Lake to leave her school and transfer to mine."

"You rat bastard."

"Damn, bro. Why didn't you tell me and how are you going to fix this?"

"I don't know. Do I go up there and be honest by telling her I'm sorry for lying, but I don't regret what I did?"

"That's one way to ensure you're single for the rest of your life," Sheldon answered.

"You could promise never to do it again," Keenan suggested and earned a glare from Sheldon that I'm sure shrunk his balls.

"I'm not sure how you could fix this," Sheldon argued. "But if anyone can, I think it's you. Just don't go up there and be all growly and mean."

They started laughing and brainstorming ways that Lake would likely tell me to fuck myself instead of forgiving me, so I backed out before my irritation got the best of me and slowly took the stairs. They didn't see the way she looked at me as if I had betrayed her. I rehearsed in my head how to apologize but none if it was sufficient. By the time I reached my old bedroom door, I was still stuck on stupid. I heard her crying and leaned my forehead against the door.

"I'm sorry. Please forgive me." My plea would never reach her. She continued to cry on the other side, and I couldn't stand being the one who caused her tears.

"Uncle Keke, what are you doing?" Kennedy inquired, surprising me. Lake's crying instantly stopped, and I knew she heard and would also know I had been listening. Shit.

I turned and found Kennedy standing at the top of the steps, smiling up at me with spaghetti sauce all over her face.

"What are you doing up here?"

"I asked you first." She giggled.

"Does your mother know you're up here?" She shook her head with a mischievous glint in her eye.

"Can you read a story goodnight?" I hesitated, torn between my hurt girlfriend and hurting my niece, but I found myself taking her hand and leading her to her room. She made me read her the same story twice before she let Sheldon clean her up for bed. The uneasy feeling that settled in my stomach when I stepped into the hall and found our bedroom door cracked had me moving quickly across the hall in vain.

Lake was gone.

CHAPTER TWENTY-FIVE

ONE MONTH LATER

LAKE

I LEFT THAT night as soon as Wendy and Daniel left for the night and Keiran's guard was down. Kennedy had chosen him to read her a bedtime story before he disappeared. I had to find out through Willow that Wendy and Daniel had stuck around, getting to know their grandsons and great granddaughter. They also confessed to giving Mitch the money, not knowing he would use it to hire men to kidnap Kennedy. Learning that almost made me go back.

Almost.

I should have been there in case Keiran didn't take the news well but then I remembered that I couldn't be his conscious

A few days after I left, I received a phone call from Cassie. She wanted to talk to me about her new friends at school now that Ryan was no longer bullying her. I couldn't tell but it seemed as if she made have developed a crush on him. I spoke with Laurie who told me she moved the girls back home since Robert was dead. She'd gotten a new job with the local hospital and had even joined the PTO at school to keep a better eye on Cassie's progress at school. She also told me Keiran had visited the day before and told her about what I did for them. I expected anger—if not or Robert then for Greg but she only said thank you before hanging up.

I hadn't heard from then since and prepared myself to never again after Greg's trial.

"Thank you for coming with me. Dash is swamped with catching up since he went back to work, and he doesn't want me alone since I'm close." Willow managed to convince me to leave my woes behind in their apartment for a day of baby shopping.

"Are you excited?"

"I like to think what I'm feeling is like an exciting terror, but I am ready to gain back control of my own body again. I think whatever future pain promised will be worth it." Her pale skin whitened more if possible, and I figured she was thinking about the birth..

I picked up a onesie that read, 'Mama's Baby, Daddy's Hatin'. "What about this?" I showed it to her as a distraction. She turned wide eyes on the tiny blue garment and squealed. After snatching it from my hand to check the size, she then threw it in her cart.

"These clothes don't have enough color or personality," she grumbled. "I'm thinking about making all of his clothes myself, but my fingers have gotten so fat, I can't even stand to look at them."

I looked down at her fingers, which were a little swollen but not enough to cause her dramatics. I knew telling her at this point that she was still a beautiful curvy delight was a waste of time, so I changed the subject.

"You said Dash is back working. How is he otherwise?" I knew getting shot must have been traumatic for him even though he'd never admit it. Guys liked to bottle their feelings until the emotional overload obliterated who they once were.

"He's had his days, but he's still Dasher." She sighed and got a faraway look in her eyes.

"*Dasher*, huh?" I teased and bumped her shoulder.

"He insisted I use his name when we..."

"Got it." I didn't need any more detail about their sex life. I've already had the front seat showing. "Doesn't it get weird since his mother also calls him Dasher?"

"Not like me." She winked, and I had a full on laugh—snort and all. "Besides, since he only lets his mother or me call him Dasher, I figured why not."

"And Santa Claus. How does he feel about being named after a reindeer?"

"Oh, God. Don't let him hear you say that. You'll never hear the end of it. Although..." She looked thoughtful as she chewed on her lip, "you did save his life so you might get a free pass."

"I didn't save his life." The regret in my voice caused her to drop her smile. I shook my head when the memory of him being shot assaulted me. "If he hadn't been trying to protect me, he wouldn't have gotten shot. It's my fault. I made him take me out there to find Laurie."

"And that woman would have died if you hadn't. Her girls would have been motherless and I know you, of all people, don't want that for them. Keiran told me about Cassie. I think what you did for her was amazing."

"I didn't do anything. She punched the kid in the

nose."

"And I bet she'll do it again if she has to. Besides, I doubt she'll have to. That kid got his lights knocked out by a girl. He'll be licking his wounds until he's thirty, at least." I laughed and we shared silence while we looked over baby clothes. "Did you know the bullet hit him half an inch from his heart?"

I felt pain near my own as I said, "No, I didn't."

"The doctor said he should have died. The way the bullet entered was clearly a direct path to his heart, but at the very last moment, it was redirected and that alone saved his life. He said he must have tried to get out of the way, or the shooter had a change of heart."

"Dash would have never done that since I was behind him and that son of a bitch didn't have a heart to change."

"Precisely. You and I both know you tried to push him out of the way, so I repeat—you saved his life, Lake Monroe."

"He weighs a ton. I barely moved him, and he still got shot."

"Doesn't matter. It was enough to save his life which was exactly what you did."

"I don't understand why he would risk his life for me when he has you and the baby."

"Because he loves you, too. We all would have done the same thing and so would you. Now, if you don't mind, I'm hungry and my feet hurt. I'm sure I have everything."

"Dash bought out like three different baby stores when he found out you were pregnant. Where's he keeping all that stuff anyway? Spare bedroom's empty."

"I wondered the same thing, but whenever I ask, he would say he found the perfect spot. Whatever that means." Willow rolled her eyes up, but then her eyes brightened with mischief. “I say we look for them.”

“I don’t know. Maybe he’s hiding them for a rea—” I stopped when I noticed a woman appear around a pillar up ahead and head straight for us. I told myself I was being paranoid, but the way she watched Willow wasn’t the casual glance of a harmless stranger. When I started to warn Willow, it was too late. She stood in front of us, blocking any escape.

“Hello, Little Tree. It’s been a while,” the woman greeted. She awakened vibes I hadn’t felt since being kidnapped by Mitch, and when Willow stiffened and retreated, the vibes became a screaming demand to run.

“What are you doing here?” she asked the woman coldly.

“Don’t worry. I’m not here for you.” She then turned her attention to me. “I’m here for her.”

“Me?” I didn’t even know this woman. I didn’t have time to form a response because she pulled out a gun and pulled Willow close.

“I don’t have time for proper introductions. Come with me, or I pump her full of bullets.” To make a point, she pressed the muzzle into Willow’s stomach. “Do you want to be responsible for what happens to this little bundle of joy?”

“I’ll go. Just let her go.”

“Very well.” She lowered the gun, but as soon as she did, she shoved Willow’s head into the stone pillar she had obviously hidden behind to wait for us. Willow fell to the ground unconscious.

“Willow!” Instinct made me fall to my knees to help her, but the feel of the muzzle pressing against my temple kept me from helping her.

“Get up and don’t be so dramatic,” she ordered. “I had to make sure she wouldn’t call for help anytime soon.”

"And you couldn't just take her phone?"

"I could have. Now let's go." She shoved the gun in my side and kept me close with a hand on my arm as we left Willow behind. I prayed she and the baby were okay. The woman had a car parked around the corner on a deserted street. "I don't have time to tie you up, but if you so much as twitch an eyebrow, I will shoot you in that pretty face."

"Who are you?"

"I'm Esmerelda. I'm sure you've heard of me."

I looked closer and saw what I missed before.

Di was a spitting image of her mother.

"Only that you're a psychotic bitch." She chuckled but then her hand whipped out to hit me across the face with a gun. I was left dazed as she acted as if nothing happened and drove away.

"Don't talk back to me, little girl."

I bit back another smart retort and fixed my gaze on the road. After we had left the city behind, I threw caution to the wind and broke the silence.

"Where are you taking me?"

"It's more like where you're going to take me."

"I don't understand."

"My daughter, girlie. You're going to take me to her."

"Why would I do that?"

"Because I'll kill you if you don't," she answered matter-of-factly. I didn't react. Maybe I was too used to having my life threatened to be scared.

"Your daughter is twenty-five years old. Why now?"

"The last memory I have of my daughter was Mario taking her from me after she was born, saying it was too dangerous to keep her."

"But wouldn't Arthur have questioned why you were no longer pregnant and there was no baby?"

"My husband was away on business when I had her. When he returned, I told him I miscarried and had her cremated." She shrugged and lit a cigarette then turned to blow the fresh smoke in my face.

"Seems farfetched."

"Men are stupid and gullible, sweetie. Haven't you ever had to lie to your man?" I didn't answer her. I turned to look out the window, reflecting on all the lies presently standing between Keiran and me. "No, of course you haven't," she laughed. "You have meek written all over you. It's why he picked you."

"You don't know a damn thing about me."

"I don't have to. You look just like her, you know."

"Who?"

"The pitiful, blonde girl he threw everything away for. I remember her well. Keiran was top stock before she ruined him. He was the best we had, and if I didn't know any better, I'd think you were her all grown up." Using my peripheral vision, I watched her take another pull on her cigarette and then glance at me with an evil smile curling her red painted lips. "Kind of makes you wonder, doesn't it?"

"Wonder about what?"

"If he's really in love with you or a dead girl."

"I guess it doesn't matter now, does it? You're going to kill me as soon as you have what you want anyway."

"I guess we'll just have to see, won't we?" I ignored her question because there was no way I was letting her get anywhere near Di. All I needed was one opportunity.

That opportunity came when we were halfway to California when my hip pinged, and I realized I still had my phone. I cast a nervous glance at Esmerelda whose gaze remained fixed on the road. Maybe she hadn't heard.

"What does it say?" she smirked.

I slowly pulled my phone from my pocket. It was a text from Keiran—Waiting for you.

I frowned at his cryptic message. Why would he be waiting for me? I hadn't heard from him since I left that night. I had expected him to hunt me down and drag me back and demand my submission, but he did none of that. He simply left me alone like I thought I wanted. When one day stretched into one month, I became hurt and angry. He was the one to fuck up this time, and I was still the one left with regrets.

"So what does it say?" she repeated.

I quickly deleted the message. "It was just an email from my school," I lied.

After missing the exam and classes for two weeks, I had to pull out of the summer term, delaying my graduation. I was lucky they weren't kicking me out altogether considering the circumstances. My arrest on campus had made the local news.

That was a joy.

I hated even the thought of showing my face on campus.

"You're not lying to me are you?"

"Why would I do that? You have a gun."

"That's right, I do, so don't try anything. Your boyfriend isn't waiting around the corner to save you, damsel."

Waiting for you.

But maybe he was... because that's what the text meant.

He was waiting for me.

I knew Keiran wouldn't have gone back to California without me. He couldn't stand the distance. That much was proven so I had no idea how he could have made it to California so quickly, but I began to breathe a lot easier and my heart didn't pound so hard.

A few hours later, we entered Los Angeles just as the sun was setting. I gave her directions and prayed I had deciphered the message correctly. Esmerelda had taken and thrown my phone from the car after she warned me not to try anything, which left me completely alone.

Maybe Di wouldn't be home, and it would buy me some time to figure out how to stop Esmerelda.

"What do you want from your daughter?"

"What makes you think I want anything from *her*?

"You're after something. What is it?"

She glanced at me with a grin and shrugged. "All right, I'll tell you. After Mario was sent to prison, he got a message to me—told me he had some money stashed for me to get away and start a new life... and wait for him." She snorted and said, "Can you believe that?"

"So if he told you where it is, why do you need her?"

"Because it's in a safe that only she has the combination to."

"And if she doesn't give it to you?"

"My daughter will obey her mother." It was my turn to snort. I rolled my eyes and turned my head toward the passenger window. I was now looking forward to when she finally met her daughter. She was in for one rude awakening.

I directed her to Di's apartment, and when the building came into sight, I stealthily looked around for any sign of Keiran.

"He said there was a house. Why are we here?"

"Di doesn't live in her father's house. If you need her, this is where you'll find her."

"Very well. Now the apartment number?"

I assumed she would take me with her and tried

not to look defeated. "Apt 305."

"Remember, I will kill you if you try anything." The last thing I needed was to be reminded, but I nodded anyway. "Good. I want you to stay here, but unfortunately, I will have to tie your hands. Would you be a dear and grab the tape inside the glove compartment?" She flicked the gun back and forth when I didn't move to obey, so I snatched open the compartment and slammed it shut again. She then took the tape and secured my hands before leaving the car without a word.

My gaze searched the car for a knife or something sharp enough to free me and came up short. Any minute now, I expected to hear the sound of gunshots or screaming, but none came. Since my hands were tied in front of me, I tried the door only to realize the child lock had been engaged. I slammed my restrained fist against the window in an attempt to shatter the glass when a knock on the driver's window surprised me. I turned and found Di looking through the window.

"Di?"

"In the flesh," she shouted so I could hear her, and I wondered how she found me. She tugged on the locked door, and I shook my head to tell her not to bother, but then she disappeared. A couple of minutes later, the driver window shattered as Di sent a tire iron through it. The car alarm sounded, and I started to panic knowing Esmerelda would be down any minute when she found Di missing.

But where was Keiran?

She hit the locks and yanked open the door, then produced a knife to cut open the tape binding my wrists.

"We need to get Keiran and get out of here. I just hope Keiran doesn't kill her."

"Why?"

"Because I called the cops."

"Why would you call the cops? You know he will kill her." As soon as I said it, a shot rang out, disturbing the quiet of the darkened garage.

CHAPTER TWENTY-SIX

KEIRAN

I WAS GETTING sick of all the fucking waiting. I never went back to our rental after Lake left me in the middle of the night again. I figured she'd want her space to think, so I forced myself to stay behind in Nevada, only to find out through Dash she never left and was bunking with them. I went after her, forgetting my agreement to give her space, but then Dash convinced me to let her do this in her own time and that my need to control her was what was driving us apart.

This morning, I got a call from Jesse about an impromptu meeting with one of our clients that wanted to renegotiate the price of their contract. I'd been halfway back to California when I got a call from Dash.

"Where are you?" he screamed into the phone.

"Why the fuck are you screaming?"

"Willow and Lake were attacked a few hours ago. I just got the fucking call. It was Esmerelda. She knocked Willow unconscious and took Lake." I swore and sped up, already knowing where she would go and what she was after. The only thing keeping me from completely losing it was that I knew I was hours ahead of them. I'd intercept her at Di's apartment.

"Is Willow okay?"

"For now. She went into labor on the way to the hospital, but they stabilized her. Someone *found* her alone on the ground," he growled. Dash rarely ever lost control, but right now, he seemed to barely hold onto it. "This is the second time she's fucked with what's mine. I want that bitch dead."

Well fuck.

I hung up with Dash and made it to LA with about six hours to spare. When Di opened the door. I didn't bother with a greeting and shoved my way inside. "If you're looking for your girlfriend again, she's not here, and I'd appreciate more than just a knock the next time you show up at my door—you know...like a hello?"

"You're mother is coming and she has Lake." Her mouth opened and closed, but then she chose to remain silent. She closed and locked the door as if she didn't know the real danger wasn't already inside.

I heard the catch in her throat. "How did she find me?"

"She needs Lake to lead her here."

"Lake won't tell her where I am."

"I know. That's why I'm going to tell her to." It was highly unlikely that she would still have her phone, but I sent the message anyway just in case. If she got it, she'd follow her instincts.

"She's not after me. She's after the money, you know."

"I know."

"What are we supposed to do when she finds out that most of it is gone? Keenan and I spent it years ago.

He built his shop, and I made daddy pay me back for each time he made me spread my legs."

"She's not going to ever get to the money because she's not leaving here alive." I hated waiting, but it was all I could do. There was a lot of highway between here and Nevada.

"You can't kill her."

I faced her and saw that she was completely serious. "Why not?"

"She's my mother?" she answered sarcastically.

"She was an incubator, not a mother, and there are a lot of people who want her dead."

"I don't care. I can't watch my mother die the same day I meet her."

"She kidnapped my girlfriend and attacked her friend for the second time, and you expect me to let her live?"

"I'm not saying she has to get away. We could just call the cops."

"I'm not calling the fucking cops."

She was starting to piss me off and I actually began to debate killing her as well as I wondered if Di was really friend or foe. Her mother likely came to do her harm, yet she wanted to protect her.

"Are you going to be a problem?" The conversation had taken a dangerous turn.

"Really? You're threatening to kill me?"

"I'm asking you if I need to."

"Look, Lake's my friend, and I don't want her hurt, but I don't think I can watch you kill my mother. You killed yours and look how screwed up that made you."

I pulled out my gun and pointed it at her head. She maintained eye contact even as I threatened her life.

"Answer me."

"No," she shouted. It was the only crack in her

tough exterior. "I just can't do this."

"Then leave."

"This is my apartment," she argued.

My patience had run out so much that the threat I spewed next took us both by surprise. "Get the fuck out, or I swear I will bury you beside your mother."

Fortunately, she was smart enough to know I was completely serious and left.

Six hours later, a knock on the door pulled me away from the window I kept watch through. With my gun at my side, I answered the door to find Esmerelda alone. "Hello, Esmerelda." Her eyes widened with panic, but then she recovered just as quickly and attempted to pull her gun. I caught it and slammed it against the molding, causing the gun to drop and then threw her inside the apartment behind me. I then slammed the door shut and locked it.

"Why are you here? Where's my daughter?"

"Your daughter couldn't watch you die so I sent her away."

"You're not going to kill me," she challenged and smiled. Her eyes shifted wildly around the apartment as she stood to her feet.

"Why the fuck would you think that?"

"Because you're a slave, and I order you not to. I'm also the closest thing to a mother you have. Can you watch me die?"

Her attempt to mind fuck me was not lost. "Think again. Where's Lake?"

"She's secure and alive, but she won't be for long if you kill me." Her smug smile was misplaced. She thought she had me until I pointed the gun in her direction and shot the floor next to her knee.

"The next one takes out your knee."

"Okay!" She held up her hands as if it could stop

me and slid away. “She’s in the car. I tied her up and left her there.” I could have killed her right then, but my ringing phone saved her life.

“What?” I snapped without checking the ID.

“You need to get out of there,” Di warned. I was ready to hang up on her when she added, “I called the cops.”

“Why the fuck would you do that?” I growled into the phone. The next moment, I heard the melodic—yet frantic—sound of Lake’s voice.

“Keiran, get down here now,” she ordered. I smiled into the phone, despite the nefarious situation, because she thought she could command me.

“Are you safe?”

“Yes.” Her voice had softened, and silence then filled the empty space between us. “Is she dead?”

“No.”

She sighed into the phone, and I wondered if it was relief or disappointment that caused the sound. “Good. Don’t kill her.”

“I can’t leave her alive.”

“And if you kill her now, you’ll go to prison.” She fell silent again, probably to let me work it out on my own. Esmerelda watched me—her smugness had returned full force.

“Very well,” I finally answered and aimed the gun at Esmerelda. I had the pleasure of seeing her smugness wiped from her face just as she collapsed.

* * *

I HEARD THE sirens and made my way down the hall and three flights of stairs to the parking garage. I opened the door to find Lake pacing angrily and Di crouched against the wall staring at the ground. Lake spotted me first and turned on me.

"What did you do?" she hissed.

I ignored her and closed in on her space until I had her face in my hands. "Shut the fuck up. If it's not to tell me you're okay, I don't want to hear it." She glared and then her body jerked. I looked down confused and realized she had been trying to knee my dick. "What are you doing?"

"Don't talk to me like that. Don't *ever* talk to me like that again," she repeated with force.

"You could have died, but you're worried about how I'm speaking to you? I was scared shitless thinking about what could happen to you."

She blinked once and then her shoulders relaxed and she sighed.

"I'm fine."

She didn't elaborate so I nodded and kissed her lips. "I didn't kill her," I admitted. I didn't have the chance to say more because it sounded as if the entire Los Angeles' police department flooded the outside streets with sirens and lights. "We should go handle that," I directed to Di, who was now staring at the closed door as if it were a foreign object.

"Di, are you okay?"

"I never even got to see her," she croaked. "I wonder what she looks like."

I couldn't help but feel sorry for her. She was mourning a woman who would sell her daughter's soul for her own personal gain. Her mother was no better than her father, but she'd never know for sure. Maybe it was better that way.

"She's not dead," Lake offered when I only continued to frown. "He didn't kill her."

She finally turned around, appearing hopeful. "No?"

"I shot her in the leg."

She looked surprised but recovered quickly. "Thank you."

I couldn't acknowledge her gratitude because I wanted to kill Esmerelda and would have if it weren't for Lake—police be damned.

"Let's go."

Everyone in the building had already evacuated and huddled in the street leading to the front entrance. I thought it was a little dramatic for one shot fired but shrugged it off and found the nearest police officer.

"Sir, you can't cross the line."

Just then, a screaming Esmerelda was brought out of the building on a stretcher and put inside an ambulance. She was then hauled away with two police cars leading and trailing it. "Check your database. She's a wanted woman, and I'm the one who shot her."

The officer, who I quickly figured out was a rookie, pulled his gun with shaky hands, and ordered me to put my hands up. I briefly saw my entire life as I lifted my hands slowly. It wasn't the possibility of prison or the gun that made me afraid, but the terrified man behind the gun. I fell completely still once my hands were up and prayed Lake stayed back. If the wind blew, he'd panic and blow me away.

Another officer cuffed me, and I gritted my teeth.

"Officer, it's my apartment and she intruded. She would have killed me, but he saved my life." Di continued to lay it on thick for my benefit, but I caught none of it. My attention was fixed on Lake. To the untrained eye, she was a picture of calm, but I could tell she was trying to keep it together.

She was learning to keep her fear below the surface.

I never even noticed when the officer took the cuffs off. I didn't hear a word he said after. I just kept watching Lake.

"Sir. Sir?" I finally tore my attention away from Lake with a growl and fixed my gaze on the rookie. "C–could you come down to the station and make a statement?"

I wanted to say no but knew I didn't exactly have that option. It was late, and I wanted Lake alone so I could erase the past couple of months, including these last few hours.

We all gave our statements and bunked in a hotel for the night. When Di slid her key in the slot, I stood in the hallway with my arm around Lake and stared even after her room door closed.

"Keiran?"

My head whipped around at the sound of Lake calling my name. "I need to talk to Di." I handed her the key card and nudged her to our room three doors down. "Go inside and wait for me." She nodded silently and turned away, but I gripped her arm to keep her there. "We *will* talk tonight," I warned. She didn't respond. She pulled her arm away, and I watched her disappear into our room.

I knocked on Di's door and waited until she yanked the door open. "This isn't that kind of party," she greeted. I scrubbed my hand down my face, still unused to her snarkiness twenty-four seven.

"I want to talk to you."

"Why?"

I shoved my way inside and slammed the door close. "Because I said so. Come on." I gestured to the bed and took a seat in the chair directly across from it. I had to turn my glare on full force to get her to obey. She huffed and sat on the bed but not before shooting me a hateful look. I decided to start with that. "Do you hate me for what I did?"

Her eyebrow raised and she said, "Why would you care? That's not like you."

"It matters because I need to know if I can trust you. Lake considers you a friend and so does Keenan. Will your mother make you forget that?"

She looked wary now and dropped her arms she had crossed. "I wouldn't hurt them, and I don't hate you—heavily irritated maybe, but I don't hate you."

"Your mother is not who you hoped she might be. I knew her growing up. She's cold and calculating. She won't love you, but she will sacrifice you first chance she gets."

"But I'm her daughter."

"You were Mario's daughter, and he sold you to how many men?"

She stood up with her fists clenched and snarled. "Fuck you."

And just like with Lake, I was fucking this up. This is why Dash handled what needed rationalizing. He had a gentler approach that I attempted to channel now.

"I'm sorry."

It was the first apology of the night. It seemed like I would be adopting them a lot before the night finally ended.

"It doesn't matter," she said. Her shoulders slumped in defeat. "I guess I'll never know for myself because she's gone again."

I considered my next words carefully. "I know you're curious about your mother, but she'll hurt you, Di, and I can promise it will hurt much worse than when you didn't know her."

"I already told you," she laughed dryly. "It doesn't matter anymore. Can you go please?" I sat there for another minute, but she wouldn't meet my gaze. She appeared lost as she fixated on a spot on the wall. I reluctantly left the room and crossed the hall to enter my own. The room was completely dark as I shed my shirt and searched out Lake through the darkness. She sat against the headboard with her knees to her chest.

"Hey," she greeted softly,

"You waited." I flicked on the lamp by the bed and her eyes immediately found my bare chest and traveled down to where I was unbuckling my belt. I heard her suck in a breath and hid the grin that pulled at my lips. I needed to remain serious for this.

"You told me to."

"I did, but I think you and I both know following directions is no longer something you can do."

"I don't want to fight with you," she whispered, and I saw what she refused to show down the street with the police. I didn't want to scare her, and the slight shiver that wracked her body told me I did exactly that.

"Then what do you want?"

"What do you mean?"

"You keep running away from me every time we have a problem. I'm not... going... to hurt you," I gritted.

"Maybe not." She looked away, and I didn't like that shit. "But I'm starting to think we can't trust each other."

My heart skipped a beat and then began a pounding rhythm that created an ache in my chest.

"You don't trust me?"

"I—" She started to answer, but then her shoulders slumped. "I don't know."

I couldn't rely on my legs to hold me up anymore, so I shed my jeans and positioned myself against the headboard beside her. "You've been lying to me for almost a year."

"You lied to me for five," she defended before I could finish.

"My point is, I still trust you more than anyone."

She replied, "I don't know what I feel, Keiran. I'm pissed at you for manipulating me and causing my best friend to leave, but I can't deny this last month has been hell. I don't think I can be without you."

"I know I couldn't let you. You may see it as controlling and maybe it is, but it's what you do to me." She shook her head and turned her body to face me, giving me a full view of how serious she was about her next words.

"You make me feel things I'm not always proud of either, but it doesn't excuse the decisions we make. I don't want you to ever manipulate my life like that. We have to do what's right for each other. *Together*," she added.

"As you wish," I answered and grinned when she flinched with surprise.

"You've been watching Princess Bride," she accused.

"I've been living with a four-year-old for the last month so I could be close to you. Kennedy convinced me to do a lot of things I'm not proud of."

"You know she practically owns your ass, right?"

I snorted. "Keenan's got it worse. He let her put Sheldon's lip gloss on him."

"No way!" She doubled over and clenched her stomach as she laughed. "She has totally turned you into pussies!"

My eyes narrowed which she caught just as I lunged. I flipped her over and flattened her on the mattress before bringing my fingers to her ribs and tickling her.

"Wait," she gasped and screamed.

"I couldn't quite hear you before. I'm a what?"

"A pussy," she blurted and wiggled to get away.

"I see you think you're too tough. I'll have to show no mercy."

"No mercy! No mercy!" she mocked and screeched.

"As you wish." Her t-shirt had risen to reveal her lace panties. My mouth salivated when I lowered my face and kissed her through the material. Her breath caught and back bowed as I kissed her again, using my lips and tongue to coax her arousal to a fever pitch.

"Mercy, please! Mercy!" she begged but then lifted her hips for more. I used my teeth to nudge aside her panties and flicked her hot pussy with my tongue.

Fuck yeah.

I stood to push my boxer shorts down, slid her own panties down her amazingly long legs, and climbed on top of her. Her legs spread to accommodate me as I settled between them.

"You want relief, baby?" I pushed inside her before she could answer, but it didn't matter because she gripped me tight and pleaded with her gaze for me to fuck her.

For too long, I've waited to get close to her like this. The initial withdrawal drove me crazy, and lonely, cold nights I spent with my dick in my hand pissed me off.

When I thrust deeper at the reminder, her hands flew above her head to grip the sheets. My attention fixated on her hard nipples poking through her t-shirt. With a groan, I tore her shirt from her body, leaned down to suck her right nipple in my mouth, and slammed inside her. Her body slid up the bed from the force, and I followed, pounding out my past frustration on her body.

She came shortly after. The aftershock of her orgasm caused her pussy to spasm around me. I didn't want to come yet. I wanted this to last. Her top half rose from the bed so she could dig her nails into my throat and kiss my lips softly. I groaned in response.

So. Fucking. Good.

It was the last cognizant thought I had before I forced myself from her hot pussy and came on her belly. She stared up at me with confusion marring her beautiful face.

"Mine." It was all the answer I had given before I rubbed my come into her skin, marking her.

"So barbaric," she mumbled. I dropped beside her, already feeling sleep trying to overcome me when I noticed my belt lying on the bed. I leaned away to remove it but then hesitated.

"Why are you still holding your belt?" she asked curiously.

"I was going to tie your hands together so you couldn't leave in the middle of the night again." She shifted, ready to run, but I caught her hand and threaded my fingers through hers and pulled her close. Her entire body was tense, and I couldn't stand the thought of my touch being the cause. "But I have a better idea."

She turned her head enough to look me in the eye. "What?"

"If you can stay the night without running, then I'll know I can trust you and vice versa." I gave in to my body's demand for sleep. My last conscious thought was that I hoped she wouldn't run.

Chapter Twenty-Seven

LAKE

I WAS THE first to wake up the next morning and used the few moments alone to watch Keiran sleep. I'd become accustomed to stealing moments like this, and it started with the first night in our apartment together. He had a nightmare that night and almost every night since.

Over time, the nightmares decreased until he no longer had them. I still liked to watch him sleep—to see his guard down and peace replace his demons.

Maybe they were gone.

Or maybe there was one left that wasn't rightfully his...

"You didn't run." His deep voice rumbled above me. I shook my head because emotions stronger than me clogged my throat. He seemed to sense it and pulled me closer for comfort, and it worked but not how he meant it to. The white sheets were around our waist, exposing his naked chest and my breast. The feel of our naked skin together was beginning to redirect my thoughts. He kissed me deeply until I writhed against him.

He abruptly pulled away with a groan and grabbed his phone from his jeans. "We should get going. Di's already gone back to her apartment." We had a five-hour drive back to Stanford.

"Before we go back and try to make sense of our lives again, I think there's something you should know."

"What is that?"

I figured out a long time ago there was no right time or way to tell him what I learned the day Mitch died, so I decided to just say it.

"You didn't kill your mother."

He stared at me, unmoving, and then his expression turned savage as he ripped away from me and left the bed, leaving me feeling cold.

"What the hell are you talking about?"

"Your father—he told me how your mother really died."

"Well then, he lied, Lake. I had the gun. I pointed it at her. I killed her!" His roar shook my core, and I instinctually wanted to huddle into a ball and make myself as small as possible.

But I couldn't do that.

He was falling apart right before my eyes, and it was up to me to keep him together and see the truth.

"Baby, listen to me." I got up and chanced walking closer. I felt as if I were sticking my head in a lion's mouth and hoping he didn't bite it off. "Listen to yourself—you had the gun, you pointed it at her, and then she was dead, but did you pull the trigger?"

"I don't remember, but I guess I had to since she died," he snarled sarcastically and moved away from me like a skittish kitten.

I followed after him, refusing to back down. "Your father had a gun, too. He pulled the trigger because he didn't think you could do it. You didn't kill her. I know you didn't and you know, too. You question that day. I know you do."

He barked a short, dry laugh and clutched his hair. "He's doing it. He's fucking with me from the grave and he's using your gullible ass to do it."

I didn't feel myself move or my fist as it connected with his jaw as hard as I could. His head jerked and he cursed before returning his enraged glare on me. My hand throbbed as I pulled it back.

"You're not going to make this go away by trying to hurt me."

"Why are you doing this?" He shook his head and hissed when he clenched his teeth.

"Because you deserve to know. You don't have to accept it today or even tomorrow. The only living person who knows about your mother's death now is you. You can either make sense of it or continue to suffer as you have, but I thought you should know.

And because I had nothing else to say, I retreated into the bathroom, locked the door, and slid down the length of it until my naked bottom touched the cold tile.

How would I ever be able to fix my broken love when he was still afraid of the dark?

CHAPTER TWENTY-EIGHT

SIXTEEN YEARS AGO

KEIRAN

"YOU'VE ALREADY DONE this many times. What's one more?"

The gun felt much too large for the hand I held it in. I'd only begun to practice with them before the life I knew changed drastically. It was loud, and my arm would always be sore after they made me shoot it. Each time I held one didn't do anything to diminish the foreign and uncomfortable feelings.

The last time I used one was still fresh in my memories. It was the first time I'd ever used one on my own, and unfortunately, I remembered my training too well.

Lily was gone.

I blinked away the tears, afraid my father would mistake them for something else. I managed to keep it steadily trained on the woman who knelt in the corner. She was much too pretty for the tears streaming down her face. Her eyes were much too bright for the sadness it held. I knew she must have been afraid to die, but why didn't she beg and plead for her life like everyone else?

"Gabriel, my sweet boy," she whispered soothingly, finally finding her voice. Her voice held an unnatural quality to it, and her eyes wide when I entered had drooped. Her whole appearance just seemed to fade. "It's okay, my little boy. Do it."

Why was she telling me it would be okay? She was the one who would die. She must have thought I was someone else. Maybe she was looking for her son.

Suddenly, I wished she were my mom.

A strange, beautiful woman who I'd never met before but felt a connection to.

"Why are you calling me Gabriel?" I lowered the gun to study her. I couldn't shake the familiar feelings and the feeling that hurting this woman would be a mistake.

I looked to my father for guidance. "Dad?"

"It doesn't matter what the bitch calls you. Do you want your freedom, boy?"

"Yes."

"Then kill her," he sneered. He took my hand and lifted the gun again, pressing my finger on the trigger. All I had to do was squeeze a little more, but for some reason, I didn't want her to die.

I shouldn't do this.

I couldn't do this.

"It's okay, Gabriel." She nodded her head weakly. The tears were endless as they fell from her eyes.

You're not Gabriel. Just kill her. You'll be free.

"I will always love you."

What?

The gun went off.

The blast was loud, but I didn't feel the pain in my arm. It reached far beyond the physical. I didn't remember squeezing the trigger. I didn't remember killing her, but there was one thing I would always remember hearing...

"Good job, son." My father's evil chuckled echoed behind me. "You just killed your mother."

* * *

I SAT IN the corner of our bedroom and watched her chest rise and fall. The soft sound of contentment was music to my ears. My lips twitched when I remembered the day she made me stop accusing her of snoring.

She shifted in her sleep and my entire body tensed. When she rolled onto her back and settled into sleep once more, I felt my body relax. I didn't want her to awaken and find me watching her.

She'd ask questions that I didn't have the answers to.

I just couldn't sleep. The nightmare of my mother's murder—when I killed her—played over and over each time I tried. I would wake up in a cold sweat.

A long time ago, I welcomed the nightmares just so I could have a chance to see her face and hear her voice. Her pain and suffering were the only memory I had of her.

"You didn't kill your mother."

Now, I kept hearing Lake's voice tell me over and over that I didn't kill my mother. I had lashed out at her in what she thought was anger, but what she didn't know was that it was real fear that made me push her away. It was fear that she was wrong, and Mitch had only planted the seed in my head to destroy her.

But as she had guessed, I had questioned that night

over and over. Each time I had the nightmare, it would become clearer.

I didn't pull the trigger.

But my mother had died.

Because *Mitch* pulled the trigger.

"Keiran?"

My gaze tore away and found Lake sitting up in the middle of our bed with our sheets wrapped around her body. I could tell she was looking directly at me, but I couldn't see her face.

My vision was blurry and I couldn't figure out why until she said, "Ar–are you crying?"

I lifted trembling fingers to my cheek in time to catch the first tear fall. I didn't understand it.

Monsters don't cry.

She was out of bed and on her knees in front of me by the time the second one fell. I could see her face a little easier now since she was so close. She lifted a shy hand to my face, and I forced myself not to flinch. She touched the second teardrop and brought her hand back to study it with wonder.

"Keiran." She exhaled. I gripped the arms of the chair when the room began to spin. "Keiran, look at me." My heart followed her command even when my head continued to question everything. I looked into her blue-green eyes and didn't find deceit. "What's wrong?"

"I didn't kill her," I choked.

"Who? Esmerelda?"

"Sophia. My... My mother."

"Oh, baby." She stood up and slid into my lap and then slid her hands up my bare chest until they rested on my tear-streaked face. "No. You didn't kill her."

I shook my head, dislodging her hands and roughly dried my face with my hands. "But I didn't save her either." I gritted my teeth when I felt a sharp pain in my chest near my black hole where my heart should have been.

"You were only a child."

"I could have done something. My father was right that day. I killed so many, so what was one more? It should have been him."

"You were born among monsters," she lifted my face when I hid in her shoulder, "but you were not meant to walk with them."

"What am I supposed to do now? Knowing I didn't kill my mother doesn't change what I've done."

"Keiran Masters, my dark prince," she touched my face again, "you find out who you really are."

CHAPTER-TWENTY-NINE

LAKE

WILLOW WENT INTO labor the following week and we were all camped out in the waiting room. Dash refused to take any chances and paid the hospital to secure a private floor for the birth. It was forty hours after her water broke and still no baby. Kennedy was well behaved despite the long hours, but it was Keenan we had to try and keep contained. He circled the waiting room with a video camera, insisting on interviews from everyone and hourly updates. He also announced he was making a documentary for when he and Sheldon had six more kids. She cut her eye at him but wisely, remained silent. I discreetly laughed at her situation because he was determined to pump her full of babies, and she was determined to ensure that didn't happen until she was ready.

I shook my head because we all knew Keenan was spoiled and would get his way sooner than later.

Eight hours later, their son was finally born. Kennedy had jumped up at the news and demanded to see her baby cousin. The nurse warned that only two were allowed in at a time, but as soon as her back was turned, we all bum rushed the room until it was overflowing.

We found her appearing half-alive and sitting up as she held onto him. Dash stood over them, staring down at his son swaddled in a blue blanket. I could see a thin splatter of copper, much tamer than his mother's hair, on his tiny head. I inched closer just as his eyes opened and inhaled as much air as I could.

He was beautiful.

"What's his name?" Keenan blurted, still filming.

"Haven Jasper Chambers," Dash announced.

"Can I hold it now?" Kennedy questioned.

"Your cousin is not an it," Sheldon scolded.

Kennedy rolled her eyes upward. "Ok, but can I hold him, Mama?"

"Not yet, Ken Doll, but when he's bigger you can."

"Daddy says I grow an inch every day. Can I hold him tomorrow?"

Everyone laughed at her impatience. "We'll see," Sheldon answered, cooing over Haven. I could see Ken wanted to argue, but the nurse came back just then.

"All right, everyone. Shoo. We have to get this little guy fed." Keiran took my hand after the nurse kicked us all out and slowly led us to the elevator. I noticed he had been silent for most of the day but had grown even more distant when Haven was born. I could see the vulnerability in his gaze when he stared down at their son, and I wondered what he had been thinking.

* * *

THREE DAYS LATER, it was my birthday and I hadn't seen one sign of Keiran since I had awakened and found his side of the bed empty. I slowly dragged myself from the bed to begin my morning ablutions. I had been in the middle of brushing my teeth when the doorbell rang. I descended the stairs with my toothbrush in hand and found Keenan and Sheldon's porch overrun with my friends.

"Happy Birthday!!!!" They screamed it so loud, Haven, who Willow held in her arms, woke up with a hitch-pitched cry.

"Well, shit," Dash muttered and took him from Willow. He brushed past me with his son and sat on the couch.

"You gonna let us in?" Keenan questioned with a lifted brow.

"It's your house, Sherlock. Why were you outside anyway?"

"Dramatic effect," he called over his shoulder and disappeared into the kitchen. I looked at all my friends standing around in the living room and giving me weird looks and glancing away just as quickly.

"What?"

"Nothing," they all answered too quickly. My eyes narrowed, but they wouldn't meet my gaze.

"Listen, has anyone seen Keiran? He's not here." I tried not to let my agitation be known, but waking up on your birthday to find your boyfriend missing after three days of distance was not the way I saw this going down.

"He had something important to take care of," Dash answered without taking his eyes away from Haven.

"And he couldn't tell me that? Better yet, it couldn't wait?" He only shrugged, but he still wouldn't meet my gaze, so it only pissed me off more.

"We came to take you out to breakfast to get your

birthday started." Sheldon giggled. It sounded forced, and I had the feeling she was only trying to take the heat off Dash.

"I'm not hungry."

"But we are, so put this on," Willow stated and passed me a garment bag she took from the coat closet. Inside was a simple white dress that would easily sweep the floor.

"Um...?"

I looked up at Willow feeling odd. It was then I noticed they were all a little dressed up for a simple breakfast.

Even Kennedy wore a baby blue dress with a bow tied around her waist.

"It's a really nice restaurant," Dash offered at my bewildered look. Keenan came out of nowhere and nudged me toward the stairs. When I reached Keiran's old bedroom, I laid the garment bag down with shaking hands.

Something was up. I just couldn't pinpoint why they were all acting so strange, but I had a feeling Keiran's disappearance had something to do with it.

I jumped into the shower and turned the hot water on full force. Thirty minutes later, after drying and curling my hair, I returned to the bedroom and stood with a towel wrapped around me as I stared at the white dress that could almost pass for a gown.

I unzipped the bag and carefully lifted it from the plastic. "What the hell was Willow thinking?" I questioned out loud to no one. The strapless gown—because I couldn't think of it as anything but—was even more beautiful without the clear plastic surrounding it. It was the tiny, pearl-like beading, decorating the bodice that transformed it from simple to elegance.

Inside the bag, I also found a white panty and garter set and thought she had gone too far, but then I reminded myself it was Willow so I would humor her. The doctor warned that it would be a while before her hormone levels returned to normal. In other words, tread carefully.

Once I finished dressing, I used the full-length mirror in the corner and stared at my reflection. Despite how bad I felt about Keiran missing on my birthday, the dress made me feel beautiful and wiped away every negative feeling I'd had since waking up.

That was until I studied how the gown teased the tops of my feet and realized I had no shoes that would go well with the dress. I hurried for the door and opened them, only to find Dash standing there, holding up the familiar nude wedges Keiran bought me for our first Valentine's date.

"Wha—How did you get these?"

"Magic happens on special days like these. You look beautiful," he whispered.

"Thank you." I took the shoes and studied them. They were hardly the best option for the dress. "They don't really go."

"He insisted," Dash simply said and kissed me on my forehead before sauntering away. I slid the shoes on and followed after him. Everyone was waiting downstairs when I made it down. Willow stood a few feet away, and when she saw me, she started crying for some reason. I tried to go to her, but Keenan pulled me in the opposite direction.

"Hormones," he muttered and led me out the door. I began to feel a nervous flutter as we drove away in separate cars. Keenan and Sheldon drove me while Dash and Willow followed behind with Kennedy and Haven. I looked down, my hands shaking in my lap, and took a deep breath.

God, get it together. It was only breakfast.

I told myself I was only upset because I still hadn't heard from Keiran.

I concentrated on the clear summer sky and thought about classes that would be starting in a few days. The arrests and the time spent in jail caused me to flunk out of my summer courses, so I was now behind a quarter to graduation.

The car slowed to a stop, jolting me from my distraction when I realized we were at the playground. I was no longer afraid of this place and the bad memory from sixteen years ago, but it didn't mean I forgot everything it represented.

The car door opened and I found Jackson standing there with his hand outstretched.

What the fuck was going on?

I took his hand and was even more freaked out when I saw Aunt Carissa standing by with her hands over her mouth and crying.

This was turning out to be one emotional breakfast. I had no idea my birthday meant so much to them. I felt inadequate because I had no idea what to say. To be honest, all I wanted to do was to go back and crawl under the covers and wait for Keiran to remember me.

"You guys are back."

I hugged Jackson and then Aunt Carissa, who finally managed to stop crying long enough to speak.

"I couldn't miss this."

"And we need to talk later," Jackson added in a stern voice. I knew they must have heard about my arrests by now. Over the years, he willingly and wholeheartedly took on a father figure role. He really was a good guy, and I think even Keiran respected him. "But first," he held up his arm for me to take, "will you allow me the honor?"

“Uh, sure.” I took his arm and looked around but everyone had already disappeared. He started walking me across the playground, and as we passed the swings and sandboxes, I inhaled as I realized we were heading for the monkey bars. “Is this where we’re having breakfast?” I frowned because Dash had said it was a really nice restaurant. “The picnic tables are over—”

My legs stopped working, and I sucked in a sharp breath when I saw the tall, familiar figure a short distance away.

Keiran stood under the monkey bars, which were decorated with blue and white flowers. A trail of flowers made a small path from where I now stood all the way to him. Dash, Keenan, and Q stood with him while Willow, Sheldon, Di, and Jesse stood to his left. A man dressed as a priest also waited at the end, and that’s when my brain finally caught up.

OH.

CHAPTER THIRTY

KEIRAN

I STOOD UNDER the monkey bars that Dash and Keenan helped me turn into our altar and tried not to look as nervous as I felt. It took three torturous days of sad blue eyes watching and wondering if I was withdrawing from her. I couldn't tell her that I had been planning the start of our future.

I realized I never even proposed to her, but there was no fucking way I could wait long enough for her to plan a wedding once I got my ring on her finger.

I guess I had Dash and Haven to thank for that.

The day he was born, I felt more than saw the instant bond between father and son. While everyone fussed over the baby, I watched Dash.

He gazed down at his son, and no matter what went on in that room, he never took his eyes from him, but then he glanced at me so suddenly, I felt like I had been intruding on an inmate moment. But then he silently showed me everything he was feeling through his tear glistened eyes. The connection was so brief because his gaze snapped back almost frantically to Haven, and he continued to watch over him.

He showed me something in that brief moment and quite possibly saved my life.

I glanced at my watch again.

She should be here by now.

"Calm down," Q said and clapped me on the back. "They'll get her here."

I had no doubt they would get her here, but what if she ran once she did? What if she decided my emotional baggage was too much to ride out? What if—

"Here they come," Di announced. She stood in a modest, pale blue dress with her hair down and her face free of makeup. She looked much younger and innocent without it—like there weren't ten lifetimes of hell built up beneath the surface.

I turned my attention to my small crowd of friends approaching and focused on getting through this. I was going to marry Lake Monroe today and truly surrender myself to her.

"Jackson and her aunt have her held up," Keenan stated as they all took their spots. I nodded and watched the opening where she would appear soon if she didn't catch on and run for the hills.

I was beginning to grow impatient and had to force the urge to go after her. When she finally appeared on Jackson's arm and stopped, I found myself fighting for control once more.

Please don't run.

Please don't run.

Please don't—

She took a step forward and then stopped. She was too far for me to see her expression, but I knew she had eyes for only me. Every hair on my body was raised as it always did whenever she looked at me. Before long, she was standing in front of me with tears flowing freely down her beautiful face.

"Keiran," she hiccupped and struggled to breathe. "What is this?"

I took her face in my hands and brought her close so only she could hear. "This is the day we meet for the first time and the rest of forever."

"I still don't understand," she cried, so I kissed her lips and prepared myself for what came next.

"You promised me a long time ago that when it was all over, you'd bring me to my knees." I let go of her face and took her hand. "I hope one will do."

I lowered myself to one knee and looked her in her eyes. "You chased away the monsters and became my reason—my forever. I'm yours, Lake Monroe. Will you marry me today?"

"Yes, I fucking will," she screamed. Just then, a light showering of flower petals rained down on us, and when she looked up, her breath caught. Buddy sat on the edge of the monkey bars with a handful flowers, sprinkling them over us. "Buddy!"

"You were my hero." He grinned.

She smiled up at him and then turned to face me, and I nodded at the priest to begin. "We are gathered together to celebrate the very special love between bride and groom, by joining them in marriage..."

EPILOGUE

ELEVEN MONTHS LATER

LAKE

DURING ALMOST A year of wedded bliss, a lot has happened. I graduated with my Masters in Education and accepted a job in Six Forks at Bainbridge Elementary. Keiran sold his part of the business back to Jesse and followed me. He's been volunteering his time to help coach the basketball team at Bainbridge High and started an after-school little league for younger kids. He didn't seem to be in a rush to figure out what to do with the rest of his life, and when he opened a joint account, I realized why. The nosy wife in me reared its curious head, and I couldn't believe how much cash he was sitting on.

When we first moved back to Six Forks, we stayed with Keenan and Sheldon while Keiran and I scoped out a home to buy, which ended up the next street over from theirs anyway. They had run off to elope a few months after we married when Keenan decided he wasn't taking any more chances. She, in turn, convinced Keenan she wanted to stay local despite his earlier ruling on her attending med school in California as planned.

Today was the best day of them all because today my best friend would marry the love of her life. Shortly after Haven was born, they moved into a beautiful home that Dash had built for their family. It was then we discovered where Dash had been hiding all of the baby stuff he had purchased. Willow, Sheldon, and I—and Keenan—all cried at the sight of the beautiful nursery.

Everything was perfect.

Until reality crash-landed and I learned our world was about to get a little bigger. I had been helping Willow with her dress when a wave of nausea overcame me, and I nearly puked all over her ivory gown. It was the most subtle thing I'd ever seen her wear, and I almost ruined it.

"Should I go get Keiran?" Sheldon asked after I finally stopped vomiting. I shook my head and closed my eyes as I leaned over the toilet. He was the last person I needed to see right now. I still hadn't found a way to tell him.

God.

I thought we'd slain all his demons.

"I just need to sit down, I think." She nodded and I followed her back out into the church hallway. Keenan walked by as the door closed behind us but stopped when he noticed my face.

"Whoa. Why do you look like that?" he frowned.

"Honey, have a brain. She's sick and you're not being nice."

"Sick?" He stroked his chin and stared at me for a

long moment. "Are you sure you aren't pregnant?"

Sheldon' stiffened at the same time I did. Her head whipped around to face me, and her jaw dropped. I felt as if my tongue had become lodged in my throat.

"I—I, uh..." I couldn't form words but it didn't matter because he smirked and walked away.

"Are you?" Sheldon shrieked. I could only nod and stare down a spot on the floor. "Does Keiran know?"

"No," I croaked. "I don't think I can tell him."

"What are you afraid of?"

"I'll lose him." It was the only thing I was afraid of now.

"That's not possible."

The door to Willow's dressing room opened, and she poked her head out. Her curls had been whipped and beaten into shaped by her mother and pulled back to show off the angelic lines of her face, which was now pulled down with concern.

"What's going on?"

Neither of us responded though Sheldon pulled us inside and shut the door. "Tell her," she nudged when the silence stretched too long.

"I'm pregnant."

Moisture immediately pooled in Willow's eyes, and then she grabbed and pulled me into a tight hug. "Is this for real?"

"I don't know what to do," I cried and she pulled me tighter.

"Do you truly believe he wouldn't be happy?"

"He'll be terrified." Just then, the door shook and a loud boom echoed around us.

"What the—"

"Baby, open up." I recognized the voice instantly and felt my blood drain. I was rooted to the spot. Breathing was no longer an option.

Sheldon growled beside me and stormed for the door. "I swear if Keenan told—" She ripped open the door and was met by my anxious husband who rudely pushed past her. Dash was behind him but she said, "You can't come in here," and slammed the door in his face.

"Keenan said you weren't feeling well." Keiran reached out and grabbed my waist to pull me close. He tucked his chin low and spoke against the side of my face. "What's wrong?" His voice was tender with fear.

"I threw up."

"Why?" The guttural sound of his voice broke me, and I was pretty certain he already knew.

"Because I'm pregnant," I stated matter of factly and looked up to meet his eyes. I needed to see his true feelings. I was surprised to find him smiling. "Wait... Why are you smiling?"

"Actually, I think we should give you guys a moment," Sheldon cut in and grabbed Willow's hand. "But don't take too long. The wedding starts in fifteen." She checked to make sure the coast was clear and then they left.

"You're smiling," I repeated as soon as the door was closed.

"I was beginning to think my soldiers were weaker than Keenan's."

"Explain please." My tone was short because this was not the reaction I was expecting. He should be yelling and making threats and storming out.

Keiran doesn't want kids.

"He's been bragging how he got Sheldon knocked up even though she was on birth control."

"I'm still not following."

He swallowed hard and suddenly looked very serious. "I want this."

"No," I argued more out of confusion than denial. "You don't want kids. You're scared—" I didn't get to finish because he had placed his palm on my stomach but stared down at his hand confused.

"I'm fucking terrified."

I didn't know how to respond because he wasn't making sense.

"So why?"

"I promised to give you everything, and I know this is what you want. So, I thought maybe I could make that sacrifice."

"That's not a reason to face your fears. I don't want a family to be a sacrifice."

"I thought so, too."

"Then *why*!" I yelled frustrated and stepped back. I wanted to believe him. I wanted a family with him.

But not if my happiness was a sacrifice that he couldn't live with.

"Haven loves Dash and Dash loves him back. He's. Just. His. Son."

"Keiran, baby, explain a little better," I pleaded. I felt just as desperate as the look in his eyes.

"I got a call from Daniel after we were married. They wanted me to know the inheritance is still in place. If I have a son, I'll inherit."

"My son will not be a meal ticket."

"I'm glad you said that because I told him if I ever did have a son, any cent given to me will be donated or burned. He seemed to understand."

"So what does this mean?"

"It means I'm not Mitch, and I never will be. I know that now. I want to be a father."

"What if one day you wake up hating me, or I wake up one day and you're gone?"

He reached out for me and I went. He needed to

touch me just as much I needed him to but he didn't stop there. He kissed my lips until I softened against him. "That's never going to happen. Even when I hated you, being without you wasn't something I could do. It's you and me forever, wife. Get used to it." I laughed until he lowered to his knees and looked up at me. "Do you trust me with our kid?"

My relief over his willingness to give our family a try was nothing compared to how I weakened at the humbled look in his eyes. "I trust you," I found myself saying easier than ever. He kissed my stomach through the dress, and I wanted nothing more than for him to continue, but a knock on the door pulled us apart. He glanced at his watch and cursed.

"The wedding is about to start." When he opened the door, we found Willow standing on the other side with her arms crossed. "Shouldn't you be getting ready to walk down the aisle?" he joked.

"In a minute... Is everything cool?" she grilled with her threatening glare on Keiran. He snorted and ignored her to wrap his arm around my waist and he pulled me in front of him. They had grown closer and by closer, I meant they agreed they were each equally important to me. Willow still tried to assert dominance over him, though, and Keiran still found it amusing.

"We're going to have a baby."

NINE YEARS LATER

KEIRAN

"PHEE. WHAT IS this?" I held up my favorite ball with flower stickers all over the surface. I almost wept when

I saw it. Keenan and Dash gave me shit the entire practice after I'd pulled out my 'pretty ball.' A few years ago I took over coaching the boys high school basketball team with the help of Keenan and Dash during Saturday morning practice.

"What do you mean, daddy?"

"What do you mean, what do I mean?"

"I *mean*," she emphasized, "what do you mean?"

"Phee." I pinched the bridge of my nose and prayed for patience. The little shit maintained a serious expression even though I was sure she was fucking with me. The universe cursed me the day he gave her my personality and her mother's looks. Maybe it was payback for the shit I gave as a kid.

At only seven years old, she was a fucking nightmare.

"Daddy, I just wanted to make it better. Don't you like it?"

"No."

"Well, I like it," she stated and walked past me, silently ending the conversation. I spun in time to see her and her evil pigtails leave her room.

Oh, hell no.

"Sophia!" I roared, following behind her. She must have run off because the hall was empty.

Somewhere near, I heard a sigh and the patient voice of my wife asking Phee what she'd done now. I followed the sound of their voices and found them in our bedroom. Lake was in bed where I left her this morning as she breastfed Nicky. He was only four weeks old and ate more than three grown men. I wasn't complaining, though. Each time I watched her feed him, it only made me want to breed her again.

One more.

And then I promised her I'd quit.

I eyed Phee faking fear and attempting to hide against her mother's side. Despite how crazy she made me, I wanted another princess. Maybe one gentle like her mother. This one was all me. I'd never say it out loud, and fuck whoever disapproved, but she was my favorite. I'd just never tell her so.

Or make any of my other kids feel inferior.

It wasn't about that.

I'd die for any of them.

"Dad?"

My attention shifted to the door where my oldest looked as if he'd just woken up. It was almost fucking noon and he got to sleep in. I couldn't even sleep past six anymore even on weekends.

"Trey! Daddy's being mean again." She left Lake and ran straight into Trey's arms, knowing her older brother would put up the biggest fight. Lake and I had an agreement that we didn't disagree in front of the kids ever. It never stopped her claws from coming out behind closed doors. They had her wrapped her finger.

Trey eyed me and I eyed him back. I could see his internal struggle because while I told him to protect her from all assholes, including me, it didn't mean I would tolerate being challenged. He finally smirked but remained silent and tucked Phee behind him, and I nodded my approval.

"Trey, why don't you take Sophia outside? She's getting restless," my wife dictated.

"Get your swimsuits on first!" I called out when he left. He didn't shut the door behind him so I knew he heard me even though a response didn't follow. He had inherited my personality as well, unfortunately.

"Why are they getting their swimsuits?"

"We're having a barbecue. Q's in town."

"What's the occasion?"

I shrugged and walked closer. Nicky had just finished his meal, which left her breast exposed. She lifted him to her other shoulder and began to burp him so as I stood over them, I ran my finger over her pink nipple.

"I want another."

"We just had one," she grumbled. I tried not to laugh but failed. It was funny how the tables have turned. I was the one against reproducing, but now I just couldn't fucking stop. Lake found and brought out the good in me... and also, my apparent fetish for breeding her.

She glared up at me. "I'm serious, Keiran. I'm not a machine."

I ignored her anger. We both knew as soon as I was able to enter her again, I'd be doing more than just fucking her, and she'd want it too.

"Would it be so bad?" I found myself asking anyway. I was selfish, but I didn't want her unhappy. When she sighed and her shoulders slumped, I knew I had her. I was grateful when Nicky burped, distracting her so she couldn't see my grin.

"Wipe that cheesy grin off your face," she said without looking up as she wiped Nicky's mouth. "You still can't touch me for two more weeks."

"Look at me," I demanded. She didn't hesitate to lift her head and meet my stare. I leaned down until my lips brushed hers. "Two weeks is nothing when you have forever."

* * *

DASH ARRIVED WITH his family for the barbecue first. Haven and Trey immediately disappeared into the shed we made into a boy cave, while Ashe, their seven-year-old daughter, and Phee already had their heads together. Dash's parents had been invited by Lake but declined. Dash and his father eventually managed to find equal ground after Dash made good on his threat and put the company at jeopardy and ultimately gained complete control from his father. He and I both knew he would never end so many jobs just to get back at his father but Cale didn't know that. I guess it went to show how much he really knew his son. They've been working on their relationship but he still hated me. Willow had opened up a modest boutique here in Six Forks. All of her designs were unique since they were handmade by her but she made a killing...despite her clothes still being weird as fuck. I would never get how kids dressed today.

Keenan arrived last with his hands full shortly after. He opened a new tattoo shop in Six Forks but never managed to do much of the work himself anymore since he was mostly a stay at home dad. After Sheldon finished medical school, completed her residency, and started her own practice she eventually agreed to give him more kids. She gave birth to twin boys a year ago. Tristan and Tobias hung from his arms as he walked into the backyard followed by Sheldon and Ken, who looked as if she'd rather be anywhere else. She was only fourteen and already moody. It made me wonder if we were this bad at her age.

"Hi, Uncle Keiran."

She also stopped calling me Keke around the time she turned eight. I wouldn't admit to anyone and if someone should ask, I'd deny it, but I kind of missed it. She grew up too fast.

"So your mom made you come?"

"Nope. Daddy said I needed to appreciate family more so here I am," she threw her arms out with a blank look, "appreciating."

I laughed and could mentally hear Lake scolding me. She would always tell me I shouldn't encourage her by laughing, but every day, I liked the kid more and more.

"Maybe it won't be so bad this time. What did you have to do anyway?"

"Well, since you asked... there's this boy..."

"Geez." I cut her off and backpedaled as quickly as possible. "I can't hear this." I walked away, leaving her standing there before she could say more. I found Keenan by the grill. Dash kept slapping his hand away when he tried to take a patty.

"The kids eat first."

"But they always get to eat first."

"Why don't you put them down? How are they ever going to learn to walk?"

"They don't need to walk. That's why they got me. Plus, what if they think someone else is their daddy?"

"You can't be serious?"

"Are you letting your daughter date now?" ?" I questioned. They stopped arguing to shoot me bewildered looks.

Keenan recovered quickly and said, "Of course not." He was able to snatch a burger off the side table since Dash's full attention had shifted to me. "She'll never get to if I have anything to say about it," he said around a mouth full of beef.

"You sure about that? She just tried to talk to me about a boy."

He immediately started to choke and spit the rest of the meat he hadn't swallowed to the ground.

"Come again?" He seemed to get a clue and unhooked the slings that held his boys, handing Tristan to me and Tobias to Dash. Without another word, he stomped off in Ken's direction.

"You know she'll be mad at you, right?"

I shrugged and smiled down at Tristan, who grinned right back.

"She shouldn't be dating."

"Geez, what is she thinking?"

I snorted. "She's a fourteen-year-old girl. What do you think?"

"What's going on?" Lake asked, walking up with Willow.

"Yeah, why is Keenan screaming at Ken about an all girl's school?" Willow demanded.

They each narrowed their eyes at us. I swear it was as if they could smell guilt.

"Keiran snitched on Ken about dating boys," Dash offered without hesitation.

"Thanks, man."

He patted me on the back as an offer of apology, and Keenan chose that moment to come back over. "I can't believe this," he growled and snatched another burger.

"It was bound to happen sometime," Lake argued.

"Yeah, when I was dead preferably. My daughter doesn't have sex."

"She was talking about a simple date," Sheldon scoffed.

"Wait you *knew* about this?" Keenan, Dash, and I all yelled at once.

Just then Phee ran toward us at full speed, saving Sheldon from answering. "When is Uncle Q supposed to get here?" she whined. She looked over her shoulder with wide, hopeful eyes. "They're still coming, right daddy?"

I smiled and looked across the yard at the glass door as it slid open. "They're coming."

NOTE

WHERE CAN I start? I guess at this point my emotional attachment to this series and the character's story told within the pages has reached its breaking point. Keiran, Lake, and the rest of the gang will always be my favorite simply because they were my first. Their story was special and misunderstood by some but worthy of telling nonetheless.

If you're wondering why Keiran took a backseat to being the hero, I think it's because I owed it to Lake. Everyone doubted whether she could shed her damsel and become the hero, including her. Keiran, at the same time, struggled with the moral dilemma of what was right so Lake stepped in to share the burden.

This may be the last book, but who is to say their story will ever truly end? I guarantee you'll see them again when Q, Di, and Jesse tell their story in a spin-off coming soon.

Interview with Keiran

If you could have a phone conversation with Keiran, what would you say/ask?

DELILAH CARO: Only one question comes to mind... when did you know you were in love with Lake? At what point was it no longer hate? Was it something she said or a particular incident?

KEIRAN: It's hard to say when it happened because whenever it did, it was hard to remember a time or possibility when I never was. It felt like a natural part of me.

BRIANA BLACK: That time you may have gotten Lake pregnant and she was freaking out, you really seemed like you didn't give a damn. What would you have done if she were pregnant? Did you want to get her pregnant?

KEIRAN: The last thing I wanted at the time was to create more monsters.

VERONICA ASHLEY: Keiran, if you could do one thing differently in your life, what would that one thing be—something you control, not something that was chosen for you. P.S. You are badass and hot as hell!

KEIRAN: I'd changed who fathered me and bring my mother back to life.

INTERVIEW WITH KEIRAN

RACHEL CAMPBELL: Keiran, back when you were tormenting Lake right after you were released, if you found out that she actually had an intimate relationship while you were locked up, would you really have killed her? You always threatened it but, at that time, would you really have gone through with it?

KEIRAN: That's the answer that might scare me the most. I guess we'll never know.

LUCY COOPER: Keiran, does it scare you that the people around you are no longer scared of you, but if anything, becoming more like you. First your brother then Willow and now Lake?

KEIRAN: I have no doubt that I have influenced decisions and actions made by my friends, but just as I influenced them, their influence turned out to be more powerful.

KRISI FULLBROOK: How does it make you feel that the one person you love has the power to make you FEAR what BREAKING her LOVE for you (Which would NOT make you FEARLESS) would leave you BROKEN ???

KEIRAN: I think you said it, Krisi. ☺

ANGIE ESQUILIN: Keiran, I know you love Lake. But if you had a choice to do things differently with her. Will you do it?

KEIRAN: Lake gave me that chance the day she took my ring and my name. I've been doing things differently since.

JAMIE BUCHANAN: Keiran, I love you. If you and Lake don't work out, can I be your Dark Princess of Bainbridge, please?

KEIRAN: LOL. Are you sure you could handle me?

HATICE SAHINER: Keiran, in high school, when did you first start to notice Lake as anything other than someone to hurt? Was there ever a time when you thought you would rather 'be her man' than 'the man who hurt Lake'?

KEIRAN: After she finally convinced me for the first time that I wasn't a monster.

LISA P. KANE: Do [you] ever worry that Lake will wonder what it would be like to have dated anyone else, since [you're] the only guy she's ever been with?

KEIRAN: I've been keeping her too busy to wonder. Besides... she knows better.

ABBY CAMACHO: Keiran, Lake told you once "Love is much more powerful than fear." At this point in your lives, what do you think about that statement? Is love powerful enough?

KEIRAN: Love brought me to my knees, Abby. I think it packs a pretty powerful punch. Through all the hate I threw her way, she remained standing. And I'm much bigger than she is. ☺

INTERVIEW WITH KEIRAN

STACEY ADAMS: Keiran, the moment Keenan found out you killed his mom, did it make you regret it, considering he's your brother?

KEIRAN: I was sorry for hurting him, but I didn't know the truth about my mother to regret the thought of killing her.

CAT HOLLOWAY: What is the most intriguing thing you've read in Lake's journal, and how do you think it affected your relationship?

KEIRAN: Learning she had a crush on me when we were sixteen. That was definitely interesting considering I was the biggest dick to her that year.

MARISOL BARRENAS: Keiran, where is the weirdest place you have done it with Lake?

KEIRAN: In my head. There's some pretty wild things that involve her in there—things she'd never let me do.

SAMOA JAHAN: Keiran, I don't mind being your side chick. Will you accept it?

KEIRAN: If I were that type of man, I'd be honored.

CAROL NEVAREZ: Keiran, have you ever been to The Container Store with Lake!?!

KEIRAN: Jesus, no. I've heard about that store. I'd sell my left nut never to have to step foot in there with her.

INTERVIEW WITH KEIRAN

NICOLETTE GUAJARDO: Keiran, I have one thing to say to you. One word. One syllable. One meaning. Hi.

KEIRAN: Hello yourself. ;-)

LUPINE BARRAGAN: Keiran, what is your biggest regret?

KEIRAN: I'll never know my mother, I'll never be able to erase the hurt I caused Lake, and I'll never know who Gabriel could have been.

SKYE JACOBS: Keiran, if you and Keenan knew that you guys were brothers from the beginning, what do you think your relationship with each other would have been like? P.S. You're one hot motherfucker.

KEIRAN: We were always brothers. Learning it was the real deal didn't make our relationship feel any different.

ROSEMARIE ADAMS: Keiran, the people around you have forgiven you for most of the things you have done. Could you ever forgive yourself?

KEIRAN: I try a little each day, Rosemarie.

MARIA WILLIAMS: What do you and Lake do in your free time? Do you guys watch movies together or go bowling?

KEIRAN: I like to teach her things... shooting, bowling, basketball... for some reason, it gets my pupil hot.

INTERVIEW WITH KEIRAN

LAURA ANDREWS: Keiran, if you could give your younger self some advice, what would it be?

KEIRAN: Don't be a dick.

AGNESE KOHN: Pick me up...

KEIRAN: What time?

JANESE: Keiran, you had a difficult time loving and being loved in the beginning. How have you changed in the last five years when it comes to love for Lake, your family, and friends?

KEIRAN: According to them, I'm still an asshole, but at least I'm tolerable. Willow wasn't there, but she tells me regularly.

NAOMI SANTOS: Keiran, as much as you love Lake, do you believe she killed your father? If so, how do you feel about her now?

KEIRAN: It was hard to believe. A part of me knew she couldn't have done it, but it angered, scared, and humbled me to know she was willing to do it. She'd gone there to kill him—that much I do believe. I'm just grateful she didn't because I couldn't live with that on my conscience. We've come a long way considering I once wanted to shatter the innocence that made her irresistible to me.

LAUREN STRYKER: Keiran, when can we expect little

Keiran's?

KEIRAN: I think the only question now is, how many more can I make before Lake cuts me off?

FEENA DON: If you loved Lake as much as you claimed, why would you never let her go?? You must've known she would've done anything for you. You're selfish, Keiran! But I gotta say, I love the way you love.

KEIRAN: I never denied being selfish man.

BRIE BURGESS: Keiran, first off: Hey, Zaddy *waves seductively*

Now, when you had Lake on the floor, knife to her throat... what were you thinking as you entered her each time? Did you really want to put fear into her or was it more about you fighting your demons and not killing her?

And how did it make you feel that she pulled a knife out on you first? Obviously, hard as a rock, but what else?

P.S. Marry me and let's make this sister wives union for real.

KEIRAN: How are you, Brie? I'm not proud of what I did, but at the time, it seemed like a good idea. I think I wanted to scare her again so I wouldn't have to kill her. She was learning not to be afraid of me, and I couldn't let that happen. But I will say this... Lake pulling that knife on me was the hottest thing I'd ever seen, and I just had to get my dick in her.

Tempting... but I'm a married man, Brie.

INTERVIEW WITH KEIRAN

LIVIA BEJKO: What's the thing that scares you most about life? Thanks for answering. Oh, by the way, you are a total jackass and more than once have deserved to get beat-up, but I still like you, you selfish, brainless, awesome-killer, perfect boy.

KEIRAN: Knowing what happened to me as a child won't die with me, and I can't do anything to stop it.

It's my boyish charm. ;-)

ACKNOWLEDGMENTS

THIS ACKNOWLEDGMENT IS unusually short because rather than picking and choosing, I want to acknowledge every single person who read, loved, hated, promoted, and worked to make this series a success.

Thank you.

What's Next?

THE BANDIT
Book One of *The Stolen Duet*

SHE STOLE MY PROPERTY

I'll never forget the night I caught her sneaking around my place. She thought she could steal from me and get away with it, but I have no intention of letting her get away at all. Mian Ross has a lesson to learn, and I'm going to be the one to teach it to her.

HE STOLE MY SON

I'll never forget the night I made the second biggest mistake of my life. It was supposed to be a simple job, but it quickly became so much more—one that cost my freedom and cost me my son. Angel Knight became my worst nightmare, and now he'll never let us go.

ALSO BY B.B. REID

Broken Love Series

Fear Me

Fear You

Fear Us

Breaking Love

Fearless

The Stolen Duet

The Bandit

Contact the Author

Join **Bebe's Reiders** on Facebook!

Twitter: _BBREID

Instagram: _BBREID

www.bbreid.com

ABOUT B.B. REID

B.B., ALSO KNOWN as Bebe, found her passion for romance when she read her first romance novel by Susan Johnson at a young age. She would sneak into her mother's closet for books and even sometimes the attic. It soon became a hobby, and later an addiction. When she finally decided to pick up a metaphorical pen and start writing, she found a new way to embrace her passion.

She favors a romance that isn't always easy on the eyes or heart and loves to see characters grow—characters who are seemingly doomed from the start but find love anyway.

Made in the USA
Lexington, KY
24 December 2016